THE LIAR'S DAUGHTER

CLAIRE ALLAN

avon.

Published by Avon
A division of HarperCollins*Publishers*
1 London Bridge Street,
London SE1 9GF

www.harpercollins.co.uk

A Paperback Original 2020

2

Copyright © Claire Allan 2020

Claire Allan asserts the moral right to
be identified as the author of this work

A catalogue record for this book is
available from the British Library

ISBN 978-0-00837-835-6

This novel is entirely a work of fiction.
The names, characters and incidents portrayed in it are
the work of the author's imagination. Any resemblance to
actual persons, living or dead, events or localities is
entirely coincidental.

Set in Bembo Std by Palimpsest Book Production Limited,
Falkirk, Stirlingshire

Printed and bound in Great Britain by CPI Group (UK) Ltd, Croydon CR0 4YY

MIX
Paper from
responsible sources
FSC
www.fsc.org FSC™ C007454

This book is produced from independently certified FSC™ paper
to ensure responsible forest management.

For more information visit: www.harpercollins.co.uk/green

To my children,
who make me want to be the best person
I can be every single day.
I love you both so much.

Prologue

Now

Joe

They've told me I'm dying. A doctor in a white coat, and a blue shirt with a stripy navy tie that had a coffee stain on it, had perched on the end of my bed and adopted a very serious expression on his face.

A nurse – who I had heard give out to her colleagues about the lack of resources on the ward and how she was getting 'sick, sore and tired of working her arse off' for too much responsibility and not enough money – had pulled the clinical blue curtain around my bed to afford me some privacy.

Her sombre expression mirrored that of the doctor, although it was clear it was a front. It was almost the end of her shift. This was a life-changing moment for me – the moment I heard I was condemned to die despite all the chemotherapy and surgery that they had been able to offer. For Katrina the nurse, with her short brown hair and ice-blue eyes, it was just the end of another shift. And she was tired. She had to do this final grim task before she clocked out and went home. She'd get a cup of tea, or coffee, or maybe a glass of wine (she seemed the type). She'd kick off her shoes and watch something mindless on the TV. She might even laugh if it was funny.

I doubted she'd think about me and the fact that I was dying. That no more could be done for me. I was already in the past tense for Katrina.

I was feeling sorry for myself, but that was allowed, wasn't it?

I wasn't that old. This shouldn't have been happening yet.

I didn't deserve this.

I wanted to scream that I didn't deserve this.

But it was like there was a tiny voice, or a chorus of voices, whispering in her ear that this is exactly what I did deserve. In fact, I deserved much, much worse.

Chapter One

Heidi

Now

The back seat of my car is full to bursting. Lily is bundled up in her car seat, asleep and blissfully ignorant of the strained atmosphere between her fellow passengers. A weekend bag, filled with pyjamas and underpants to be laundered, a toilet bag containing a razor, toothbrush, soap and shaving foam sits beside her.

A plastic 'Patient's Property' bag sits in the footwell. It's loaded with boxes of medication, dressings, instructions that I will have to will my postpartum brain into reading and understanding once we are back at Joe's house.

I won't call it home. It ceased to be my home the moment my mother died – also from cancer. Unlike Joe McKee, the man who has played the role of my father for the past twenty-one years, she didn't deserve it.

'Did you lift my slippers?' Joe asks as I help him ease his seat belt on. He is still sore – still tender from the operation to try to remove the tumour found in his lung. Except that they found it had company, all through his body. 'Riddled with it,' he said, sadly, when he told me.

'Yes, I lifted your slippers. They're in your bag, along with your pyjamas and dressing gown.'

'There was a book in the locker. Did you . . .'

'Yes, I lifted it as well. And packed it. Along with your prayer book and your reading glasses.'

He nods. 'I wonder how many more books I'll read,' he says, to himself as much as anything.

'You know what the doctor said,' I tell him. 'Take it one day at a time.'

'Those days are still numbered, though, aren't they? I doubt I'll see the spring.'

He looks out onto the bleak, grey car park of Altnagelvin hospital, on the very outskirts of Derry, Belfast in one direction and the city centre in the other. The sky is almost as dark as the tarmac below us. Heavy and angry-looking. It seems apt.

Joe has always liked spring. More so as he grew older and found comfort in God. 'A time of renewal,' he would say as the evenings stretched and the temperatures crept up.

I know as well as he does, there'll be no renewal for him this year.

'You never know,' I say, even though we do know. Odds are he'll be gone before the seasons change.

He shakes his head slowly, looks ahead. 'Some things you feel, Heidi.'

I switch on the engine, nudge the car into first gear.

'It's not a lot of time, is it?' he asks. 'To do all the things I need to do or to make things right.'

Joe McKee could have a whole other lifetime to live and it wouldn't be long enough for him to make things right. There's a time in a person's life, if they are truly, truly wicked, when they move beyond the point of redemption.

I stay quiet. If he's looking for some sort of absolution, he's looking in the wrong place.

Ten minutes of a silent drive home later, we pull up outside his house. The house my mother owned, which in turn will belong to me when he is gone. This is where the first almost ten years of my life were blissfully happy. My mother created a loving, warm and magical childhood for me.

Then she died.

Even all these years later, there are times when that realisation hits me like a punch to the gut.

The world has never seemed fair or right since.

'Will we get you inside?' I ask Joe.

He nods. 'I'm tired.'

He looks pale, his eyes red, dark circles around them. The effort of the short journey has worn him out. He looks wretched. It's almost, but not quite, enough to make me feel sorry for him.

'Sure, we'll get you in and to bed then,' I say. 'Just let me take Lily in first. I don't want to leave her here in the car on her own.'

He nods. 'Of course not.'

I open the door, carry Lily, who is thankfully still sleeping, through to the living room in her car seat and allow myself a few seconds to take some deep breaths. I'm shaking, I realise, but it's not from the cold. I count my breaths in and out until the shaking lessens. I tuck Lily's blanket around her, stroke her cheek. Note how she is filling out, changing. Only five months old and already I can see shades of the little girl she will become.

I do not like being here with Joe. Even in his frail condition, I still feel scared to be close to him.

I've tried to have as little as possible to do with him, especially after I moved away to university at eighteen. But somehow, and much to my shame and self-hatred, I still find myself unable to cut him from my life entirely.

It will be nigh on impossible now, not without appearing to be cold and uncaring. Not without telling people all the things that happened. The things I've tried so hard to bury.

The thought of how much he will rely on me over the coming months make me feel sick to my stomach.

'It must be nice in a way,' the nurse at the hospital had said, 'to care for him now. After all he did for you after your mother died. There aren't many men who would take on the responsibility of someone else's child like that.'

Joe had told her he had only done what any decent person would do.

But Joe McKee doesn't have a decent bone in his cancer-riddled body.

The sweat is lashing off me by the time I have helped Joe upstairs and into bed. I do not like the feel of him leaning his weight on me as I help him up the stairs. I do not like helping him slip off his shoes and socks and lift his feet into bed. He is complaining of the cold, even though the heating is on full and the extra oil-filled radiator in his room is pumping out a dusty, dry heat.

I pull an extra blanket from the airing cupboard and put it over him, offer to make a cup of tea. 'It might bring you round a bit,' I say. I feel I'm speaking the words from a script of what a good daughter should say to an ailing parent.

'It might, aye,' he replies. 'That would be nice, Heidi.'

He makes a move as if he is going to pat my hand and I pull it away quickly. The gesture makes him flinch, but I won't have any physical contact with him that isn't strictly necessary.

I catch him looking at me, his face sorrowful. I wonder if he'll say it, now. The words he's never said in all these years. 'I'm sorry.'

'Maybe . . .' he starts. 'When I've had a rest, maybe you could call Ciara for me? She should know how ill I am. Or maybe you've spoken to her already?'

Ciara. Joe's daughter. His real daughter. The one tied to him by biology. The one he left behind when he moved in with Mum and me all those years ago. She has never forgiven him. Or me, for that matter. We don't speak. I can't remember the last time I saw her face-to-face.

'I've not spoken to her yet,' I tell him. I understand why he thinks it would be easier for her to hear from me first, so I know I'll have to do it. Regardless of the state of her relationship with her father, she has a right to know he is dying. 'But I will. When you wake up. You look exhausted.'

'That's what dying will do to you,' he says with a sad smile.

I don't return it, I just nod and leave the room, head for the kitchen, where I disseminate his various medicines into boxes and baskets for easy access while waiting for his tea to brew.

I've long since given up any idea of religion, but while I'm waiting for the kettle to hiss and rattle, I wish there was a godlike figure I could pray to for the strength to get through the next few weeks without wanting to throw myself off a bridge or put a pillow over his face.

Chapter Two

Heidi

Then

I first met Joe when I was seven years old. He was already sitting at the table in Fiorentinis Ice Cream Parlour on the Strand Road, looking around him at the old photos and pictures on the wall, when my mother and I arrived.

'I've someone I'd like you to meet,' my mother had said.

I remember that she looked happy. That her eyes seemed to sparkle. She'd put on make-up and I could smell she was wearing her favourite perfume – the kind she saved for special occasions. She'd even let me have a little spritz on my wrists. I remember that I was happy for her. Her excitement was contagious and yes, I was a little nervous, too. But that was okay, my mother had told me. It's okay to feel nervous about meeting new people.

I liked the cocooned world my mother and I shared. Just the two of us, with Granny and Grandad popping in occasionally to check on us. To fuss. To ask if we had everything we needed.

My mother's response was always the same. 'Sure we have each other and that's all that we need,' she'd smile.

My grandmother's eyes would tighten so that I could see the fine lines of wrinkles spread out across her face. 'You know I worry,' she would say.

'There's no need to,' my mother would reply.

And there wasn't. We were happy. We had what we needed. A small house with a garden big enough to play in. Food in the cupboards. And if I needed new shoes or a new school coat, or sometimes just because Mum thought we deserved a treat, she would reach into the tin tea caddy on the top shelf of the corner cupboard in the kitchen, lift out some money and treat us.

Occasionally, the topic of my father would come up. Usually around Father's Day, or after we'd watched some schmaltzy family movie. My mother would tell me, as gently as she could, that my father had moved away before I'd been born. 'He wasn't ready to be a daddy just yet,' she'd say, and sometimes there would be a sadness in her eyes about it. 'But that was everything to do with him and nothing to do with you,' she'd tell me.

I suppose I knew she was lonely sometimes. She would read romance novels and sigh, and I knew most of my friends had both their parents living together. I suppose it was understand-able my mother might want to find a partner too, even if she said that we had all we needed to be happy between the pair of us.

But if I was nervous that day in Fiorentinis, it was nothing compared to how nervous this man, Joe, appeared to be. He was fidgeting in his seat and, as he stood up to say hello, he almost knocked over his teacup.

I was as shy then as I am now. I stayed close to my mother, my hand gripped in hers, my cheek pressed against the soft fabric of her coat.

'Heidi, this is Joe,' she said. 'He's a friend of mine.'

The man smiled, extended his hand towards mine. Dark hairs crawled from the cuff of his jacket. They looked like spiders. I cuddled in closer to my mother.

'Heidi, say hello,' she said, an urgency in her voice.

He withdrew his hand and sat down. 'She doesn't have to if she doesn't want to. Isn't that right, Heidi? I'm a little nervous, too.' His smile was kind.

The tightness in my chest eased as he lifted his teacup and sipped from it. I dared to take a step away from the safety of my mother's long, green woollen coat.

'I know it's cold and rainy outside, but maybe you'd like an ice cream anyway? Since we're here?' he asked.

'You'd like that, wouldn't you, Heidi?' My mother's voice was more relaxed again, too.

I nodded.

'How about we get them to make you the biggest ice cream they've got?' he asked and my eyes widened at the thought. There was little that seven-year-old me loved more than ice cream.

'With jelly?' I asked, because jelly came a close second.

'Lots of jelly,' Joe said with a wink, and I smiled at him and then at my mother.

The smile on my face was mirrored on her own. Then I noticed how she looked at him. How her smile was different when she was smiling in his direction. It was how those men and women smiled at each other on the front covers of her romance novels. She was falling in love. I knew it at once.

It was only when he came back from ordering and reached out to hand me the giant ice cream he was carrying that I noticed the glint of a gold ring on his finger.

I may have been only seven, but I knew what that meant. And I also knew he wasn't married to my mother. He was grinning at me. Telling me he asked for extra sprinkles. I could sense Mum beaming at him from beside me. I knew she wanted me to smile, so I did. I remembered my manners just like I'd always been taught, and I thanked him and ate the ice cream. I pretended it didn't suddenly taste a little sour.

Chapter Three

Heidi

Now

I wonder what the official protocol is when it comes to saying no to a dying man. Is it an out and out no-go area, or is it okay in some circumstances?

I chew the nail of my left thumb while I try to build up the nerve to call Ciara.

Alex, my husband, tells me getting her involved might be a good thing. She may be able to lessen any burden on me. Which sounds great, but still I'm not so sure. I'm not sure I have enough emotional energy to deal with a second toxic relationship just now.

I sigh as I realise that despite my misgivings, I have to do this. I just have to suck it up.

Alex is at least sitting close to me as I call Ciara's number. I draw a little strength from him. My hands are shaking, my tummy tight. Even the sound of her voice makes me nervous.

I take a deep breath. Remind myself that she is an adult now.

As am I. I'm a wife and mother, for goodness sake. I should be able to speak to another grown woman without losing my nerve.

But the truth is Ciara has always intimidated me. At times she has utterly terrified me, if I'm being honest. She was the loud to my quiet. The tall to my short. The confident to my terrified. The angry to my sad. She was always bigger and badder and more able to dominate a room than I ever had been or ever could be. She's the kind of person who can shred your self-confidence to ribbons with just one look.

I hear a soft voice say hello in a calming Scottish lilt. 'Hello, Ciara's phone.'

I'm momentarily thrown. 'Hello,' I stutter, 'I'm . . . I'm Heidi Lewis. It's about Ciara's father, Joe . . .'

I hear an intake of breath. An awkward 'uhm', which tells me what I suspected. This phone call will not be welcomed.

'Is she there? I need to speak to her about him.'

'One moment please, I'll check,' the voice answers, efficiently as if she is speaking to a business associate.

Perhaps Ciara is still at work. Maybe this isn't the best time to call. I think about hanging up. It would be easier and I'd have a good excuse to do so.

I'm just about to take my phone away from my ear and end the call, when I hear the calming Scottish lilt replaced by a brusque Derry hello.

'Ciara?' I say, to be sure.

'Yes. It's me. Heidi, what can I do for you?'

She sounds as pissed off now as she did as a truculent teenager. I revert to type and feel inadequate. My tongue feels heavy in my mouth. I feel unable to form coherent sentences.

'Erm, are you still at work? Because maybe, you know, this would be a call better taken later, a conversation . . . you know . . . to have when you're free to talk.'

I sound like an imbecile.

It annoys her.

'I'm at home,' she says, her voice terse. 'What is it?'

'It's your father,' I begin. I wait for an interruption that doesn't come. 'He asked me to call you. Look, Ciara, maybe this really is a conversation better had face to face.' I realise I don't want to tell her. I don't want to have to be the one to say those words to her.

'I'd rather you just spat it out,' Ciara says. 'What is it? Does he need money? Has he met someone else?'

I take a deep breath.

The easiest way to do something you really don't want to is to do it quickly, like tearing off a plaster. That's what my mother would say, so I say the next sentence quickly. Probably too quickly. The words rattle off my tongue.

'It's nothing like that. Ciara, he's not well. He's just been in hospital for surgery and well, the news isn't good. It isn't good at all, I'm afraid. And he has asked me to call you to let you know he'd like to see you if you'd be willing.'

There's a pause. 'Are you telling me he's dying?' Ciara asks, as forthright as she always was.

I nod before saying, 'Yes, Ciara. It's cancer. He's been given maybe three to six months, at best.'

The phone line goes quiet. I wonder if she has hung up, take the phone from my ear to see if the call is still connected.

'Good,' she says eventually, although I hear a trace of emotion in her voice that wasn't there before. 'Good. He's dying. Good enough for him.'

'Ciara . . .'

I start to talk but the line goes dead. She has hung up. I sit staring at my phone, my face blazing, wondering how I tell Joe what has just happened.

Chapter Four

Ciara

Now

'Dinner's ready,' Stella calls from the kitchen.

I don't answer. I'm staring at my phone, trying to process the conversation I've just had with Heidi bloody Lewis. The golden child. It had to be her to tell me, didn't it? It couldn't have been anyone else. He couldn't have spoken to Mum and got her to break the news. No, he was always one to go for maximum impact. Maximum distress.

The bastard.

Anger wells in me and I throw my phone at the sofa, watch as it bounces off the cushion and hits the solid wooden floor with a crack. I'll have broken the screen, in my anger.

'Good enough for him,' I'd said to Heidi. It had been my gut reaction, to feel angry and shocked and think fuck him for getting her to contact me only to tell me he was dying.

He is dying.

My father, for all that word really meant to me, is dying.

'Ciara,' I hear Stella, 'are you still on the phone, only the pasta . . .'

She walks into the room, glass of white wine in hand, and looks from me to the phone on the floor and back to me again. The glass is put down on the table and she is across the room beside me before I can figure out what to say to her.

'What is it?' she asks, her eyes searching my face for information that I'm still trying to process.

'He's dying,' I say, thinking about how the words feel on my tongue. How they sound in my voice. Alien. Weird. Melodramatic.

Her eyes on mine, her blue eyes, deep and dark and able to see the real me. 'Oh, sweetheart,' she says, one hand gently caressing the side of my face. It's her sympathy, not the news of my father's terminal illness, which brings tears to my eyes.

'The bastard has cancer,' I tell her.

One tear falls and she brushes it away with the pad of her thumb.

Stella knows I have a complicated relationship with my father. Or had. We haven't had much of a relationship at all in at least ten years. I've been more than happy about that.

'He wants to see me,' I say as she leads me to the sofa. All thoughts of dinner, or glasses of wine or the movie we had planned to curl up on the sofa to watch, are gone. 'He asked Heidi to call me. Not enough balls to even call me himself.'

That angers me. Maybe it shouldn't. Maybe he is now just a frail old man facing a death sentence and I should give him some leeway; but then again, when did he ever give me leeway for anything? He walked in and out of my life, leaving damage in his wake without so much as looking back. So much damage.

'Do you want to see him?' Stella asks.

Only she could ask that question and not have me bite back at her. She understands me in a world where it feels like no one else does.

I shrug. 'I don't know. Maybe. Maybe I'd like to tell him exactly what I think of him.'

'Or maybe it would help you find your own peace and move on a bit?' Stella asks. 'But, you know there's no right or wrong in this? You do what you want to do. If you want to see him, I'll come with you. If you want to tell him to go to hell, I'll hold your hand while you do it.'

I brush away a second pesky tear, take a deep breath. I'll be damned if he can force me to make a decision like this quickly. Who does he think he is to get his mousey little minion to call me and ask me to come over?

'Is there much wine left in that bottle?' I sit back and ask Stella.

'Not much,' she says. 'But there's a second bottle in the fridge and I'm sure there's another bottle of something in the rack.'

'Okay,' I say, sniffing and sitting up straight. 'That dinner we spent all of fifteen minutes cooking is going to be absolutely ruined if we don't eat it now. So, I say we eat. I don't want to waste any more energy today thinking about that man.'

Chapter Five

Ciara

Then

I was an only child and I was deliriously happy in my only-child status. I was never lonely. I had lots of friends. We lived in a busy street in the Creggan Estate – a proudly working-class area on the west bank of the River Foyle.

There was always someone to play with. Come rain or shine we would be riding up and down the streets on our bikes, or on scooters or roller-skates. We would play 'padsy' or 'tig' and occasionally a gang of us would disappear en masse into one of our friends' houses to watch a movie and eat crisps and biscuits.

I'd seen how friends with a houseful of siblings didn't get the same treats that I did. Or the same attention from their parents, either. I was the apple of both of my parents' eyes – but at heart I was always a daddy's girl.

Right up until the day he left.

At thirteen years old, I experienced the worst, most painful, heartbreak of my life.

It didn't make sense. I thought my daddy loved me. I was his special girl. I trusted him never to hurt me. But then he left – on a Thursday afternoon. I came back from school to find my mother perching on the edge of the sofa, a cigarette in her hand and a tautness to her posture that screamed that something was wrong. Being thirteen, my first thought was that I was in trouble. I braced myself for her to launch into some rant about my messy bedroom or the three pounds I'd nicked from her purse that morning. I expected her to use my full name and though my heart sank at the thought of the rollicking I was about to receive, I was already preparing my best eye-roll and 'But, Mammy . . .' response.

'Sit down, pet,' she said.

It was the 'pet' that threw me. She was hardly going to give out yards to me if she was using 'pet'. I felt a knot in the pit of my stomach.

'Look, there's no easy way to tell you this, Ciara, so I'm going to come right out and say it. I want you to know that I love you very much. And your daddy loves you, too. You're not to doubt that, ever. Okay?'

There was a strange buzzing sound in my ear. I could feel something build up inside of me, a burst of adrenaline that made me want to fight or run. I dug my fingernails as hard as I could into the palm of my hand to try to ground myself. I'd seen enough corny movies to guess where this was going.

'Daddy has moved out,' she said, the shake in her voice belying her true feelings. 'It was a mutual decision and it's just that we don't make each other happy any more.'

'Where has he gone?' I asked. I needed to know where I could see him. When I could see him.

My mother's face coloured. She sagged momentarily before straightening her back again. 'He's gone to live with a friend,' she said.

Of course it wasn't long before I found out that friend was another woman, and that woman had a daughter.

My father had left us to go and be with another family. A family he'd known for less than a year. A family with a daughter for him to love.

My teenage heart hurt so much that I cried until I threw up.

Chapter Six

Ciara

Now

It's two days since Heidi called and I'm now standing, with Stella, outside the front door of my father's house. It's less than ten minutes' walk away from our riverside apartment, but it might as well have been another country for all these years.

I have avoided the shops I know he frequents. Stayed away from the library where he used to work, and where he still liked to spend his mornings drinking strong tea from polystyrene cups and reading over the day's papers.

He holds court there, talks to everyone who comes in. Shares his stories of old Derry and snippets of local history. It's laughable for the man who barely looked at a book when he lived at home with my mother and me. Once he left, he transformed himself. Discarded his working-class persona entirely, lost himself in books. Went back to college. The few old friends he still deigned to spend time with gave him the nickname

'The Professor' because he was considered so learned. He enjoyed feeling superior to them. He enjoyed revelling in their new-found respect for him.

Learned and respected. It galls me to this day.

I feel Stella give my gloved hand a little reassuring squeeze.

I see lights on through the stained-glass panelling of the front door. It might be the middle of the day but it's dull and dark, and January has us firmly in its grip. The darkness is as oppressive as this house looming over us. Semi-detached. With a big back garden. There was a wooden swing set there when I first visited all those years ago – a sure sign of wealth, along with a phone in the hall that didn't have a lock on it to stop anyone from running up a big bill.

I'd felt intimidated then, but that was nothing compared to how I feel now.

'I'm not sure I can go in,' I say to Stella.

'You know you don't have to, but you've come this far. And look, if it feels all wrong, you never have to come back again. Focus on that.'

I squeeze her hand. There's no way I could be here without her by my side. 'Okay, then,' I say. 'Here goes nothing.' I reach up and rattle the brass knocker, and it's not long before I hear footsteps clacking along the tiled floor and see the shadow of a person approach.

I've not seen Heidi in as long as I've not seen my father. She was only a teenager the last time our paths had crossed, in her second year at university. She'd come home for the Christmas break – wherein my father had made a disastrous attempt to have us all round for drinks. I shudder at the memory.

Looking at Heidi now, she looks as if more than ten years have passed. Her face is pale. Tired-looking. There are dark circles under her eyes, and her hair, which clearly could benefit from a wash, is pulled back in a tight ponytail, which does her no favours. Her roots need touching up, I notice. There's a lot of grey there for a woman still in her twenties.

She pulls an oversized grey cardigan around her small frame, wrapping her arms tightly around herself as she does. Her body language screams that she is deeply uncomfortable with this situation.

She blinks at me as if it is taking her some time to put a name to a face. I know I look different now – but not that different. And she had been aware that I was coming.

'Heidi?' It is Stella who breaks the silence – coming to my rescue as she always does. 'We spoke on the phone. I'm Stella, Ciara's partner.'

I watch for any sort of reaction on Heidi's face at the realisation that I'm gay. It has never been something I've advertised. It's no one's business but my own, and Stella's, of course.

Heidi barely blinks. She looks from Stella to me and then takes a step backwards to allow us in. 'Please, come in, both of you,' she says, her voice quiet. 'It's nice to meet you, Stella,' she says. 'And it's good to see you again, Ciara.'

I smile at her because it is what is expected. We both know that what she has said is a lie. It's not nice to see each other at all. I think we could have quite happily existed without ever seeing other again and been perfectly happy.

I hear the cry of a baby, look to Heidi.

'That's Lily,' she says. 'My baby. She's due a feed. If you'll excuse me. Joe's sleeping just now, but I'm sure he would be okay with you waking him.'

'Maybe we'll just wait a bit,' I say.

She nods, looks anxiously towards the living room door where the cry is becoming more persistent. 'Well, you know where the tea and coffee are, why not make yourselves a cup?' she says, and with that she scurries, mouse-like, into the living room, closing the door behind her.

I lead Stella to the kitchen.

'So that's Heidi,' Stella says as she sits down and I switch the kettle on to boil.

'It is indeed. Although she is much more mouse-like than before. And she was pretty mouse-like then.'

'It must be hard for her, with a new baby to look after and Joe to be minding,' Stella says as she looks around the room, taking in the slightly dated décor. I bristle. I do not want to be any part of a 'poor Heidi' narrative. I saw and heard enough of it over the years to be done with it for good. I'm not so much of a bitch that I don't accept she had it rough to lose her mother at a young age, but she has led a life of privilege, and him – my father – he chose her over me. Not just once. But time and time again.

I don't answer Stella. I just make the tea, rattle around the cupboards for sugar. This house is familiar and yet it isn't. It's quieter. Darker. Colder. I think briefly of the angry teenager I had once been. I can almost hear echoes of her stomping up the stairs or slamming the front door. My heart aches for her a little. I wish things had been different.

I turn to hand Stella a cup of tea. I see her shudder.

'Are you okay?' I ask.

'Hmmm, uhm, yes, I think so,' but she doesn't look it.

'You know you're a terrible liar, don't you?'

'Never mind me. It's nothing. I'm being silly.' But I notice she is holding on to the mug of tea for dear life.

'Stella?' I raise an eyebrow.

'Honestly,' she says, 'it's nothing. Someone just walked over my grave. If you could find me a biscuit I'd feel much better.'

I look at her for a moment, sure it's more than that, but I know her well enough to know she won't be drawn any further, so I start to rummage for biscuits in this house that has never been my home.

This has never been a place where I was made to feel particularly welcome.

As a teenager it had felt as if every time I'd visited here I was reminded of just how much I was no longer the centre of my father's universe.

I'd asked him once if I could put some posters up in the spare room – the room I slept in every time I visited. He shook his head. It wouldn't be right, he'd said. He didn't want Natalie to think he was making assumptions. It was still her house, he said. He was just a guest. I didn't understand it, not really. Not at the time. Natalie was always so welcoming. Annoyingly so. She was desperate for me to like her, but that was never going to happen. Not when she had taken him away from me.

I'd left my pyjamas there once, about six months after my father moved in. It was shortly after Natalie took sick, I remember that. I remember I felt, momentarily, sorry for her. I wanted to help more. To do more. I folded them and stashed them under the pillow, waiting for me to pick them up and put them back on. When I came back the following week they were folded and neatly placed in a plastic carrier bag on the end of the bed.

'Now's not the time to make changes,' my father had said. I always wondered who decided that. Was it him? Or was it Natalie? Regardless, I felt a renewed hatred towards them both.

I find a pack of Bourbon creams, pass them to Stella and sit down, the only noise around us being the ticking of the big clock in the hall.

'Do you want me to come up and see him with you?' Stella asks, splitting the biscuit in two.

I think of all the things I need to say and want to say and shake my head. 'I need to do this on my own.'

His room smells of dust and stale breath and illness. The curtains are drawn tight and an electric radiator is pumping out heat into a room that feels oppressively warm. I feel myself break into a sweat.

He is small in that bed of his. So small that for the briefest of moments, I question if he is there at all. I look behind me, half expecting to see him come out of the bathroom larger than life, as imposing as he ever was. Tall, sturdy, full of bravado and his own self-importance.

As my eyes adjust to the darkness, his new shape becomes more apparent. Illness has shrivelled him. He's curled on his left-hand side, his duvet and blankets folded up to his chin. The cancer has carved hollows in his face. His skin sags limply over his bones, grey, thin, wrinkled. His hair is now more salt than pepper.

I step forwards. Slowly. Quietly. As if he might jump up at any moment to shock and surprise me. He doesn't shift. I contemplate leaving. I could close the door. Lie to Stella that I've spoken to him and we have nothing more to say to each other.

But I can't lie to Stella. I don't want to. It's not what we're about. She knows almost everything about me.

He shifts, just a little, a loud sigh accompanying the movement followed by a small groan of pain. My heart quickens. I should let him know I'm here, but what do I say? Do I say 'Daddy', or 'Joe', or 'You bastard'?

I feel tears prick at my eyes. I have to hold in a low groan of pain myself. I'm not sure who I want to cry for most right now. Him, or the little girl I was, who was so hurt all those years ago.

'Dad,' I say softly. 'It's Ciara.'

He should know, of course. I'm the only person who has ever called him 'Dad'. Despite their many years together, Heidi has never given him that title. He stirs. I can almost hear his bones creak as he does so. He's still a relatively young man,

26

only in his early sixties, but the way in which he tries to pull himself to sitting in his bed is more fitting to a man much older. I wince at the sight of him – the thinness of his hands as he reaches out to lift his glasses from the bedside table and put them on.

'Ciara?' he mutters. 'Open those curtains. Let me see you.'

I fall into the role of dutiful daughter quickly, to my annoyance, and pull open the curtains. Not that it makes much difference. The gloom outside is such that the light barely lifts in the bedroom. I reach over and switch on the bedside lamp instead.

Then I sit at the bottom of the bed. Far enough away that he cannot touch me. I have drawn my lines. I have to. Self-preservation is everything.

'I didn't know if you would come,' he says, his hand shaking as he reaches for a glass of water from the bedside table.

I lift it and hand it to him, watching him take a few sips before I take it from him again.

'I didn't know if I would come, either,' I say. There's a harshness to my voice that makes me feel both proud and ashamed of myself.

'Well, I'm glad you did. And Heidi told you, did she? My news?'

'That you're dying? Yes.'

He winces a little at the word dying, as if my uttering it will summon the Grim Reaper sooner.

'If I can get over this operation, I might get back on my feet again,' he says. 'For a while anyway.'

I nod. I don't know what he expects me to say.

'Ciara, I don't have much time, but I wondered if I might have enough time to make things right with you. We've wasted so many years. If there's any chance at all that we can even start to reconcile . . . it would mean more to me than I can say.'

I wait for him to say he's sorry. I will him to say it. I've wanted him to say it for twenty years. Surely now, when time is running out, when he says he wants to reconcile – when he wants that more than he can say – surely now he can force those words out.

Maybe, if he does, I can think about a reconciliation. He's scared now – I can see that in his eyes – in the way he looks at me. I need to know if he is really interested in acknowledging the pain he caused, or if he's just scared of the judgement he'll face from his God.

'Heidi says you have maybe three months. Six at most,' I say, picking imaginary fluff from the blanket on the bed.

'I'll not see six,' he says. 'I feel it. I can feel it getting closer. The cancer's spreading.'

I look at him. There's so much I want to say that I don't know where to start. I could quip that the cancer started to spread a long, long time ago. But I don't.

'I'm scared, Ciara,' he says, his voice weak. Pathetic.

I close my eyes. Just once, Dad, I think. Just say sorry once.

I can feel tears prick at my eyes. A well of emotion I know wants a release rises up in me. It's a mixture of anger and grief and fear. I'm that thirteen-year-old again having her heart broken, asking her daddy to say he loved her enough to stay and that he was sorry that he ever hurt her.

I swallow them down and look him straight in the eyes. He will not see me cry. He will never know how much he hurt me, or how scared I was.

'I'm not sure what you want me to do about that,' I say, not caring in that moment about the icy tone in my voice.

Chapter Seven

Joe

Now

I don't like being in this house alone any more. I used to enjoy the silence. I'd be happy lost among my books, or out in the garden. Now, no amount of books can distract me from the knowledge that my body is giving up on me.

I should have known I wasn't well. Maybe I did and I was in denial. I've felt myself slowing down for the last few months – having less energy, less drive. I was foolish to think, or hope, it was merely my age.

Time is running out and I don't know what's ahead of me. Will it be a painful death? Will I just slip away? What will be waiting for me on the other side? I'm a believer, of course. I believe in a God who forgives all sins when the sinner repents, but is there is a cut-off point in His tolerance for wrongdoers? Are some sins unforgivable?

Ciara has been so cold with me. I'm not sure what I expected. A hug? A tearful reunion? It's been almost ten years or more since we last saw each other. Ten years since she said I was no longer part of her life and never would be again.

I suppose I expected some sign of love. That she cared. She's not the thirteen-year-old girl I moved out on any more. She's a grown woman, old enough to know that adult relationships aren't always straightforward. She should have a bit more savvy by now. Then again, maybe I don't deserve to be forgiven, by Ciara or by God.

Maybe I'll ask Heidi to call Father Brennan for me. Get him to come to the house and provide some spiritual counsel. I'm too sore and too tired to get out of this bed save to shuffle to the bathroom and back again. I'm definitely too sore for a trip to chapel.

What will he think, though, if I tell him? Will he stay impartial as priests are supposed to? Will he dole out the penance of a couple of Hail Marys and Our Fathers and all will be forgiven, or will he never think of me the same again?

The clock in the hall is ticking loudly. I used to find it a comfort – a constant companion on quiet afternoons in front of the fire, reading my books with a cup of tea at hand.

Now, though, it's just reminding me that every second passing is one that I won't get back, and brings me one second closer to facing the judgement of God.

Forgive me, Father, for I have sinned.

Chapter Eight

Heidi

Then

Ciara's face was incandescent with rage. Her blue eyes narrowed. Her mouth set in a snarl. She was lashing out, swiping at him with her arms while he tried to subdue her.

I was standing in the corner. If I could have pushed myself further into it, disappeared through a crack in the plaster, I would have. I was cradling my favourite doll and trying to understand what was happening. My mother was trying to coax me to come and sit beside her, but I'd never seen such rage before and it scared me.

Ciara was angry and Joe was doing his best to mollify her. Although she was thirteen – tall and lanky with a smattering of teenage acne – she started to cry like a baby. To cry the way I wanted to cry at the sound of their raised voices.

'You can't make me be friends with these people!' she howled. 'You can't make me like them. I don't want to be here. I want to go home. LET ME GO HOME!'

She kicked him square in the shins and he let out a roar of pain, while she darted around him and made for the front door. Quick as a flash he went after her, blocking her escape.

'Ciara, pet, there's no need to react like this. Natalie and Heidi just want to spend more time with you.'

'Heidi! What kind of a stupid name is Heidi? Does she live up in the mountains with her granda or something?'

I shrank into myself. I was all too aware of my literary name-sake, but most people had told me how pretty my name was. How unusual. They didn't mock me – not like Ciara was mocking me.

'She's a nice girl,' I heard Joe soothe.

'I'm a nice girl, too,' Ciara yelled, 'but you've left us, me and Mammy, for them. And they let you. Mammy says they're homewreckers.'

'That's enough,' I heard Joe say. It was probably the first time I'd heard real sternness in his voice. 'I understand that you're angry, Ciara, but there's no excuse for such rudeness. Things aren't as simple as your mother would have you believe. We'd fallen out of love with each other a long time ago.'

'That's crap!' Ciara blustered. 'Mammy still loves you. She told me. She cries all the time.'

I glanced at my mother, who was pale. She looked as if she might be sick. I felt as though I might be sick too. I didn't like that Ciara was calling my mammy names. I didn't like that my mammy was being painted as a bad person. She wasn't a bad person. But Ciara looked so sad and scared, and angry.

'Loving someone and being in love with someone are two different things,' Joe said. 'I'll always love your mother, but I'm in love with Natalie now. And she needs me.'

'We need you!' Ciara wailed.

'Not as much as Natalie does,' Joe said and I felt my mother stiffen beside me.

'Joe,' she said, a warning edge to her voice. 'Now's not the time. She's upset. She has a right to be upset.' I saw her give a small, reassuring nod to Ciara, but her face was blazing as if she was embarrassed, or ashamed. As if she had done something wrong.

'Sweetheart, they need to know. They need to know why I have to be here with you,' Joe said. His voice was thick with emotion. 'When you're older, Ciara, you might understand more. I love Natalie, and she's sick. Very sick. And I need to be – no, I want to be – here for her, and for Heidi, because we don't know what time we have left.'

I heard my mother sob as Joe crossed the room and took her hand. I saw the shock and hate on Ciara's face.

Mammy squeezed my hand tight. I heard a small groan, barely perceptible, leave her lips. 'Joe!' she said in an angry whisper before nodding her head in my direction.

I felt as if the ground had just shifted under my feet and things were never going to be the same again. My mammy was sick. They didn't know what time they had left. What did that mean? Did that mean my mammy was dying? No, that was impossible. It was unthinkable. I remember putting my hands to my ears to block out the noise, but it was already too late. The damage had been done. The words had been said and they couldn't be taken back.

Chapter Nine

Heidi

Now

Alex sits on the edge of our bed, taking off his shoes. They clunk to the floor and he kicks them out of his way before standing up to undress.

'That wasn't as bad as it could have been,' he says.

'It wasn't great,' I say, stroking Lily's head as I give her one final feed before bedtime. 'It was awkward.'

He pulls his T-shirt over his head, exposing the fine smattering of hair on his chest, before he pulls back the duvet and climbs in beside me.

'It was always going to be awkward,' he says, leaning over to kiss me on the cheek and then to kiss Lily on the top of her head. 'You haven't seen her in what, ten years? And when you do, it's not under the nicest of circumstances.'

'I suppose,' I say, unlatching Lily from my breast and putting her on my shoulder to try to get her wind up.

'She seemed upset after she saw him,' he says. He'd arrived

while Ciara was upstairs and had sat with Stella until I finished breastfeeding. 'Do you think she'll get involved in his care?'

I shrug. 'I hope so, but I don't know. And that girlfriend of hers wasn't giving anything away.'

'Stella? She seems nice,' he says. 'They seem to be happy together.'

And they do. I saw how Stella had looked at Ciara when she had come back into the room, how she'd held her hand and mouthed 'are you okay?' before I had the chance to ask after her. I saw how Ciara placed her head on Stella's shoulder as they sat together, letting her usually impenetrable guard down for just a moment or two.

'Are you okay?' I had asked as if I hadn't witnessed the interaction between the two of them.

'What do you think?' Ciara had said. Or snapped. It felt like more of a snap.

'It must be a shock for you, all of this,' I added, trying to be polite.

'That's one way to describe it,' she sniffed, looking around the room. 'This house hasn't changed much over the years.'

Her judgement, even though it wasn't the house I lived in, and even though I had no say over the decoration of it, made me bristle.

'Joe's very set in his ways, you know,' I said.

'Actually, I don't know. The man's a virtual stranger to me.'

I felt chastised again and with each answer from her I could feel myself shrinking back into the little girl I was all those years ago who was afraid to speak.

'I'm sorry things have been difficult for you,' Alex said, and it took me a moment to register that he was talking to Ciara and not me. I realised then, as she looked him up and down, that I hadn't even introduced them.

'This is Alex, Heidi's husband,' Stella said, getting in ahead of me with the formalities.

'Oh God, yes, sorry,' I said. 'I should've said.'

'I was able to figure it out myself,' Ciara said, looking at me with something akin to disappointment on her face.

Why was I so useless, so socially inept?

Alex spoke, making up for my tied tongue and awkwardness. 'Look, we appreciate this isn't easy. But we want you to know you're welcome here any time you want. If you want to spend more time with your father. We can get you a key. Heidi is here most days at the moment, helping, but if you'd rather have time alone with him then I'm sure Heidi wouldn't mind.'

'Can Heidi not speak for herself?' Ciara asked.

'I can,' I answered, blushing at having my social ineptitude called out so openly. 'But what Alex has said, it's true. Whatever you need . . .'

'I don't *need* any of this,' Ciara had said, waving her hand around, signifying the house around her and the entire situation. I watched Stella rub her hand, tenderly, soothing her. 'I need to think about it. I'll be in touch.'

Now, with Alex beside me in bed, I can't stop replaying the entire conversation over and over in my head and forensically picking it all apart. Her words. Her tone. The looks she shared with Stella, and Alex, and me.

'You don't think Ciara was sharp? Nasty and bitchy?' I ask him just as Lily produces a momentous burp that rattles her whole body.

'Not overly, Heidi,' he says. 'Given the circumstances. I'm sure she doesn't know her right from her left at the moment.'

'You really don't think she was off with me?'

He shakes his head. 'No, I don't. Honestly. I think she's a person dealing with some pretty major stuff and it's clearly stressing her out. But I don't think it's necessarily aimed at you, personally. Try not to overthink it.'

He takes Lily from me and lays her in her cot before climbing back into bed and switching off the bedside lamp. 'I'm worn out,' he yawns, turning onto his side away from me. 'Try to get some sleep. It will all feel a little more manageable in the morning.'

He drifts off within seconds – I listen to the pattern of his breathing change. I wonder, how can he not have noticed how she was with me? Her resentment dripped from her every word. I'm not overthinking. I'm not always just overthinking.

Chapter Ten

Ciara

Now

Mammy sits wringing her hands together. 'I knew it. I knew there was something wrong and he wasn't telling me. I could feel it in my waters.'

My mother has never stopped loving my father. She might say she has, but her feelings are written across her face every time she hears a mention of his name.

'I didn't think you saw much of him any more,' I say.

She blushes, looks down at her hands, where she still wears the plain gold wedding band he put on her finger almost thirty-six years ago. 'I don't. Well, not much really, but I stopped mentioning it to you because it only seemed to annoy you. I can't believe it, Ciara. He's dying.' Her voice breaks, but she composes herself quickly, taking a deep breath. 'And he wanted to see you? That's good, isn't it?'

'Mammy, he has always wanted to see me. It's me who hasn't wanted to see him and I'm not sure that's changed.'

She bristles.

'He's a dying man, Ciara. I'm sure all he wants is to make things right. You know he adores you. The pair of you were so close when you were little. "Me and my shadow," he used to say. I'd be jealous of it sometimes, you know. You were my little girl but you much preferred going on long walks out the back roads with your daddy than you did baking with me or playing with all the dolls I bought you.'

'Well, I never have been a very girly girl,' I say.

'No, I suppose you never have been,' she says, looking me up and down as if she still can't quite get her head around my gayness.

'But I'll tell you this, Ciara McKee, once he's gone this time, that will be it. There won't be any more chances to say the things you want to say, or hear the things you need to hear. Not everyone gets the chance to know when their time is coming. It's hard, but it's a blessing in its own way. Don't spend the rest of your life wishing you'd said or done something differently.'

The only thing I wish I'd done differently was not to let him have so much power over me and my happiness. Letting him manipulate me and hurt me. And this? Now? The desires of a dying man, this was a masterstroke in manipulation.

'I know I raised you well, Ciara,' my mother continues. 'I know I raised you to be the caring, loving woman you are now. I can't tell you what to do . . .' Her sentence trails off.

She doesn't need to finish it. She is right, she can't tell me what to do, I think. Not that it will stop her.

'For all his faults, he's family,' she says. 'And goodness knows he doesn't have much of a family around him what with your auntie Kathleen being over in England. So maybe he needs us, and he needs you most of all.'

'He has the golden child,' I say petulantly – and I'm immediately annoyed at my childishness. 'Did you know she has a baby now?'

My mother nods. 'I do. And I know as well as you, Ciara, that wee girl doesn't do well under pressure. It would be cruel to leave her to manage all this on her own.'

'It's not as easy as all that, Mammy,' I tell her. 'I have my own pressures, too. Do you think work will be okay with me announcing I'm taking reams of time off to care for an estranged parent?'

She sniffs, shakes her head. 'You practically run the place for them, Ciara. You're owed time off. Take it.'

'That's the problem,' I tell her. 'I do practically run the place. They need me there.'

'Oh, for goodness sake,' she says, in full flow now. 'It's only an art gallery. It's not like you're CEO of a major company or a brain surgeon or something.'

I bristle. It may not seem like much to my mother, but running the small, independent gallery is my passion. Has been for years. But now's not the time to argue with her about the importance of the arts. Nor is it the time to tell her that yes, I may well be owed time off, but I've things I'd much rather be doing than spending that precious time off with a man who I can't stand to be near.

'All I'm saying is, he's your father. He needs you. You need to be the bigger person here.' My mother cuts through my thoughts, neither listening to nor understanding what I've been saying.

I carry a tray laden with a bowl of chicken soup from a tin, a slice of wheaten bread, a glass of milk and an apple. Mammy has already expressed her disappointment to me over the phone that I didn't make the soup from scratch. I'd rolled my eyes so hard I'd given myself a headache. Was it not enough for her that I'd booked a few days off work after all, leaving a nervous assistant to oversee the installation of a new exhibition?

'He's lucky he's getting anything,' I said down the line to

40

Stella, my phone on speaker as I heated the soup and took a spoon from the drawer.

'You know your mum. Always a little bit extra,' Stella said, trying to lift my mood. 'It's obvious she's never tasted your soup before!'

'I make a lovely soup,' I told her. 'Just not for estranged family members.'

'So I take it you won't be sharing your lunch with Heidi, then?'

'She's out,' I'd told her.

She'd scarpered out of the door with that baby of hers in a buggy almost as soon as my foot had crossed the threshold.

'Can't say that I blame her,' Stella said, who'd said the previous day there was something about the house that gave her the creeps.

'It's a feeling,' she'd said when I pushed her to explain further. 'It's hard to put into words, but that house feels sad. Like bad things happen there.'

'Bad things do happen there,' I'd said. 'It's never been a happy place for me.'

'I think it goes deeper than that,' she'd said, 'but look, never mind me. I'm probably just away with the fairies again.'

I replay that conversation in my head as I reach the top of the stairs. Stella has always been intuitive. She jokes that in olden times she would most likely have been burned at the stake for being a witch.

She's right about the creepy feeling under this roof though, especially in this dimly lit hall, the ticking of the clock echoing around the quiet house.

I've kept all conversation with my father functional so far today. Did he need anything? Should I freshen his water? Plump his pillows? Did he need anything picking up from the chemist?

He'd asked me to return some library books for him, pick him a few he had reserved behind the desk. I'd jumped at the chance. Of course I didn't think that in doing so I'd have to listen to the simpering librarian behind the desk wax lyrical on what a wonderful man he was and how he must be a great father. I nodded, made relatively non-committal noises. She'd become misty-eyed.

'A terrible tragedy. He's so young still, and such a good man. They say God takes the good ones first,' she said. 'You must be beside yourself at the news.'

I'd been so, so tempted to tell her that I wasn't beside myself at all at the news. That I'd spent more time than I'm proud of wishing he was dead. A wicked voice inside me wanted to scream: 'The sooner the bastard is in the ground the better.'

I didn't, of course. And for now I'm doing what my mother wants me to do. I am being there for him. Smoothing waters, even though I know no matter how calm the surface, there is an undercurrent threatening to drag me down at any moment.

I take a deep breath. I won't let that undercurrent win today. I plaster something akin to a smile on my face and carry the tray into his room, where he's sitting up in bed, reading a newspaper, his glasses perched on the end of his nose. He needs a shave, but I'll not be offering to help with that. He looks much brighter than he did when I first saw him three days ago. There is some colour back in his cheeks. He smiles back at me. Or leers. It strikes me that there has always been something about his smile that makes me feel uncomfortable.

'Here's your lunch,' I say, sitting it across his lap and making sure he has everything he needs.

I don't want to be in this room with him any longer than I need to be, so I turn to leave.

'Ciara?' His voice is thin and reedy – thinner and reedier than it probably needs to be. 'Come and sit with me. Just while I have my lunch. Then you can get back to hiding downstairs again. Or you can go home. But just give me five minutes of your time, please.'

'Okay,' I say, instantly wishing I had the guts to say no.

'Why don't you sit down, instead of standing there and growing tall? You're tall enough already.'

'I'll go get a chair,' I say.

It might be a good idea to have one here anyway, for visitors. Not that there have been many, by all accounts. Despite his supposed status in the community, the house has been remarkably quiet according to Heidi. All those people who he holds court with, chats to in the street, in the library. They're not really his friends, are they? Where are they now?

'Sure, there's no need for that,' he says. 'You can sit at the bottom of the bed.'

I hesitate. I remind myself that I'm an adult now and I have my own voice.

'I'd rather just get a chair,' I say, clenching my fists tightly to try to stop myself from shaking. Without giving him the chance to argue further, I go and get a chair from the spare room, place it just far enough to the right of his bed that he can't reach it, and sit down. I've left the bedroom door open. I can leave at any time I want, I tell myself.

I watch and listen as he slurps spoonfuls of his soup into his mouth while he tries to make small talk. It's all inconsequential babble that infuriates me. He wants me here, he says, but he doesn't seem to have any intention of saying the things I need him to say.

As soon as he takes his final mouthful and washes it down with the last of his milk, I lift the tray from him and walk from the room, not looking back.

'Would you not just stay another few minutes?' I hear him ask, but this time I find my voice.

'No. I've done what you asked. I have to leave now.' I don't wait to listen to any response – I just get down the stairs and out of the house as quickly as I can.

Chapter Eleven

Heidi

Now

Joe's not getting better. Not the way the doctor's hoped, anyway. I mean, of course, we know that ultimately he is going to die. But they did expect him to recover from his surgery well enough to enjoy some sort of quality of life, for some amount of time.

He's still confined to his bed, six days after coming home from hospital. He doesn't even want to try to manage the stairs, to sit in the living room and maybe watch some TV. He complains he is in pain. He complains he feels sick. He complains he is too tired. He complains he can't sleep. He complains his cup of tea is too hot. Or too milky. Or he wanted coffee instead. He complains the room is too stuffy. Or it's too cold.

It's a constant barrage of complaints, which I feel I have to swallow down. Because he's sick. Because he's dying.

I've tried – I'm still trying – to rally the troops, so to speak, to get help. I've spoken to some of Joe's friends. Asked them if they could maybe take a shift on, a morning or afternoon, or an hour even of looking after him.

They've mostly been too busy. They work. Or they mind their grandkids. Or they have plans but they'll 'see what they can do' and disappear off the radar.

With every 'Sorry, I'd love to but can't,' I feel myself crumble a little.

This house has started to make me itch. I only have to get to the bottom of the drive and I can feel my skin prickle. Everything here is heavy and there are shadows everywhere.

We have, at least, managed to secure a care package for Joe. From next week, carers will visit for fifteen minutes each morning and fifteen minutes each evening to help with personal hygiene and the like. It's not much, but it's something, and I cling to it.

So far Alex has been on hand to help Joe shave every second day. We've put a stool in the bathroom, where he can sit while he brushes his teeth, and each morning I bring a basin of warm water, soap and fresh towels to Joe's room and he washes himself as best he can.

He needs a shower. I know that. But he'll have to wait for that.

Ciara has visited twice. Stayed for a few hours. Seemed to be in the foulest of all moods while she was here. It doesn't help with the atmosphere, so I tend to avoid her. Use the time she's here to get outside and breathe in some fresh air. I walk the length of the quay along the river over and over again with Lily in her pram, waiting for the peace and calm to wash over me that's supposed to come with getting out and about. I'm still waiting.

'Look,' Dr Sweeney says as he sips tea from a good china cup, the kind kept for company. 'He's feeling a bit down, you know. That could be what's hindering his recovery in and of itself. I know the prognosis isn't good, but we need to do what we can to get him to make the most of what time he has left.'

45

I'd nodded, because it was expected. But 'we' all know that 'we' means 'me'.

'He says he gets panicky at night, in case he's unwell and there's no one here to help him,' Dr Sweeney, who has been our family doctor for as long as I can remember, says.

'There's always someone here 'til gone eight,' I say defensively. 'And then I'm here before nine in the morning again. He has a phone. He can call if he needs me.'

I want to add that I'm doing as much as I can. I don't actually want to do any of it. I'd spent the bare minimum of time with him before this illness and I'd very much like it if it was still that way. But of course, I keep quiet.

'Maybe, but he's a frail, sick man. I'm not one to tell you all what to do, but it might be worth talking with other family members about a rota for overnight care. Even in the interim, until he rallies a bit.'

I can't help but roll my eyes. 'Other family members' – as if there's a queue. As if I haven't been spending the last few days calling everyone I know remotely connected with Joe to try to ease the burden on my shoulders.

'I've a young baby to consider, you know,' I tell him. 'But I'll mention it to Ciara. There aren't many more options.'

'You're a good girl,' Dr Sweeney says, a master at being patronising. 'And for what it's worth, babies are very adaptable at this one's age. As long as they've a bed to sleep in at night they don't mind too much disruption to their surroundings.'

I resist the urge to tell him to piss off.

Thankfully he leaves a little later, after eating the better part of half a packet of biscuits and dusting the crumbs onto the floor. As I close the door behind him I hear Joe call from the bedroom and I climb the stairs, each step feeling heavier and harder than the last.

'Yes, Joe?' I ask, opening the door just slightly and peeking in.

'Was that Dr Sweeney talking to you about night-times?' he asks, his face a picture of perfect misery.

'It was.'

'I don't want to cause you girls any more trouble,' he says, 'but it's so hard here being on my own, with only my thoughts to keep me company after you all go home to your happy families.'

'It must be,' I tell him.

'I'll not be round to be a burden on you all for much longer,' he says.

'I'll talk to Ciara,' I say.

'Kathleen said she might come over from England,' he says. 'Maybe you could call her for me. Tell her I'd like to see her. She might listen to it better from you. Come sooner, you know?'

'I'll do that, Joe,' I say, putting my hand to the door to leave.

'Heidi . . .' His voice is soft, setting my teeth on edge. 'Could you pray with me?'

I grip the door handle a little tighter, feel the beginnings of the fight or flight fear set in.

'I've things to do,' I tell him.

'Just a wee decade of the Rosary,' he says. 'It won't take long and it would mean the world.'

I glance out of the door, I don't know why. In the vain hope, perhaps, that someone will come and rescue me. There is no one there, of course, just as there has never been anyone there.

'Please,' he says.

I nod, cross the room and sit on the chair close to his bed. He lifts his red rosary beads and starts to pray, stopping only to encourage me to speak up when I'm too quiet.

I parrot the words, the rhythm and familiarity of them providing no comfort at all. Tears are sliding down my face.

'Pray for us sinners, now and at the hour of our death . . .'

Chapter Twelve

Heidi

Now

Thankfully, I don't have to lay the guilt on too thickly before Kathleen agrees to fly over from England. She'll be here as soon as she can get it all arranged. Maybe her visit will give Joe a bit of a boost, she says to me.

'I'll ask my friend, Pauline, if I can stay with her,' Kathleen says.

I tell her she's welcome to stay at the house, not adding that it would be great if she did so that she could take care of the overnight minding that Dr Sweeney seems to think her brother needs so badly.

'I wouldn't want to get under anyone's feet,' she says, and even though I tell her it would be no imposition, she is firm in her resolution to stay with Pauline.

She stayed here, in this house, back then, when I was a child. For a few months, before she moved to England, if I recall correctly. It was, I think, about a year after my mother died. So

I had been maybe ten or eleven. I can't quite remember. We'd had a strange, strained, relationship. At times she was so loving and caring towards me, I felt as if I never wanted her to leave. I realise now that a part of me was longing for someone to fill the hole my mother had left, but also instinctively knew no one could. I was so lost without my mother, though, I grabbed on to every act of affection tightly.

But then, at other times, Kathleen would look at me as if I was completely incomprehensible to her. An alien child. I'd see no trace of warmth or love. Those times were scary.

I've often wondered if she knew what happened under this roof, if she had any suspicions at all. It's hard to believe she didn't, but it's worse to think that she might have and did nothing about it.

Even though she says she will stay with Pauline, I decide to make sure the two spare rooms are ready. Joe is sleeping and Lily is napping in her pram in the living room, so I decide to kill the time productively. One used to be my old bedroom and the other a guest room. At least they'd be in a decent state for anyone unlucky enough to get landed with an overnight shift.

If nothing else, it gives me something to distract me from my own thoughts, which have a tendency to slip towards darkness and despair a little too often for comfort these days. It's best just to keep busy, I tell myself.

I can't remember the last time I set foot over the door of my old bedroom. God knows when anyone was last in it. There's no doubt it will need to be aired and dusted, especially if there's a chance Lily will have to spend a night here with me.

But even walking to the far end of the landing makes me feel a sense of horrible foreboding and when my foot lands on the squeaky floorboard – the floorboard that used to act as my warning signal – my body tenses.

I take a deep breath and open the door, feeling the cold air hit me. The room has a damp feel to it. A musty smell. I need to air it but it is much too cold to consider opening a window just yet. I shiver and switch on the overhead light, the bulb giving just one pathetic flicker before it pops and dies. I reach for the switch to the bedside lamp instead and thankfully it turns on, although it must be the weakest wattage known to man. A dim, yellow glow lifts the darkest corners of the room but I wouldn't say it is in any way light. Stubbing my toe on the foot of the bed, I swear as I walk around to plug in the small oil-filled radiator that sits by the desk.

We can probably fit a travel cot in here for Lily if the need arises, but apart from that there is only enough space to walk around the bed, open the chest of drawers or sit at the small school desk. Still scored with my childish graffiti, it sits under the window.

An unpleasant burning smell rises from the radiator and I curse myself for not thinking to dust it off before switching it on. I grab an old towel to give it a wipe while I look in the airing cupboard for any suitable bedding to dress the bed with. I decide I'll bring my own, buy new stuff if I have to. I don't want anything he has slept in touching me.

The room doesn't feel like my room any more, although the echoes of my childhood and teenage years are still here, down to the remnants of Blu-Tack still clinging to the walls, where posters once hung.

Sitting on the bed, I look up and see the dolls, which were once the most important thing in the world to me, on the shelf of the far wall. Four of them. Porcelain, pale-faced, dressed in Victorian-style clothes. Ciara hated them. Said they were ugly and gave her the creeps. But when I was younger they were a vital link between my mother and me. She would buy me one each Christmas. 'A little girl deserves a very special doll,' she

50

would say. I'd nod. I loved them. Especially Scarlett, a doll with the darkest black hair and green eyes, in a green velvet gown. She reminded me so of the actress Vivien Leigh in *Gone With the Wind*, my mother's favourite movie, so Scarlett seemed the most apt name.

I can hardly believe I've left her here. I can't believe I reached an age when I am embarrassed by her and the others, too embarrassed to bring this vital link between my mother and me to my new home. I'll get some bubble wrap, I vow. Wrap them up and take them to our house, even though it's small with not enough storage space. We'll find somewhere for them. Maybe Lily might want them when she's older.

I wonder what her granny would have made of her. What she would think of me as a mother. My heart aches for her. Then again, my heart always aches for her.

Chapter Thirteen

Heidi

Then

I was nine and three quarters when time ran out and my mother died.

I remember her death in snapshots. Like looking at old pictures. Moments in time captured forever in my mind, the minutes and hours between just a blur.

It's as if I hear a click of some imaginary camera and I'm in my bedroom listening to a raised voice from the room two doors away. It's not an angry voice. It's something else – something that makes my stomach tighten and my heart hurt. It belongs to my granny, I think, or the smiley nurse who has been visiting each evening. She always gives me lollipops. The taste sours in my mouth.

Click.

'Mammy's in heaven now.' The nurse isn't smiling any more, but her face is soft, sad. Her mouth downturned.

Granny's face looks strange. Twisted. Changed. Her eyes are

red – so red that the blue of her pupils looks almost too bright, like there are lights shining on them or something. She doesn't look like herself any more. I don't think she'll ever look like herself again.

Joe wanders around the house, lost. He seems to stand a lot. Like he has forgotten how to sit down. He looks so sad. He looks how I feel. As if a part of him has died, too.

Click.

I'm on the stairs and I can't understand it. They say Mammy is in heaven, but I know she's in the living room. Lying in that box. I've seen her through the door. It's definitely her. I want to ask how can that be her if she is in heaven, but I'm afraid to. I don't want to make my granny cry again.

Click.

'Who's going to mind me now?' I ask.

Granny is crying. She pats my hand.

'Am I coming to live with you and Grandad? You'll have to get a new house with a bedroom for me.' I'm momentarily lost, wondering what my new bedroom will look like.

'Well, here's the thing,' she says. 'You know how Joe has lived here for the last year helping your mammy and you?'

I nod.

'And he loved your mammy for a year before then?'

I nod again.

'Well, he loves you so much that he is going to stay here and look after you,' Granny says with a smile that doesn't reach her eyes. 'Your mammy talked a lot about it, you know. With me and with Joe, and we all thought it would be easier for you if you were able to stay here. In your own house, in your own room with your own toys.'

I don't want that. He's not my daddy. I don't even like him. Not really. I was nice to him for Mammy. He'd moved in a year ago and everything with Mammy had changed. She spent less time with just the two of us. More with him. And then she got sick.

He doesn't know how to look after me. He doesn't give me cuddles like Mammy did. He doesn't bake me cookies like Granny does.

My lip wobbles. I feel tears settle in my eyes and I'm trying so hard not to blink and let them fall.

'Your grandad and I will always, always be here for you, darling,' Granny says, her voice cracking a little. 'But we're not as young as we used to be. And Grandad doesn't keep well. I'm sure you'd much rather stay in your own house, among your own things, anyway. All your toys. Sure, Grandad and I don't have room for toys.'

'But if you got a new house . . .' I say, trying to keep the pleading tone from my voice.

I watch as Granny shakes her head. 'I'm so sorry, pet. We can't do that. I wish we could, but you will be fine with Joe and we'll always be close by. Always. I promise you.'

'But Joe's not my daddy,' I stutter. 'He wasn't even married to Mammy. He's not my family. I can't stay with him!'

I notice she's crying and guilt swoops in. I don't want to make her cry any more, so I stop talking.

'It will be okay, my angel,' she says through her tears and I will myself to believe her.

Click.

'You have to be brave now.'

He's sitting beside me. My little hand dwarfed in his. His hand is clammy. Sticky. People have been coming and going to the house all day and it's stuffy in here. There's a smell of strong tea and cigarette smoke. People keep looking at me with funny expressions on their face. Telling me I'm a great girl. They bring me sweets and treats as if it's my birthday.

I want to ask them why.

Click.

Granny tucks me into bed. I don't want to sleep. Not with Mammy downstairs in that box. Who is sleeping in her bed? Is Joe there? Who will be there if I wake up in the night? I lie awake, afraid to close my eyes. Will they put me in a box like Mammy, too? Tell everyone I've gone to heaven?

Click.

I'm sitting on my bed and my grandmother is pulling the hairbrush through my hair. She's distracted. The brush keeps catching on knots. It hasn't been brushed properly in a few days. Still, I'm a brave girl. I don't cry out. It seems such a babyish thing to cry about. Especially now.

She has a new dress for me to wear. Black. With ribbon. I hate it. Mammy would never have made me wear something like this. She knew I loved running about in jeans and a T-shirt. Playing in the garden and getting covered in mud.

Click.

A church. It's cold. Everyone is crying and looking at me as if I'm the one making them sad. I want to tell them I didn't do anything wrong. I didn't hurt Mammy. I swear I didn't! But Granny has told me to be on my best behaviour.

'I won't be able to cope if you don't behave,' she said.

I'm angry. I want to tell her I always behave. I'm always good. I always do exactly what I'm told.

Click.

He sits on the edge of my bed. His jumper smells of beer and stale cigarettes again. It makes me feel sick, as if I might throw up. The last people have left the house. Why has it been a party? Cake and sandwiches and the grown-ups drinking. Someone singing and laughter ringing out every now and then. My mammy is dead. I don't understand.

I pull away from him as he tries to hug me. I don't want him near me. I'm fed up with grown-ups. His hands are still clammy.

'You're not to worry. I'm not leaving you. I'll make sure you're okay.'

I hold my tears inside me, give in to his hug. I'll be a great girl. And a brave girl.

Just like Mammy would want.

Chapter Fourteen

Joe

Now

There's not a single person in this world who hasn't made a mistake. Who hasn't done something they are ashamed of. Anyone who denies this is a liar.

I've not always done the right thing. I've absolutely done the wrong thing a few times. Some of these things for the right reasons. Or I thought so at the time.

Like when Natalie was sick. She was in so much pain. So wretched. It hadn't been that hard to get my hands on some extra morphine for her. I suppose things weren't as rigid then as they are now.

I was trying to help. I still believe I did help. I took her pain away, and then I stayed because even though I knew it was good and humane that her suffering was over, I was still overcome with guilt.

Each and every time I saw Heidi look up at me, her eyes wide, her face pale. Her grief too painful to watch, I wondered if I'd done the right thing. I'd taken a mother from her child.

So I stayed. Did what Natalie had wanted. She'd begged me, you see. 'Make sure Heidi is okay,' she'd say, knowing her own parents weren't fit to look after the child. Natalie was so terrified that Heidi would end up in care. Bad things happened in care, she said.

She'd had faith in me. She was foolish, too. I tried to be good, but I was – I am – only human and I am flawed.

But I've fought my demons. That has to count for something, doesn't it? I rehabilitated myself. Found God. Asked for His forgiveness for what I did to Natalie. What I did for Natalie.

And I lived a good life. I thought it would make a difference, but in the end it seems it doesn't matter what you do for people, it's never enough.

No one realises how hard this is. What a burden it is. Temptation is everywhere. Urges don't just go away, you know. I had to content myself with looking and not touching, but I did that because I wanted to prove I could change.

I was prepared to wait for forgiveness. I've been very patient, but time is running out and now I think there's a cruelty to them that they aren't prepared to let go of.

How do they not see how hard it was for me, too? How it ate me up inside? Because it did. I hated myself for years. It almost destroyed me, almost drove me to suicide.

I was a victim, too. I didn't ask to be born this way.

I wasn't perfect. I did so much for them that they will never bring themselves to acknowledge.

The selfish, spoiled little bitches.

Chapter Fifteen

Ciara

Now

Auntie Kathleen is far changed from the confident, fashion-conscious, funky auntie who I hero-worshipped through my childhood and into my teen years.

Looking at her from across the living room in my father's house, I feel shocked at her distinctly middle-aged appearance. She can't be any older than her mid to late forties, but she dresses like someone in their late fifties or sixties. Gone are the short skirts, the big hair, the coloured tights and bright make-up. Instead, a woman with the same salt-and-pepper hair as my father sits in sensible black trousers, a pale pink jumper over a crisp white blouse and black shoes, which owe more to comfort than style, on her feet. The only jewellery she wears is a pair of pearl stud earrings and her plain gold wedding band. She wears no make-up and I can't help but notice that her eyebrows could use a good reshaping.

She's smaller, too, than I remember. A remnant of the person she was, or am I just remembering it all wrong? Sometimes I don't know what I remember any more.

She looked lost when she arrived at the airport. I'd gone to pick her up and had been waiting for her at arrivals, when I saw this rather wretched-looking creature walk through the security doors blinking as she glanced around. She looked pale, tired and old, and she'd promptly burst into tears when she saw me.

'I can't believe it,' she'd said over and over, to the point where I wanted to scream at her to stop talking.

She was quieter in the car, lost in her thoughts for a while. Then she asked about me. About Mum. About Heidi. How she was coping.

'She is okay, isn't she?' Kathleen asked. 'You know, stable?'

'She seems to be,' I said, which was the truth. I don't think I was ignoring any warning signs just because it suited me to have Heidi doing the lion's share of looking after Joe.

'Because we have to be careful,' Kathleen said. 'You know she's fragile.'

Yes, I knew Heidi was fragile. Everyone kept reminding me, not that I needed telling. For a year or so when she was a teenager our entire existence had revolved around 'poor Heidi' and her fragility.

'She's a different person now,' I said, as if I knew her well enough to comment authoritatively on her mental wellbeing. 'Her husband seems to be lovely and she's focusing on her baby.'

Kathleen made a noise that was at best non-committal. 'I don't know,' she'd said. 'I wouldn't want to push her too far.'

I'd tried to draw her further on what she meant, but she clammed up. Refused to say any more. Frustrated, I'd switched on an audiobook through the car's Bluetooth system and tried my best to lose myself in it as we drove the rest of the way home.

Of course, when Kathleen had finally seen my father, she'd collapsed into a paroxysm of grief. 'My poor big brother,' she'd wailed, pulling him into a hug and then apologising as he'd winced from the pain. I'd winced, too. The show of emotion ringing hollow in my ears.

But she's calmer now as she stands in front of the fireplace, orating on palliative care and family responsibility.

'Perhaps we could put our heads together and think of things that might encourage him out of that bed and back into the world for another bit. Maybe we could get him to make a bucket list. You know, things he'd really like to do while he can. We could try to make them happen.'

She seems so determined she can make a difference. That taking him on some poorly thought-out adventure might save him that I almost feel sorry for her.

She's also assuming the rest of us have the same desire to have him around for as long as possible as she does.

'Do you have any ideas?' she asks to the silent room.

I see Heidi bow her head like the shy girl in class desperately hoping the teacher will have forgotten she exists and skim past her. I feel a sense of dread build as her gaze falls on me.

'Ciara?'

'Dad and I aren't very close,' I tell her, which of course is a gross understatement. 'I've no idea what he might want to do.'

To my annoyance, I feel the warm glow of shame rise in my cheeks.

'He's still your dad. You must have some ideas.'

I know when I was little he liked books and gardening. He liked being the centre of attention. He liked people thinking he had brains to burn. Country walks. Talking about himself. Wildlife documentaries. Hurting people. Manipulating their feelings. Leaving.

'I don't know,' I say, shaking my head. 'Maybe a drive to the beach. A visit to the museum,' I say with a distinct lack of enthusiasm.

'We could try to get him down to the library, to see his old friends,' Stella suggests and I could kiss her for trying.

'I was going to take him out for a pint, if he was well enough,' Alex offers.

Heidi stays silent.

It's all pretty mundane as far as a bucket list goes, but at least it feels doable, and without too much effort or time spent with him.

'Those are all great ideas,' Kathleen says, nodding a little too enthusiastically given the dull nature of our suggestions. 'I think it's worth really focusing on the fact that the thing he needs most of all right now is all of us pulling together to support him. I know you girls are young and have enough going on in your lives, but in the great grand scheme of things it really doesn't amount to an awful lot of time. Then he'll be gone and you'll never have to think of him again.' Her voice cracks as she looks at us all.

Auntie Kathleen induces guilt well, raised as she was in the thrall of Irish Catholicism. But for the same reasons she will be crippled by her own guilt, too. She hasn't been a frequent visitor over the years, leaving for England some sixteen or seventeen years ago and rarely making the journey back, even when a flight could be bought for less than a bus fare.

'We should probably help him get his affairs in order,' a quiet voice from the other side of the room speaks up. 'I'm sure there are lots of things he needs to tie up. Financial matters. His belongings. If he has a will . . .'

I stiffen, looking at Heidi, who stares right back at me.

'I don't know if we have to worry about that just yet,' I say, even though a part of me is impressed that little mouse Heidi can squeak, after all.

'Well, I think we do. We can dance around it all we want,' Heidi says, 'but we know there will be upset when he's gone. I'd rather we're all prepared for it. I'll be hoping to get this house on the market as soon as possible.'

I hear Kathleen gasp. Even Alex can't hide his shock at the manner in which his wife has spoken. I'm shocked myself. Simpering Heidi who has been at his beck and call all these years. It strikes me for a second that this is actually how she has been since I first visited. Restrained. Cold. No hint of personal grief.

'I don't think that this is the time or the place for this discussion, sweetheart,' Alex says, looking at her, a confused expression on his face.

'This is exactly the time and place for it,' she says, her voice growing in confidence. 'I want everyone to be very clear about what will happen after. This is my house, as outlined in my mother's will, and when Joe is dead, I will be selling it. As soon as possible. I'll do my bit by him while he is alive, but that's it.'

I feel Stella reach out and take my hand, but my fist is clenched tight.

'I'm sorry if anyone finds that upsetting, but that is the way of it. And it's better to be honest and prepared than to deal with more upset after his death. The lines are very clearly drawn.'

'Heidi.' Alex puts his hand on her knee as if to quiet her.

She pushes it away.

'No, Alex, I'm not being insensitive. I'm being honest. Someone has to be honest about this all. We're all dancing around, afraid to say what needs to be said. Joe is not a nice man. He's not a good man. He has been a cuckoo in this nest for too long.'

Kathleen looks as if she has been slapped squarely around the face. I watch as she stands up and walks out of the room.

I can hear the sound of her crying just as I hear her climb the stairs.

I can hear Stella asking if I'm okay, but it's almost as if I can't quite understand what I'm feeling any more.

Heidi gets up and storms out of the room, Alex following her. I hear the back door open and I just sit and try to process everything that has just been said.

But I can't escape the truth. I might be shocked at Heidi's outburst, but she is only speaking the truth. My father is not, and never could be, a good man.

The only person I'm truly angry at is him.

Chapter Sixteen

Heidi

Now

I have stopped, dead in my tracks, at the edge of the lawn in the back garden. I swallow a lungful of the damp night air, shuddering as I exhale. I've not realised until now that I am shaking. The sound of heavy footsteps on the gravel behind me makes me jump. I brace for impact. For a clip to the back of the head. For admonishment that I had run away and good girls don't run away.

Good girls show gratitude.

Good girls behave.

'Your mother would have wanted you to behave, that's what would have made her happy.'

My breathing changes, becomes shallow, short gasps at the air that feels moist and heavy and cold. It's as if I am consuming coldness and it is filling my veins until my shaking becomes more violent.

Maybe Alex is right. Maybe this isn't the right time or place, but I'm struggling to hold this all in now. I'm struggling with the weight of keeping quiet, of talking about bucket lists and making him happy.

Joe McKee does not deserve to be happy.

He does not deserve to leave this world peacefully, thinking he is absolved of all of his sins.

The steps grow closer. Heavy breathing. I sense anger. I feel it grip me.

'Heidi.' Alex's voice is hard and cold.

I turn to look at him – see disappointment and anger in his eyes.

'Was there really a need for that?' he asks.

I blink back at him. My usual reaction is to say no. To apologise. To push down at the feelings and all the memories that weigh heavy on my chest every single day. But it feels different now and I want to tell him. I want to tell him everything – even though it will change our lives. I want to be brave.

'Yes,' I tell him. 'There was a need for it. All this, what we're doing, Alex. It's all bullshit. While he lies up there, being waited on hand and foot. The people he hurt are running themselves into the ground trying to make his last few months bearable.'

'You keep saying that,' Alex says. 'That he hurt people. That he is a bad man. But why, Heidi? He's a bore, for sure. He takes advantage of your good nature. He holds political and religious beliefs that I don't agree with it. But a bad man? He raised you for years. He didn't have to.'

I open my mouth to tell him. Know it would shut him up. But then, what if it changed how he thinks of me? Would he be angry that I've kept it from him? And all those people, Kathleen included, who thought I was mad, that I was a naughty little girl who told lies for attention, would they tell him all about the girl I was? The trouble I caused?

The fire I started. If I close my eyes I can still taste the acrid smoke as it started to choke me. Still remember heavy hands, pulling me away. Still remember kicking out at them. I just wanted it all, myself included, to burn.

How could he look at me the same if he knew it all? At best, he'd see me as a victim. At worst, he would see someone who had been driven to madness. Would he ever be able to trust me to be alone with Lily? I know I had struggled while pregnant with those same fears – fears that were allayed for me the moment she was placed on my chest and I knew I'd do everything to protect her. To protect my family.

I feel a bubble of shame and grief and anxiety rise up. I see Alex search my face for an answer, but it's not one I can give right now. Not without ruining everything.

'You're right,' I say, and I know my voice sounds funny. Angry. Frustrated. 'You're always right.'

And still he searches my face for signs of the truth and I just look at him, not daring myself to talk, until he gives up. He throws his hands in the air, then plunges them deep into his pockets as he turns away. 'I think I hear Lily,' he says. 'I'll go check on her.'

I know as well as Alex does that Lily isn't making a noise, he just needs an excuse to leave. I stay in the garden, even though it is starting to rain. Fat drops of ice-cold rain land on my face, stinging me where my skin is rough and sore from the tears I didn't even realise I had been crying.

They start, as these things do, slowly at first. Little drops. Warning signs leaving me enough time to get inside if I want to. It's like they're telling me to go. To run. Take shelter. Now they come in greater numbers, but still I know I can get into the house relatively untouched if I just move. But I can't move. I'm frozen in the middle of all this and the rain rushes at me, soaking me through to the bone until I am so wet, so icy cold that the hailstones that have started to fall don't hurt. I am untouchable. I don't care about the storm. I have always been right in the middle of one.

Chapter Seventeen

Heidi

Now

I offer to make Alex a cup of tea when we get home. He refuses, says he is tired and takes Lily from me and goes upstairs. We barely spoke on the drive home and I can't shake the feeling that everything is slipping out of my control.

I'm tense and even though my body aches with tiredness, I know I've gone past any notion of sleep, so I make myself a cup of very milky tea and curl up in front of our gas fire watching the faux flames flicker and dance. Ironic, really, that I can find flames comforting.

Well, ironic or worrying. One of those.

I think of the chain of events that led to that point – when I ended up in hospital, missing the second semester of my first year at university and having to start all over again come the spring.

Did it all start that day in Fiorentinis? Or the day my mother died? Or was it the first time he came into my room to 'comfort' me?

So much is blurry now, you see. After all these years. But some details are crisp and clear in my head and they never leave. The senses of things. Smell. Touch. Pain.

I shake my head, trying to shake all those memories from it. If only it were that easy.

But it's not, of course. And it's only going to get harder over the next week and months. I have to find a way to cope, otherwise I'll not only push Ciara and Kathleen further away, but I'll also push Alex away. That is truly unthinkable.

I have to stop taking my anger out on other people. Even people such as Ciara and Kathleen. People I'd tried to make like me all those years ago. People I'd wanted to love back then, but who never loved me back. I owe them no loyalty, but they aren't responsible for what Joe did any more than I am.

Eventually I drift off into something approximating a sleep, only to be woken at 4 a.m. by a hungry baby in need of a feed. When I've satisfied her needs, I climb into bed beside my husband and whisper to his sleeping form that I love him, and our daughter, more than he could ever understand.

When morning comes, I apologise to him for being insensitive. I tell him I'm stressed but I love him. He pulls me into a hug, kisses the top of my head and whispers that he loves me and just wants me to be happy. I stop myself from crying. I just plaster on a smile, tell him I am happy and send him on his way to work.

I have the same fake smile plastered on my face when I arrive at Joe's house and offer an apology to Ciara and Kathleen, which I'm making to try to smooth the waters.

'I'm sorry if I came across as clinical and cold last night,' I say, trying my best to maintain eye contact even though it is almost physically painful to do so. 'This is difficult. For us all. I was feeling stressed and I didn't mean to upset anyone.'

They nod and we sit in uncomfortable silence until we hear

the tinkle of the bell Kathleen gave Joe to summon us when he needs anything.

Ciara is first to her feet. I take the break in the awkwardness as a chance to move myself.

'I'll peel some potatoes for dinner. There's chicken and veg there, too,' I say, getting up and going to the kitchen, where I pull the bag of spuds from the vegetable rack and look for the peeler.

Kathleen is behind me before I've had the chance to shed even one slice of skin from the mud-covered potato in my hand.

'Can I ask you something, Heidi?' she says, and I turn to watch her sit down, wincing as she does so, on one of the kitchen chairs. 'My knees,' she says, rolling her eyes. 'Seems all that road-running has left them in a bad way.'

I mumble something sympathetic and wait for the big 'something' she wants to talk to me about.

'Why do you hate him?' she says eventually, her eyes sad. 'You always did. All those years when he just tried to look after you. You made it so hard for him, you know, but he never gave up on you. You never give him credit for that. I know he's not perfect. Believe me. But does he really deserve to be hated?'

I blink at her. I don't know what to say. Can she really not know?

I shrug, feeling a tingle of nervousness start at the top of my spine, enough to send little shockwaves through my head.

'That's it?' she says with a strange laugh. 'A shrug to explain it all.'

I shrug again, scraping at the potato with the peeler, not realising that my finger has moved perilously close to the blade. One strike and I take a layer of skin with it, yelping as I do so.

The sight of blood, which comes before the sting of the cut, makes me feel woozy.

Kathleen, sore knees and all, jumps to her feet, forces my bleeding finger under the running tap, and I watch the water turn pink, mingling with the soil from the potatoes as it hits the steel surface of the sink. I watch it. I feel the pain bite. I'm reminded of a release. Of a coping mechanism. Kathleen pulls my hand from the water, wraps a clean piece of kitchen towel around it, squeezing tight. So tight it's painful.

'Hold that for a bit,' she says. 'We'll get a proper look at it in a minute. Does Joe have plasters?'

I nod to the thin cupboard beside the cooker, where Joe stores an old tin first-aid box.

'I . . . I'm sure it's just a scratch,' I stutter. 'I was . . . I was distracted.' I can see the crisp white kitchen towel start to colour with my blood. I need to sit down.

'You certainly were,' Kathleen says, pausing for a moment, looking at me intently.

She hands me some more kitchen paper, then sets about fishing in the first-aid tin for a suitable dressing.

Chapter Eighteen

Joe

Now

They've all been to see me today. My 'family', for what they are. The daughters who don't seem to care too much. The sister who hovers around me. Fidgets as she talks. Babbles. Annoys me. The drippy husband. Talks about going for a pint. And that woman – the deviant my daughter is with. I can barely look at her, never mind tolerate her faux sympathy.

All these conversations take place that mean nothing but seem to teeter close to the edge of something else.

The day has been painfully long. Bookmarked with the times when I'm allowed to take medication to make everything go fuzzy again for a while.

I've tried to read a little, but my eyes won't focus for long enough – and I'm finding myself having to read and reread the same passage over and over again. None of it making sense.

Every now and again I hear raised voices. The cry of that baby. A phone ringing. Doors closing and opening. A whole world carrying on within earshot, but excluding me all the same.

The rain is getting heavier outside. I can hear it batter against the windowpanes. It's a noise I used to find comforting. But not now. Now, I can hear that there is a storm brewing.

I take my medication. Feel it numb me and lull me to sleep, only to wake with a jolt. With a feeling of pressure. Choking me. Making me gag.

It's said your life flashes before your eyes in the moments before your death. That your electrical synapses fire, pulling memories from the innermost depths of your brain and flooding your senses with them.

There are no flashbacks now, but I know that I am dying.

I know there is no way out.

There are no visions of long-lost relatives reaching out to me between dimensions.

There is no angel of death to help me move between worlds, either. There is someone here, of course, but this person is no angel. They're not guiding me towards a soft beam of light. There is no sense of peace.

No sense of forgiveness or redemption.

There is just fear. Disappointment.

Grief that it has all come to this.

I fight, even though I'm weak. I had been sleeping, but now I feel the weight of something on my face. A pillow, perhaps. It's soft but it's not malleable. There's no give in it. No matter how I turn my head, it is there and it won't move.

There is a fierce, unquenchable burning in my lungs and a pressure on my chest. Is someone kneeling on me? Has someone placed a weight on me? I'm pinned down. Is there more than one person in this room? I'm trying my hardest to orientate myself to the space around me, but I can't. I try to cry out but I can't. I can't breathe. I can't make a sound. I hear a voice I can't place, muffled, almost drowned out by the increasingly loud thumping of my heart. I can't tell if it is man, woman or beast. It feels as if my chest will open, my lungs explode or burst into flames.

The Devil, I think, the Devil is in this room and I can feel his flames threaten to engulf me. I know where I'm going and all those years of kneeling at the altar rails haven't made a difference.

'Repent, then, and turn to God, so that your sins may be wiped out,' the Bible says. Maybe God knew what I wouldn't admit – the sin was always in me.

I want to breathe. I need to breathe. I need oxygen. I need to live.

I am trying, thrashing. My hands are fisting the bed sheets trying to gain purchase on something, on anything, on this life. The voice again, indistinct, muttering words I cannot hear. But they are not words of love. I know that much.

This person is weighing me down, I realise, jabbing their bony knee into my chest, close to a wound that's not yet healed, that I can feel start to pull and strain against the pressure. Everything is tearing. Everything is burning and still they don't stop. They keep going. I try to suck air in, even the smallest amount. Just enough. I just want enough. I don't need more. I just want to live.

But I can feel it all slipping away. A dizziness washes over me, tingling. A sensation, almost as if I'm floating, as if I could just drift away. And the pain stops, you see. My lungs stop burning. I stop needing to breathe in. There is a moment of relief.

Of false hope.

There is a moment where I'm between this world and the judgement that awaits me.

Then the darkness stretches out in front of me.

74

Chapter Nineteen

Heidi

Then

Joe McKee was a clever man. He was very good at making people believe he was a nice person. I learned that very quickly. People always smiled when they saw him in the street. They would stop to talk to him, and he would listen intently to their news and offer his nuggets of wisdom, or reassurance or condolence as appropriate.

I quickly lost count of the number of times I heard people say: 'You're a sound fella, Joe,' and they'd pat him on the back. Sometimes they'd slip a shiny fifty pence piece into my hand and tell me to treat myself to something. They'd give me a sympathetic look and pat me on the head. I'd smile and thank them, because that was what was expected, but I never bought sweets, not with that money. That money always felt like a consolation prize.

I'd started to think that the whole world must have known was what happening in my house. That they couldn't be oblivious to the fact that I was a troubled child, that something was badly wrong. I started to think that they either didn't care or maybe, worse than that, this was something that happened to all little girls and just nobody ever talked about it.

Like how nobody ever talked about the fact that Santa wasn't real. I learned that one quickly too, the year my mother died. Instead of the lovingly wrapped pile of presents under the tree, there were some books and a selection box. New underwear wrapped up in crinkly Christmas paper. Pants and vests. Nightdresses, when I preferred pyjamas. A board game, something we would have to play together, because I never, ever asked anyone to come back to the house with me. I was too scared to. Imagine they found out? Imagine if he hurt them, too?

No, it was better to go it alone. And I had my dolls for company. And I had my growing collection of fifty pence pieces, which I saved in a spare Trócaire box I'd taken from school. If I saved enough, maybe I could get a plane ticket and fly away to America or somewhere. Then I'd write to my granny and grandad and tell them I was safe and happy, and maybe they would come and visit me.

I'd never tell Joe, though. Never, ever tell him where I was.

So it broke my heart, and my spirit, the day I came home from school to find Joe standing in the living room, in front of the fire, the Trócaire box, used to collect money for charity during Lent, on the mantlepiece.

It was May, I remember that. It had been a sunny day. Warm. I'd made a daisy chain at school and I was still wearing it around my neck when I got home. I had a sense of things being, maybe, possibly okay. That things were going to be okay.

Then I saw him. Saw the expression on his face. Thunderous. Not the smiling, genial 'sound fellah' everyone thought he was.

'Would you care to explain this?' he said, thrusting the box at me, a picture of a starving African child, eyes wide, staring at me.

'I was just . . .' I was trying to think. How to tell him I was saving to run away. How I never wanted to see him again. Or what to say so he wouldn't know my plan, after all. That I would still have a chance to get away with it.

But I didn't get past those three words.

'You were just what, Heidi? Stealing? From a charity? From these starving children?' He thrust the box at me, so close to my face that I closed my eyes in anticipation of an impact that didn't come.

'That's not what . . .'

'I know people feel sorry for you, poor little girl, having lost her mammy.' He spat the words at me. I felt flecks of his spittle hit my face, his coffee-tainted breath fill my nostrils. 'But this! This is despicable. I have never been more ashamed of anything in my life. After all I've done. After all I do and you steal from a Christian charity from people who have nothing?

'Maybe you'd like to live out there, Heidi, starving, sick, alone. Then you might stop being such a selfish, moody little bitch! May God forgive you for what you've done!'

He grabbed me by the arm so tight that I feared it would break and he hauled me through the house, the Trócaire box in his other hand, and into the street. He let go only to open the car door and then he practically threw me into the back seat, my head colliding with the sill of the door as I fell. The skin of my bare legs burned against the hot leather of the car seat and I tried to curl up.

'Sit properly, girl, or so help me!' he hissed, of course keeping his voice low enough that no neighbour out mowing their lawns or soaking up the sun could hear the vitriol with which he spoke.

He wouldn't tell me where we were going, and I dared not ask more than once. Soon we were at the parochial house and he was hauling me from the car, my daisy chain breaking and falling to the ground, trampled over by his heavy shoes as he dragged me to the door.

'Now, Heidi, you are to tell Father Campbell what sins you have committed and you are to beg him for his forgiveness. You wicked child, it's a good thing your mother is dead so she doesn't have to be humiliated by how badly you've turned out.'

Father Campbell was an old school priest. Small, round, hunched with his white hair that seemed to sprout as much from his nose and his ears as it did from the top of his head. He didn't ever speak during Mass, he bellowed as if he had the power to bring forth hellfire on command. Every child I knew lived in mortal fear of Father Campbell and I was no different.

My legs were wobbly beneath me, my arm aching from Joe's tight grasp as he dragged me towards the large wooden door of the parochial house. I couldn't help but cry, even though I was trying so hard to be brave. I always tried to be brave no matter what, but this . . . It was beyond me.

I prayed with all my power that Father Campbell wouldn't be in. That Father Brennan would answer the door instead. He was young then, new to the fold, considered to be approachable. He told funny stories when he visited us at school. I might have a chance of him believing me.

But it wasn't Father Brennan who answered the door. It was Father Campbell, who glowered at me from beneath his heavy-set eyebrows as Joe told him of his deep shame at finding the 'stolen' Trócaire box and money in my room.

I don't know which scared me most. The abuse I took from Father Campbell, who told me hell had a place waiting just for nasty little thieves like me – a place where I would be shown no mercy for stealing from innocent, starving children. Or the fact that Joe handed over my savings, my escape route from all this, to Father Campbell and my hope of getting away was gone.

The beating I got back at home could not have broken me more than the loss of that money. The beatings I knew I could take as long as I knew I could get away some day.

Of course, what followed the beating was worse. The creaking of the floorboard and Joe, his face a picture of misery at my door, telling me he was sorry. That he had done it only for my own good, you see. I had to learn. I had to be a good girl. Then he crossed the room and even as I cowered from him, he climbed into the bed beside me.

Chapter Twenty

Heidi

Now

'The roads will be icy,' Kathleen says. 'You'd better be careful if you're heading out in it.'

She has barely spoken to me since our earlier conversation in the kitchen and the drama of me cutting my finger. She keeps looking at me, though, and I don't like how exposed I feel.

'I think maybe I'll stay here tonight,' she says to no one in particular. 'The chances of getting a taxi won't be great.'

'We can drop you to Pauline's,' Alex offers.

I don't give out that dropping her to Pauline's will take us at least ten miles in the opposite direction of home.

'I wouldn't want to put you to any trouble,' she says, her voice meek.

'It's no trouble at all,' Alex says.

'You're very kind,' Kathleen says, yawning again.

She's exhausted. We're all exhausted. None of us are sleeping well. I can tell just by looking around the room. Dark circles and bags under our eyes. Pale skin, bodies stiff with tension. We're no further forwards in coming up with a cohesive plan about Joe's care, but we are at least faking an air of mutual respect. No, not respect. Tolerance. We are tolerating each other.

'You go on,' Ciara says. 'We'll stay here tonight, Stella and I. In the spare room.' She looks me square in the eyes as she says this.

Is she marking her territory on this house? Still sore from my outburst yesterday. I've apologised so there's nothing I can do, or am willing to do, to appease her further.

'Well, we should get going, then,' I say, more keen than ever to get away from this house and the stifling atmosphere.

'I'll get Lily from upstairs,' Alex says, standing up and stretching before going to get Lily from my old bedroom.

I don't want to be left alone with the others, so I set about packing up Lily's things and putting my coat on. I'm in the hall, cramming a pale pink blanket into the top of her changing bag, when Alex appears at the top of the stairs. His face is pale, his eyes wide. He isn't carrying Lily and for a moment I feel my heart sink to my stomach and fear grip me.

'Lily?' I mutter. 'Where's Lily?'

I feel my head start to spin. Why doesn't he have Lily? The look on his face. Something bad has happened. My knees start to go beneath me. He can barely speak. He shakes his head slowly.

I think I might throw up. It feels like minutes, hours even, are passing when really it can only be a second or two. Then he speaks.

'It's Joe,' he says.

A guttural cry breaks forth from my chest – and it's not for Joe. It's borne of relief that Lily is okay. Ciara comes out of the hall to see what the fuss is about.

'What is it?' she asks, her eyes darting between Alex and me.

'He's dead,' Alex says, matter of factly, as if he can hardly believe what he is saying. 'Joe's dead. I'm so sorry.' There is a tremor in his voice now.

Joe McKee is dead. I inhale deeply.

In that moment everything is still. The ticking of the clock is the only thing to punctuate the silence. I can almost feel Alex's words, and the realisation of what they mean, move around the room, around the house. They wash over us all, and they start to sink in and the noise builds slowly. Kathleen wails, quietly at first, but her cry increases in volume and intensity within the same breath. Ciara calmly, maybe too calmly, asks Alex to repeat himself, and she's already moving towards the stairs as if she needs to see it for herself. Stella is calling her back. Alex is looking at me, watching for my reaction, perhaps. I'm frozen to the spot. I dare not move, or hope . . .

Ciara pushes past Alex, knocking him flat against the wall. Stella is following her up the stairs, pleading with her to slow down. Kathleen has slumped to the floor and she is keening, rocking backwards and forwards. She is muttering something. The words of a prayer or something that I can't quite hear over the buzzing in my head. Alex moves to her and not me, sitting beside her and wrapping his arms around her.

'It looks very peaceful,' he says, his voice shaky. 'He looks very peaceful. He must have just gone in his sleep. I'm so sorry.'

I watch them as if I'm watching a TV show. Without emotion. Without a feeling it is real.

I hear a shout from the top of the stairs. A cry out. A 'Daddy' – it's the most vulnerable I have ever known Ciara to be.

Stella appears at the top of the stairs, her face as ashen as Alex's. 'I think we should call an ambulance,' she says.

'But if he's dead . . .' I blurt. My voice sounds funny.

'I think it's still protocol,' she says.

'And Dr Sweeney,' Kathleen says, her voice thick, trembling with grief.

'It's very late,' I say. 'And a bad night. I'm sure the ambulance crew can do what's necessary.'

'Dr Sweeney won't mind. He's a friend of the family. Joe would want him to be here. He would want to be here,' Kathleen says, her voice borderline hysterical.

'Okay,' I say, 'I'll make the calls.' Anything to calm her down.

I half walk, half stumble through to the living room, dig my phone from the changing bag I've carried in with me. The same pale pink blanket is still poking out of the top of it.

I make the calls. I hardly recognise my own voice as I speak, and then I sit and wait to feel different.

I always thought the minute he was dead, my shame would die with him. But I feel it niggle as I climb the stairs. It has mutated, though. This time, some of it comes from the fact that a tiny spark inside me feels alive for the first time in twenty years.

Chapter Twenty-One

Ciara

Now

My teeth are chattering. The room – his bedroom – is still much too warm. It's not the temperature that is making my teeth chatter, or my body shake. I'm sitting on the bed – his bed – the bed I refused to sit on over the last few days, and I am looking at this familiar face before me.

It has changed. Slackened in death. Even though he is still warm, I can see the colour, what little of it there was, leave his face in front of me.

Alex said he looked like he was sleeping. He doesn't. He looks dead. What he was, who he was, is gone.

I hear voices downstairs. Cries from Kathleen. I'm aware Stella is hovering, unsure what to do. She puts a hand on my shoulder and I shrug her away. Probably too harshly.

'I just . . . need a moment. Please,' I say. 'On my own with him.'

She says 'of course' and she leaves, pulling the door behind her until it's almost closed tight.

I look at my father's face again. See traces of me there. The same shape of nose. Pointy chin. I think of all the things I inherited from him. Not just his looks, I think. Or his love for books.

I think – no, I'm pretty sure – I inherited some of his badness. Because while I know I'm in shock and I know he's gone, I know there's a justice to it.

Joe McKee never should've had a chance at a bucket list. He never should've had anyone sitting around his bedside, trying to figure out how to support him.

He didn't deserve to be waited on. To be able to creep his way back into our lives. To guilt us into feeling sorry for him when he never, even once in his sad and miserable life, felt sorry for the pain he inflicted.

He'd been given time to say sorry. I'd waited for him to speak up, but he hadn't. He'd only tried his old tricks all over again. Manipulating me. Us.

My father deserves to be dead, I think as I see how he lies in his bed, seemingly peaceful. There is something so false about it all.

I hope wherever his soul is now, and I have my suspicions about that, it is in torment. It deserves to be. He should've died all those years ago, in the fire that Heidi started. He should've burned. I look at his body, the warmth draining from it, and I whisper, just as I hear the front door open and the tramp of paramedics on the stairs, that I hope he never finds a moment's peace.

And suddenly, all of this is outside of my control. Paramedics are in the room. Followed by Dr Sweeney, who takes my hand and solemnly offers me his condolences.

Questions are asked and I answer them. As best I can. People come and go. Auntie Kathleen, who sits rubbing my father's hand as the paramedics fill in their paperwork. Stella makes tea.

Alex hovers. The one person who doesn't come near the room is Heidi.

'It's probably better for him,' Dr Sweeney says. 'In the long run. I know it's an awful shock now.'

I nod and make the right noises and say the right things, but I'm starting to wish they would all just get on with it. Take him away. Load him onto a trolley and into the back of the ambulance, or get the undertakers to collect him. I can't escape the reality that he is already starting to decay. With every minute that passes, I start to believe that this is real. That finally he is gone.

I want his physical remains to be gone, too.

I need him to leave.

'It will be okay,' Stella says, appearing beside me.

I want so much to tell her it already is.

Chapter Twenty-Two

Heidi

Now

There's a uniform for grieving. I don't think I've ever thought of it much before, but now, standing in front of my wardrobe trying to find suitable items in black to wear over the coming days, I realise that it exists.

I glance down at my stomach, still loose and flabby following Lily's birth five and a half months before. It's hard now to remember it swollen and tight. It's hard to imagine the smiling, wriggling baby lying on her play mat beside me ever living inside me.

I find a simple shift dress, loose and forgiving, which I'd worn to a friend's granny's funeral, and decide it will do for now. Thick black tights, flat shoes and the grey cardigan from the back of the door complete the look.

I wonder if I should put make-up on. I don't think I've worn make-up since Lily was born, but the black clothes will make me look even more washed out. I resolve to put on a little but not too much. I pull my hair into a loose ponytail, aware that it is still falling out in clumps. The joys of a post-pregnancy body.

I wish we didn't have to go through this process. The Irish wake. Two days and nights of mourning over a coffin sat in our house. Several days of making sure he's not left alone, bowing to tradition and superstition. Several days of handshaking and nodding and passing around cups of tea, snifters of whisky for the 'oul fellahs', before we can bury him and I can start to bury so much more.

I wish we could leave him in a funeral home. Visit only when we want to – if we want to. Keep a distance from it all. I wish I'd never have to think about Joe McKee again.

I glance at the clock. It's twelve thirty. We've said we'll be back at the house by two. There will be furniture to be shifted. Someone will have to go to the community centre and see if we can get a loan of some chairs for visitors coming to the wake and a tea urn to keep the fresh cups coming. There will be sandwiches to make . . .

I feel overwhelmed and sit down on the edge of the bed and focus on Lily, who seems to be enraptured with the discovery that she has feet.

The bed dips as Alex sits beside me and takes my hand. 'We'll get through it,' he says and I lean my head on his shoulder.

'Do you think people will think we're awful for not having the wake here?' I ask, looking around me.

'In a boxy two-bedroom new build with a tiny baby to mind? No, I don't think people will.'

I take a deep breath. 'I know I shouldn't care what people think, but I do.'

'Do you think any less of Ciara for not offering to hold the wake in her house?' Alex asks.

I shake my head. Of course I don't. But that's different. Ciara is different. No one would expect it of her, even though she was his biological daughter. Me, though? I've been told for the past two decades that I'm so lucky that Joe stayed to look after me. That I must owe him a debt of gratitude.

Those people don't know the truth, though.

I glance down at Lily again on the floor. Her eyes meet mine and she breaks into one of her heart-melting smiles. I feel a wave of emotion rise up in me and I start to cry, immediately annoyed at myself for not holding it together. I can't fall apart – not at this stage. I just have to get through the next few days, then this whole ordeal will be over.

'I'll put some soup on,' Alex says. 'You need to eat something, keep your strength up. I'll take this little madam with me too, so she doesn't distract you further.'

He reaches for our daughter and lifts her tenderly into his arms. Her smile is instant, her head curling in against his chest. His love for her is so pure it makes my breath catch in my chest. I reach over and stroke the soft, fair, fluffy hair on her head. I know I'd do anything to protect her. To keep her safe.

The phone rings downstairs. It has been ringing all morning and each time I have jumped. I'm tired and it's too loud. Too shrill. The voices on the other end of the line too false. More wanting to know the gossip than genuinely sympathising. The news hasn't taken long to spread. It never does. Not in Derry. I want to pull the landline out. Most people I know don't have them any more anyway.

I hear the low tone of Alex's voice as he answers. His words muffled and indistinct through the closed door. I hear his feet on the stairs, watch the door for him to open it and impart whatever news he has. So and so sends their sympathy. If there is anything they can do, et cetera, et cetera.

But his face looks different when I see him. It's as if he has faded in the few minutes we've been apart. He is pale. Looks shaken. I don't like this. It reminds me of his face last night, when I saw him on the stairs.

He takes my hand. I fight the urge to pull it away. I know, just know, something is wrong.

'That was the undertakers,' he says. 'There will be a delay with bringing Joe's remains back.'

'Why?'

'He didn't say exactly. Just that something had come up.'

An uneasy feeling washes over me. 'And you didn't ask what exactly?'

'He said they just needed to check some things. That's all.'

I bite my tongue. It won't endear me to Alex if I say what is going through my mind, which is that there can't be much to check given that it's pretty clear he's dead.

'Did he say how long?' I say instead.

'No.' Alex shakes his head. 'He said he'd be in touch.'

'Well, what are we supposed to do?' I snap. I feel fidgety. If I have to endure his wake, I'd rather get on with the enduring. I'd rather get to the 'moving on' part.

'Do your best to relax, maybe. Enjoy the calm before the madness of the wake starts.'

I immediately dismiss that idea. There's no way I can relax. Not when I don't know what is going on. There is no calm and there never has been when it came to Joe.

'Maybe I'll go over to the house anyway. Get a head start on things. No doubt Ciara will be there already,' I say.

The thought of her poking around the house I grew up in makes me uncomfortable, even though it's a long time since it felt anything like a home to me.

'It's not a competition,' he says gently.

The rational, adult part of my brain knows that. Another part of me thinks that it is very much a competition and always will be between Ciara and me.

90

Chapter Twenty-Three

Heidi

Then

I remember holding my pencil. It was red. One of the thicker ones they used to give you in primary school to help with your handwriting. I'd done my homework. Written my sentences using my best handwriting and finished my sums.

I had closed my copybook and slipped it back into my satchel. I was sitting at the kitchen table and he was humming. I can't remember the tune exactly. I'm not sure I ever knew what it was. But I remember that the noise irritated me.

He was doing a little dance as he set about making dinner. As if he didn't have a care in the world. As if nothing had ever hurt him. I couldn't understand how he could be happy. I wondered if I'd ever feel happy again. Mammy was dead more than a year, but it still hurt as much as it did the day she died.

I lifted the jotter my granny had bought me, just for scribbling in, and started to draw. Dark streaks of deep grey lead on the paper. Pushing down so hard that I thought I might tear through several sheets at once.

It helped to release some of the anger that was inside me.

I gripped the pencil tighter – my knuckles white with the effort – and flipped the page over and started to write:

I hate Joe McKee
I hate Joe McKee
I hate Joe McKee

I jumped when his hand landed, thick and heavy, on the table beside where I was scrawling. I felt him loom over me until I could feel his breath – warm and smelling of tea – on my cheek. He was right beside. So close that even while he wasn't touching me, I could feel him as if he were.

'You hate me?' he asked.

I didn't flinch. I was scared, but a defiance had crept over me that day and I refused to show it.

I didn't answer. I just kept writing those four words over and over again.

His hand moved, covered mine, pressed down so hard that not only could I no longer write, but also so that I could feel the pencil pressing painfully into my fingers.

'You hate me?' he said again, his tone more menacing.

I would not break. He would not break me.

I mustered as much bravery as I could and said 'Yes' in a voice that didn't shake as much as I feared it might.

'All I have ever done,' he hissed, 'is take care of you. And love you when no one else wanted you. You're just an ungrateful little brat.'

He stayed close. His breathing heavy. I could feel the skin of his palm turn clammy, could feel the sweat on my hand – a hand that was pinned on the table.

I was only a child. Only ten when that happened, but I wasn't stupid. I promised one day I'd make him feel as trapped, as helpless, as I did.

Eventually he loosened his grip, took the notebook and tore it into pieces before dragging me through to the living room, where I could watch it burn in the fireplace.

He couldn't burn my feelings, though. He would never be able to do that.

Chapter Twenty-Four

Heidi

Now

It's only been a few hours since we were last at this house but it already feels as if everything has changed. The energy is different. I can feel that he is gone. I stop for just a moment – taking a deep breath, revelling in how fresh the air feels in a house that has been oppressive for so long.

Alex must mistake my shivering for a wave of grief. He wraps his arms around me, holds me and kisses the top of my head. I stand still and let him believe what he needs to.

I hear the slam of a car door and turn to see Ciara walking up the short drive towards the house, hand in hand with Stella. Tiredness is written all over her face, I suppose, but then none of us slept well last night.

'Has the undertaker been in touch with you?' I ask as she walks through the door and slips off her coat.

She nods, fidgets a little, pulling the sleeve of her cardigan down over her hand. 'I don't know what it's all about. I thought it was just a matter of them . . . you know . . . preparing his body.'

'I'm sure it's nothing to worry about,' Stella says, rubbing her girlfriend's arm. 'Don't let it upset you, anyway. At least we have a bit more time to get things organised here.'

'True enough,' Ciara says, her eyes darting around the house as if she is seeing it for the first time, even though we'd all been here for most of the night.

Stella speaks next. 'Where should we start?' she asks, taking off her coat and hanging it at the bottom of the stairs. 'I'm not familiar with all your traditions over here, so just tell me what to do and I'll do it.'

Stella is very practical by nature. No nonsense. I'm glad to have her around. Ciara gives her a small smile. It lasts just a moment or two before she turns to look at me with a more serious face. Her expression reminds me of how she looked when we first met – full of teenage angst and intransigence.

'Well, Heidi, what do you suggest?'

I don't know what to do any more than Stella does, if truth be told. I avoid death rituals. I saw enough of them as a child that I blanked them out. I stare, unspeaking, at her.

'Well, where do you want to have him laid out?' Alex asks, stepping close to me and taking my hand. 'Do you think the front living room would be best? If so, I'll start clearing the furniture.'

I could kiss him for taking charge. Stella is not the only person who can help in a crisis.

'That's fine with me,' Ciara says.

'Grand. I'll get started on that, then,' Alex replies.

'You can't do that on your own,' I say. 'I'll help.'

'How about I help Alex?' Stella asks. 'I'm sure you and Ciara have enough to be doing elsewhere.'

Ciara and I look at each other, neither of us sure what else we should be doing at all but sure that whatever it is, we don't want to be doing it together.

'That would be great.' Alex speaks for me again.

It isn't lost on me that both Alex and Stella are talking slowly, as if giving instructions to truculent toddlers. There is an air of broken eggshells all around us and we're all being careful not to tread them further into the ground.

'Mum has the refreshments under control,' Ciara says. 'She knows a caterer and wants to help.'

Ciara's mum, Marie, has always been kind to me. Unlike her daughter, she doesn't seem to hold me partially responsible for her husband leaving her. I'm glad of her offer of help.

'And she has been talking to Kathleen about the funeral,' Ciara continues. 'Kathleen has very definite ideas about what she wants. I imagine it doesn't matter to you that much,' she says. 'Besides, it will free you up to call the estate agent and get the house on the market. Do you want to do that now, or is it time enough to wait until he's actually buried? It might get a little awkward showing people around and seeing a coffin in the living room.'

I'm not sure which is my most overriding emotion: shame, embarrassment or anger.

'Sweetheart,' I hear Stella say gently.

Alex is quiet. Ciara stands and stares at me, waiting for an answer. She's not letting me get away with it. She wants to break me down just like her father did.

But I won't let her. I'm not a child any more. I won't apologise or cower.

'After the funeral is fine,' I say, my voice steady.

Ciara glares at me, waiting for more maybe. But she won't get it. Not about the house, anyway. I slip into organisation mode, trying to remember all the things we did twenty years ago when it was my mother's turn to be laid out in the front room. Of course I was so young then, my memories are hazy at best.

'I think maybe we should be closing curtains. Find somewhere to place the candles from the undertaker. Do people still cover all the mirrors?'

Seeing that she's not getting a rise out of me, Ciara shrugs. 'I'm not sure. I'll check.'

She takes her phone from her pocket and starts to search for 'wake traditions'.

'It seems a lot of it is up to us,' she says. 'But maybe we should go and look in his room,' she adds. 'Strip the bed, open the window at least and air it out. See what medications need to be dropped off at the chemist. Then we can close the curtains again. Or the blinds at least. I think we maybe should cover the mirror in the room he'll be in,' she says.

I don't really want to go into that room again, but I'm determined not to show any weakness in front of Ciara.

'Okay,' I say. 'That seems a good place to start.'

'Will you two be okay?' Stella asks.

She's keeping her voice light, but I know both she and Alex must be scared we will tear lumps out of each other given the chance. It wouldn't be the first time, of course. It had become physical on occasion when we were younger. Ciara had been stubborn and I had been angry, and grew angrier every day until I couldn't hold it in any longer.

'We will,' Ciara says. 'We can do this together,' she says gently to me. Her sudden change in demeanour – the shift from bitchy to supportive – is so fast that I feel wrong-footed.

Ciara crosses the hall and takes my hand in hers. I have to resist the urge to pull away. I have to stay in control and not be manipulated by her rapid mood swing.

I let her lead the way up the stairs, not pulling my hand away. I can play her game.

★ ★ ★

His room is dark. No one has opened the curtains; the light has been switched off. It smells of stale air with a faint undercurrent of something medical; disinfectant perhaps. I find myself standing for a minute or so just inside the doorway. Ciara has let go of my hand and she walks in and briskly pulls the curtains apart, the stream of light showing the dust motes in full flight.

This was where it all ended. It feels more real now than when the paramedic told me he was very sorry for my troubles. Or when the priest prayed over Joe's body, or when the doctor made it all official.

That had been much less of a momentous declaration than it should have been. A life over, acknowledged with a shake of a head and a scrawled signature on some paper.

My lungs struggle to suck in the stale air of the room and I feel a weight of something akin to grief hit me directly in the centre of my chest for the first time. It's a physical sensation that I have not expected. It makes me feel as unsettled as Ciara's mood swings.

I half walk, half stumble to the bed, where I sit down and close my eyes, trying to find my breath.

I feel the mattress dip beside me. Ciara is sitting down.

'It's so strange, isn't it?' she says. 'After all these years . . .'

Her words hang in the air. I don't know what to say to her. How to respond.

Slowly, as my breathing returns to normal, I open my eyes. The room looks different in the light. Dated. I can't remember the last time he had the painters in here. If ever. There's a fine layer of dust on the chest of drawers. The mirror on the front of the wardrobe is smeared and smudged. Should I have cleaned for him? Or cleaned more? Should Ciara have?

An indentation in the shape of his head still exists on the pillow his head was resting on. The sheets are pulled back. His bedside table is less dusty, but it is cluttered. A glass of water, half empty, a straw poking from the top of it. A couple of boxes of tablets, which I lift and set on the chest of drawers. I'll put them in a plastic bag shortly. Some loose change and a box of tissues. Some crumpled and discarded. His reading glasses, unfolded, the arms pointing upwards. A packet of Werther's Original, three discarded wrappers from the sweets he had eaten. I pick up the detritus, drop it in the bin. I open the drawer on his bedside locker and slip the sweets and the change in. I'm not sure why I do this. He won't be coming back for them later. A leather-bound diary, burgundy, and a pen are among the scarce contents of his drawer.

I feel wrong doing it, but not wrong enough to stop. Sitting on the edge of the bed, I open the diary, my heart contracting as I see the familiar loops and swirls of his handwriting. It's this year's diary. There aren't that many entries completed, but I see that he has dutifully filled in his contact information.

'What's that?' Ciara asks from across the room.

'His diary,' I say.

'Well, I don't think you should be looking at it,' she says.

The harsh tone is back in her voice. I'm more familiar with this version of Ciara than with the Ciara who held my hand walking up the stairs.

In three or four steps she crosses the room and snatches it from my hands.

'He deserves his privacy, you know,' she says. 'Even if he's gone.'

I mutter an apology, feel shame burn at my face.

Ciara walks back to the other side of the room, opens the wardrobe with the smudged mirrors and places the diary high on a shelf. She closes the door with a rattle and turns the bronze key in the lock, which she then puts in the pocket of her dress. The message is loud and clear. I have overstepped the mark.

'Ciara? Heidi?' I hear Stella's voice from downstairs before I have the time to react.

We walk to the landing and look down the stairs.

There are two police officers standing in the hall, looking directly up at us.

Chapter Twenty-Five

Heidi

Now

'Can we help you, Officer?' Ciara asks.

'Perhaps if we can have a sit-down we could chat,' a tall man, his face solemn, says. 'I'm Detective Inspector David Bradley, and this is my colleague Detective Constable Eve King, from Strand Road police station.'

My heart thumps.

'Has someone been hurt, Officer?' Stella asks.

My stomach lurches.

'This is in relation to Mr McKee,' he says. 'And really it might be better if we sit down.'

Ciara leads the way into the living room. The furniture has been pushed against the walls, some dining chairs lined against the window. Space has been cleared by the far wall for a coffin. For his coffin. So that mourners can file in and pay their respects, leave a Mass card, say a prayer, look at his body, embalmed and laid out looking like a waxwork of the man he was.

I perch on one of the dining chairs, leave the soft seats for DI Bradley and DC King. Alex hovers beside me before sitting down. Ciara and Stella hold hands and sit on the sofa.

'If you could let us know what this is about,' Ciara speaks, 'because we're expecting to hear from the undertakers and we want the house ready for the return of my father's remains.'

DI Bradley takes a breath and looks at each of us. 'I'm afraid there will be a further delay to the release of your father's remains. Following discussions with Mr Steele, the undertaker tasked with making all funeral arrangements, and Dr Sweeney, your family physician, we have decided that in this case there is cause for a postmortem examination to be done.'

My heart races.

'But why? He was ill. The doctor said it was one of those things. This is ridiculous,' Ciara says, anger evident in her tone.

DI Bradley pauses for a moment, as if he is checking that Ciara's rage is spent, then speaks. 'While preparing your father's remains, there were some marks to his body that warrant extra investigation. I should stress, at this time, this is a formality. It's our duty, and the duty of the coroner, to investigate anything that may explain your father's sudden death.'

'He had terminal cancer. He was recovering from major surgery. That's what caused his sudden death. Dr Sweeney said so.' Ciara is on her feet, dragging her fingers through her hair. 'This is ridiculous.'

'I'm sorry you feel that way,' DI Bradley said gently. 'However, it's policy in cases such as these.'

'What kind of marks?' I ask. All eyes turn to me. 'You say Mr Steele found marks, what were they? What does he think may have caused them?'

'I don't have that particular information at hand, and it would be remiss of me to say anything more until after the postmortem. Any findings will be for the coroner to determine.

We appreciate this must be very distressing for you all,' DI Bradley says.

Ciara snorts. 'Well, that's okay then,' she snaps. 'Take my father and carve him up all you want. It's okay as long as you appreciate how difficult it is for us.'

'Sweetheart,' Stella says gently.

Trying to smooth the waters again, I imagine.

Ciara's face crumples at the softness of her tone and Stella pulls her girlfriend into a hug while DI Bradley and his colleague watch. I'm sure they are used to this. To seeing grief — raw and angry — in front of them. I wonder how many times they've had conversations as distressing as this before.

I hear Alex speak next. He is standing in the doorway looking pale and tired and worn out. 'Is there a suggestion of foul play?' he asks.

All eyes are on him, Ciara even breaking from her embrace with Stella to watch, as he speaks.

DI Bradley shifts in his seat. 'As I've said, it wouldn't be appropriate for me to comment at this stage, but we are looking at all lines of inquiry.'

'So that's a yes,' Ciara says. 'Jesus Christ. This is ridiculous.'

The woman who had been introduced to us as DC Eve King clears her throat. 'We'll keep you informed every step of the way. Should a family member wish to come to Belfast with us while the postmortem is carried out, this can be facilitated.'

I'm aware I'm not openly reacting to any of this. That I am sitting here numb, listening. I'm trying to take it all in. Foul play? Really? What must they think of me?

'For our records, would you mind if we asked a few questions?' DC King asks.

Ciara throws her hands to the air as if she can't believe what is happening.

I mutter a quick, 'We'll do what we can to help,' knowing that it wouldn't really matter if we minded.

She takes a pen and notepad from her pocket. It feels so serious, so formal.

'Can I ask who was in the house last night with Mr McKee at the time of his death?'

'We've been through this already,' Ciara says, but there is less fight in her now. She is sagging and sits down on one of the armchairs, her head in her hands.

'All of us,' I say. 'That's me, Heidi Lewis. My husband, Alex Lewis. Ciara, and Stella Brown, Ciara's partner.'

'My aunt, Kathleen Douglas, was here, too,' Ciara says. 'My father's sister.'

'And where is she now?' DC King asks.

'Staying with a friend. She was very distressed. Dr Sweeney gave her some tablets to help her sleep.'

The policewoman nods. 'And it was you, Mr Lewis, who discovered that Mr McKee had died?'

Alex nods. 'I went to check on him just after eleven and I noticed he didn't appear to be breathing. I checked his pulse, but he was gone.'

'And who was the last person to talk to Mr McKee?'

I shrug. It's hard to know. We'd all been making our way up and down the stairs over the course of the evening to take care of him. Or to take care of Lily. Or to use the bathroom. It was all muddled.

'I'm not sure,' I say and DC King looks to Ciara, who shrugs, too. 'We were all in and out with him during the evening.'

'Okay,' Detective Constable King says before taking contact details for us all.

There seems to be an awful lot of red tape in this 'just a formality' business.

'What happens now?' Ciara asks.

'Well, your father's remains will be taken to Belfast, where the postmortem will be carried out. There are no facilities for this to take place closer to home, unfortunately. We should have preliminary results fairly quickly and we will keep you informed.'

'Will his remains be released afterwards? Might it still be today?' I ask.

'That depends on the results of the postmortem,' DI Bradley interjects. 'But we will keep you . . .'

'Informed,' Ciara butts in.

'If you could, Officer, that would be appreciated,' Stella says, the lilt of her Glasgow accent softening the tension.

'We are very sorry for your loss,' DI Bradley says as he stands. 'By all accounts Mr McKee was a well-liked man.'

Ciara nods. All fight seemingly gone. I don't. I don't react at all. I don't stand up or follow the officers to the door to let them out. I think I'm afraid my legs will give out from under me if I even try to stand.

Chapter Twenty-Six

Heidi

Now

I'm afraid to speak, afraid to ask questions. I watch the door as if someone will walk in with answers. I watch my phone. I do my best to stay out of Ciara's way, but I hear the rumblings of a heated conversation between her and Stella behind the closed door of the kitchen. I look out into the street, to where the light is already fading, and I wonder if people are peeking out from behind their own curtains to see what is going on here. Surely they must be wondering why his remains haven't been returned yet, why the official period of mourning has yet to start. Did they notice the unmarked police car earlier?

I try not to think about the 'unexplained marks' that DI Bradley spoke about. Try not to think about how police are looking at all lines of inquiry or however he worded it. I definitely try, unsuccessfully, not to think about 'foul play' that may or may not be suspected or what that might mean. Except that someone else may have been so angry with Joe that they may have done the one thing I have spent my whole life wanting to be brave enough to do.

I push those as far to the back of my mind as I can. That way madness lies.

I go back to hovering. Waiting. Ignoring any phone call that isn't from the police or the undertaker. Ignoring text messages asking what the arrangements are.

People are talking.

Gossip spreading.

There's nothing we can do to control it.

I think about the postmortem. Try to imagine at what stage in the macabre proceedings things may be at now. Marie has gone to Belfast. None of us could face it. A friend has driven her because she is much too distraught to have driven herself. I have long suspected she still harboured some feelings for her ex-husband. God knows why.

When she'd heard none of us were planning to go to Belfast, she'd insisted on going, determined that Joe should not make the journey alone – as if he hasn't gone way past being able to care. 'He deserves to have his family with him,' she had said. There was no hint of judgement in her voice – just sadness.

They'll definitely be in Belfast now. This could be the moment that first incision is made. A straight line, diagonal, under his collarbone. Like you see on TV. Is it like it is in the movies? Solemn and respectful. Or is it all in a day's work? Another body on a slab to be carved and dissected. Another set of lungs to examine. Mottled skin to be sliced, blood and tissue removed and tested.

Thinking about it is making me sick. My stomach gurgles. I don't know if I need to eat something or throw up. Perhaps a lungful of air will help.

I make a cup of milky tea, which I'm not sure I can stomach, and walk around the frost-covered back garden. In the dusk the frost sparkles, a reflection of the glow of the lights on in the kitchen. I try to focus on that while I wish I hadn't given up smoking when I was pregnant with Lily. A cigarette would be perfect just now.

I hear footsteps and turn. Alex is at the door, his own cup in his hand. It will be a black coffee. Extra strong. He drinks too much caffeine, I think in passing. Wondering how fast it makes his heart beat. Would they be able to see his addiction if they carved out his heart in a postmortem and examined it?

'How're you holding up?' he asks, putting two cushions on the patio chairs so that we can sit down more comfortably.

I pull a face. One I hope conveys that I don't have the first notion in the world how I'm holding up.

'It's scary,' he says. 'That they think someone might've hurt him.'

I nod.

'He wasn't a very good man, was he?' Alex asks.

I look at him and he is staring at the grass. He needs a shave and a decent sleep. Probably something to eat.

'No, he wasn't,' I say. 'He wasn't what people think he was.'

I feel shaky. This is a conversation I suppose I need to have, but don't want to.

'What was he like, Heidi? I mean, what was he really like?'

Alex's eyes are on me now, looking into my eyes. And there's this place inside of me that is so filled with pain and so in need of healing that I almost tell him. I almost explain how Joe hurt me. Abused me. Raped me. Yes, raped me. That word – that experience. How he messed up every sense in my head of what love and family meant. How he broke me and then couldn't understand why I was broken. It's the same place that wants me to stand up and applaud that he is dead.

But I see sadness in my husband's eyes, and fear. It strikes me that maybe, just maybe, he thinks I was the person who left

108

the unexplained marks. That he should have seen it coming. And once he thinks that, and once people start looking – because they will start looking, and they will find out just what happened on that Christmas ten years ago – they will conclude, without question, that I killed Joe McKee.

I'm the most likely suspect. And it terrifies me to consider that my husband may realise this.

I keep Alex's gaze. 'He didn't know how to be a father. Not to Ciara and not to me. He was cruel and selfish. I'd have been better off in care than in this house. It breaks me to think things would've been so different if only my grandparents had been well enough to take care of me. Or if my mother had known what he was really like before she died.

'They were together two years and he never dropped his perfect persona with her. It was only after she died that he showed himself for what he was. It destroys me that she trusted him to take care of me. It even made me really angry with her for a long time. I wondered how could she have been so blind and so irresponsible? And then I was angry with my grand-parents for not taking me in anyway. Even with their problems. I'm not saying I was perfect, Alex. I was an angry teenager. Mixed up. But he? He was evil.'

Alex nods. I can see his eyes fill with unshed tears. I've said more to him than I ever have before. Before I'd just say we were never close. That we never really bonded. That Joe was strict and, at times, controlling. All of which had been true. And it had been enough for him not to question me when I told him I preferred a wedding away on a beach in Italy, just the two of us and some friends. That I had no need to have a father figure walk me down the aisle. That I made my duty visits to Joe, but no more. Until he became sick and it all changed.

'I'm so sorry,' he says.

'What for?' I ask him.

He opens his mouth to speak, but we hear the back door open and Ciara steps out – a mug of tea or coffee in one hand and her e-cig in the other.

'I'm not disturbing anything?' she asks.

Alex shakes his head. 'No. No, of course not. Actually, I was just going to go and check on Lily.'

'Might be a good idea. I think I heard her crying a few minutes ago.'

I bristle. 'Could you not have told us?'

'I am now,' she says matter-of-factly as she draws on her e-cig and releases billows of steam into the cool air. 'It doesn't do babies any harm to cry it out now and again. They have to learn to self-soothe,' she says.

'I think that's for us, as her parents, to decide,' I say as we rush back to the house.

'Well, I didn't know where you were. For all I knew you were upstairs with her.'

She steps out of the way to allow us to walk back into the house, but not far enough that my throat doesn't catch with the rancid smell of whatever it is she has been vaping.

'Heidi,' she calls my name and I shoo Alex on, even though I can't hear Lily crying now.

I turn to look at her. She looks like she has the weight of the world on her shoulders and she's about to unload some of it in my direction.

'What do you think they'll find?' she asks.

'I have no idea,' I reply.

'Don't you? I mean trouble in this house seems to follow you around.'

I don't like her tone. I don't like where this conversation could go. I certainly wasn't prepared to help her go there.

'As I said,' I repeated, walking past her, 'I have no idea what they might or could find and I'm not really in the mood to discuss it with you further. We're not children any more, Ciara. I'm not some wee girl desperate for you to like me, or treat me with an ounce of decency. I can walk away from you at any time I choose and I'm choosing to do that right now. My child needs me.'

I don't wait to see if she has anything else to say, but as I climb the stairs to find Alex and Lily, I feel my nerve go a little and some old demons swoop in.

Chapter Twenty-Seven

Heidi

Then

I'd always wanted a sister. I'd tried to build a relationship with Ciara in the haphazard way a nine-year-old tries to build friendships with anyone. I shared my sweets. (She didn't like toffees.) I let her play with my dead mother's make-up, even though I really wanted to keep it in a box to use myself when I was older. I gave her a bottle of perfume, one that Mum only used occasionally so it didn't hurt too much to part with it. I offered her a loan of my dolls, even Scarlett.

She'd pulled a disgusted face. Said the dolls were babyish. Creepy. Like they were watching her. She told me no one played with dolls like that any more. I was a freak, she said, who no one loved.

But I still wanted Ciara to like me, and I wanted to be happy. I knew what happy looked like and felt like. I had been happy when my mother was still alive. I also knew sadness. I lived with it every day then. Knew it inside and out; so I knew Ciara had sad written all over her. If we could just get along, wouldn't it be easier on us both?

I saw how wounded she looked when Joe turned his attention to me and not her. When she saw the latest book or jigsaw puzzle he'd bought me when she came to see us. He was forever promising her he would get her something 'the next time'. Of course the next time never came and Ciara's hatred for me grew. She never knew the presents were bought out of guilt, or to try to buy my silence about what he was doing. She never knew I hated those presents.

I wanted to tell her so many times that it wasn't my fault he'd left her family. And that I never asked him for anything. No books, or jigsaws. Certainly not to stay in this house with me and look after me. I didn't want him.

I'd act up more in front of Joe when she was around. Try to make him cross so he would favour her over me. It didn't seem to work.

I can still remember the dejected look on her face. Her grey-blue eyes cast downwards, her mousy brown hair falling over her face. The sleeves of her sweater pulled down over her hands.

But when she looked up, it wasn't him she glared at, but me. Because it was my fault. I existed and worse than that I seemed to have become the apple of her daddy's eye. If only she knew what that meant and what he did.

It didn't seem to matter, though. Nothing did. Nothing I tried or did or said made a difference. The lines were well and truly drawn.

The only thing I could do to protect myself from being hurt further was to start hating her as well.

Chapter Twenty-Eight

Heidi

Now

'He'll be back soon,' Kathleen says over and over to whoever enters the room and we nod as if we haven't already heard her say it at least ten times. She has a large industrial kettle bubbling with boiling water ready to make as many cups of tea as necessary and a huge pot of home-made vegetable soup on the go. For when he is home. For when the mourners come.

She's still a little dazed, probably still has traces of whatever tranquillisers Dr Sweeney gave her last night in her system. She asks the same question over and over again. 'What exactly did the police say?'

Her repetitive questioning is starting to grate on me, though. Each question ties a knot tighter in my stomach. I don't want to think about what the police might find, but I can't escape it with her constant commentary. That's without even taking into account the conversation Ciara and I had in the kitchen, when she made it clear where her suspicions lay. I know she will have no qualms at all about using my past against me if the police need to ask more questions. My secrets could all be laid bare.

The need to get away washes over me again and I feel it settle on my chest. I will my breath to stay settled, my heart to not race and my inner panic to stay contained, but I know I'm fighting a losing battle.

I make my excuses in a room where I'm sure no one is really listening to me and climb the stairs, past his room to my old bedroom. Two doors away from Joe's room. On the left-hand side of the landing.

We'll be sleeping here tonight, in this room. I don't want to, but I'm nervous about leaving Ciara alone in the house. I don't trust her. I don't want to leave her here to start telling anyone who calls to the house, be it mourners or the police or nosy neighbours, just how much 'trouble' followed me around.

I wish Alex was here, but he has taken Lily out for a walk around the block in her pram. I think he feels as hemmed in as I do and he doesn't even know a fraction of what went on this house.

I sense that something's wrong as soon as I walk into my bedroom. Not quite as it should be. There is a feeling that someone has been in here. Looking through my things, perhaps. Looking for something to use to pin Joe's death on me. Planting evidence. An uneasy feeling prickles at the back of my neck. 'You're being paranoid,' I whisper to myself.

But then I see that there are only three porcelain dolls on the shelf, where there should be four. Scarlett isn't standing where she should.

I spot a whisper of green velvet poking out from under the legs of the chest of drawers. On my knees, I reach under the drawers and pull her out, skirt first.

Her face, once perfectly porcelain, flawless with green glass eyes set against the palest of skin, is a mess of sharp edges and dust. Someone has very deliberately applied brute force to her face and crushed it. She is broken beyond all hope of repair.

I touch my hand to the crooked edges where her cheek is now hollowed out, her green glass eye forced inwards, and yelp as the sharp porcelain slices the side of my hand. Watching the blood pool then drip on her clear white skin, I wait for the stinging sensation to take hold.

When it does I allow myself to cry, but only a little. I'm scared. I'm scared that someone – most likely Ciara – is deliberately targeting me. Someone is pushing me because they know that I do have a breaking point.

Someone is creating their own narrative of whatever happened in this house and they firmly believe, or want people to believe, that I snapped. That I killed Joe.

They want me to snap again. To show myself in all my flawed, unhinged, damaged glory. But I won't do that. I'm better now. I can control my emotions. I have a husband who loves me and a daughter who needs me, and I won't show either of them just how broken I was.

Broken just like Scarlett. She may be only a doll. A stupid remnant from my childhood to anyone looking in. But she is the last one my mother bought for me. She is symbolic of happy times – more innocent times. And the one person left alive who knows this more than anyone is downstairs right now painting herself as a grief-stricken daughter.

I reach into the pocket of my cardigan, pull out a spare tissue and wrap it around my hand, feeling my nerve endings throb and sting, a welcome distraction from the sick feeling in the pit of my stomach. I look down and see there is blood on my cardigan and more has run up my arm, leaving a red tide in its wake.

The door to my room opens just as I reach for the handle

and Alex is there, Lily in his arms, looking first at me, my eyes wet with tears, my cardigan stained with blood, then at the broken doll.

He glances to my hand, the tissue I have held to my cut already becoming sodden with yet more blood. I don't think it's a deep cut, but it doesn't seem to want to stop bleeding, or throbbing with pain.

'Jesus, Heidi, what happened? Are you okay?'

'I'll live,' I say, trying to give him a watery smile, which I'm sure looks less than convincing. 'I don't think Scarlett will, though.'

'What happened? Did you drop her?' he asks.

'No. I found her like this. Half hidden under the chest of drawers. Someone broke her and then tried to hide the evidence.'

'Someone?'

'I'd put my money on Ciara,' I tell him.

His eyes widen just a little. I want to take Lily from him, to hold her, but I know my hand is still aching. Still bleeding. I lift one of her muslin cloths from her changing bag and wrap it around my hand.

'I'll need to clean this out to get a good look at it,' I say.

'You don't really think it was Ciara, do you? Don't you think it might have just been knocked off the shelf by a breeze or something? These things happen. It doesn't have to be malicious.'

'There's no breeze in here,' I say, wanting him to be on my side. No, needing him to be on my side. 'Look at how her face is smashed in, Alex. That doesn't come from a tumble from a shelf!'

'But if she hit the drawers on her way down,' Alex says, lifting the doll and carrying her back to where I found her. 'Look, there's debris on the top here.'

There is a small smattering of porcelain-coloured dust, a few chips. But I'm still sure that someone has done this deliberately.

Or am I? I look at Alex and he has a look of sympathy, or pity, or something in his eyes.

'I'm not making it up,' I tell him. 'You think I'm unhinged, don't you?' I ask, aware that right at this moment, my hand bleeding, my eyes red with tiredness and tears, I do in fact look unhinged.

'I think, Heidi, that you're exhausted and stuck in this strange limbo that would drive anyone to distraction. But accidents do happen.'

I don't know if there's any point in arguing back. What would it achieve, after all?

'Look, maybe you'll feel better after we get that cleaned and you can have a rest. I'll go and get the first-aid kit and we'll get you sorted, then you can grab a few hours' sleep. I'll wake you if we get the call about Joe. I'll see if maybe this doll can be repaired, too,' he says, gesturing at Scarlett, but I know she's beyond fixing. No amount of glue and patience in the world will put her back together again.

Chapter Twenty-Nine

Ciara

Now

I shouldn't have had that third cup of coffee. I'm jittery now and my heart is thumping. I wish I still smoked proper cigarettes, not these pathetic vape devices. I wish I could have a drink right now. God, I wish I could smoke a joint. I wonder if anyone would notice if I rifled through my father's meds and found something to give me a suitable hit.

I'm not a drug user. Not really. Cannabis doesn't really count, or the odd discreetly acquired prescription med. And I need something to take the edge off.

The police had walked in and turned everything on its head. 'We will be here to support you,' they said before leaving and offering absolutely no support, just the fear that they would find out 'foul play' had been involved in my father's death.

Dr Sweeney had been happy to sign the death certificate. That should've been the end of it. He knows what he's doing, after all. We thought we'd just move on to the wake and the funeral and then with the rest of our lives.

But now everything has changed.

I'd love to just block it all out, but I'm sure it wouldn't look good if I was stoned out of my head either. I suck on my e-cig, hoping for a hit of something it can't give me, and pinch the bridge of my nose. I'm tired. Really tired. Maybe Heidi had the right idea of going for a sleep, but I sense Kathleen is on the point of unravelling and I feel it's my responsibility, for my sins, to support her. To contain her.

I should probably eat something, I think. I've not had anything since last night. I've not been hungry, but now my stomach is growling and I realise if I don't at least try to eat something there's a good chance I'll be sick.

I can't face the vat of vegetable soup Kathleen has made, so I decide to make some toast and put on a pot of tea as well. The panacea for every ill, it seems.

Comfort food, I realise. I need comfort food.

I hear someone come into the room and turn to see Alex walk in, looking just as pale as the rest of us. He's an attractive man, I suppose. Not my type, of course, but I can see he is handsome. Tall, thin – possibly a little too thin – with thick dark hair that he wears just long enough that it has started to curl a little at the ends. He wears glasses, a modern dark-rimmed pair, and is in need of shave. He's not quite rugged, but he screams 'nice guy'. He has a decent job, dresses well. He's fairly sociable. I wonder what he sees in Heidi. How he fell in love with her. She has never had any redeeming qualities, in my eyes. Quite plain-looking, quiet, spoilt. I very much doubt he knows all about her past. I'd seen the fear flash in her eyes when I'd mentioned it earlier.

'I was just going to get myself a glass of water,' Alex says. 'Heidi's still sleeping.'

'I'm putting on a pot of tea. Making some toast, if you'd prefer that?'

'I think I've reached tea saturation levels for the day,' he says. 'And I grabbed a burger when I was out earlier. Walked as far as McDonald's.'

'Oooh, a Big Mac would hit the spot right now,' I say with a wry smile, relieved to have just a hint of a normal conversation.

'I've brought the first-aid kit back,' he says and I notice for the first time the blue box in his hand. 'Can I get past you to put it back in the cupboard?'

'First-aid box? Did you hurt yourself or something?'

He sighs. 'No, it was Heidi. She cut her hand.'

I raise an eyebrow, wonder if she's up to her old tricks. Alex looks weary again.

'One of the dolls in her room was smashed. She cut her hand trying to clean it up.'

I have the good grace to blush and thankfully he doesn't seem to notice.

'She's very upset about it,' he says. 'It was one of the dolls her mother got for her.'

'God Almighty.' I hear Kathleen's voice from outside of the room. 'The man who raised her is dead and she doesn't shed a tear, but she's in bits about a doll. That girl! There was always a want in her.'

'I'm sure she is upset about Joe,' Alex stutters. 'It's just, you know, her link with her mother?'

'He was a parent to her longer than her mother was,' Kathleen declares before sitting at the table.

Alex doesn't respond. He just looks extremely uncomfortable with her outburst.

'Is it a bad cut?' I ask. 'Did you find what you needed in the first-aid box, because I can always take a run out to Sainsbury's and pick up anything else you might need? It might do me good to get out of here for a bit.'

'I don't think it's particularly deep. But it did bleed a lot,' he says. 'It seems okay now and she's sleeping. I think it will do her good. She's getting herself so wound up, which is understandable, but you know, it's not good for her.'

I raise an eyebrow, wonder if Alex does know just how bad things can get when his wife gets wound up. Does he know what she is capable of?

'I think we all need to keep a special eye on her,' I say. 'She's very vulnerable, isn't she?'

The look on Alex's face tells me this is news to him. I wonder if I've said too much.

'In what way?' he asks.

'You mean you don't know?' Kathleen says incredulously. 'She must've told you.'

Alex bristles. 'If she'd told me I wouldn't be asking questions now.'

'Your wife was a very troubled young woman,' Kathleen says. 'But maybe you should ask her about it. I don't think it's our place to say.'

Alex looks to me. 'What does she mean?' he asks.

'As she says, it's something you probably need to talk to Heidi about. And, you know, it was a long time ago and she's been stable for a good while now.'

He looks alarmed. 'Stable?'

'That probably makes it sound worse than it was,' I say, aware that it was actually that bad. 'She struggled a lot, you know, after her mother died. It was to be expected, I suppose. And maybe we should have seen the signs faster, but she was just so angry and paranoid and didn't want to talk to any of us . . .'

The last bit wasn't exactly true. She may well have wanted to talk to us, but we – and especially me – didn't want to talk to her. She was a freak who'd stolen my father. I thought he deserved the hard time she put him through.

Just as I think she deserves to have that stupid doll of hers smashed to pieces. I'm not proud of myself for that, but it was either that or take my anger, grief and fear out on her.

Chapter Thirty

Heidi

Then

The poor pet. Is it any wonder she's acting up? Losing her mother so young. Joe's a saint taking her on. Honestly. No one would blame him if he just walked away.

The whispers from the mammies in the school yard weren't long in reaching my ears. And acting up? I wasn't doing anything. I was just wandering around the playground on my own, rattling a stick against the railings.

Sure, when Kathleen had called for me to come on now, it was time to go home, I'd pretended not to hear her, even though her voice was high and scratchy and everyone else seemed to have gone quiet.

But that wasn't acting up.

I just didn't want to go home. Truth was, I didn't know what home was any more. All I knew was that the only place I'd ever remembered living my whole entire life didn't feel so safe and cosy now.

But if I said anything, anything at all, what would become of me?

When I did see Granny she seemed so sad all the time. She'd visit at least once a week, but she was never really present. Not the way she used to be. It seemed as if she'd given up on life. Grandad's health was deteriorating. She was struggling. There was even less chance than before that they would be able to take me in. 'Oh, wee doll, as nice as it is to see you, it's like a knife to my heart at times. You're so like your mammy was at that age,' she would say and break into fresh tears. The last thing I wanted to do was to make her life any harder than it already was. Speaking up would've done that.

I already felt guilt-ridden just for reminding her of my mother, but that wasn't my fault. I couldn't help how I looked. Maybe if I cut my hair I'd look different. That's what I was thinking the night I took the big scissors and hacked at my ponytail. I watched my curls fall to the ground. One strand followed by another, followed by another.

Maybe if I looked less like Mammy, Granny wouldn't be so sad. She wouldn't cry when she saw me.

Maybe she would invite me to stay more and I could show her what a great help I could be with Grandad, and that I didn't take up much space, or eat much or need her to spend money on me.

Maybe if I looked less like Mammy, Joe wouldn't look at me the way he did. He wouldn't cross the landing at night-time to 'see if I was okay' and 'offer to tuck me in'. He mightn't tell me how beautiful I was and how I made his heart happy.

He wouldn't call me his special girl.

Joe had been horrified when he saw what I'd done to my hair. He'd called for Kathleen, who was living with us at the time, and her mouth opened wide in shock like a cartoon character.

'Oh, Heidi, what have you done to your lovely curls?' she asked.

I looked downwards. Yes, maybe I'd got carried away with the scissors. I didn't mean to cut my hair so short, but at the same time, I could see that it had got to Joe and that gave me a sense of satisfaction.

'Can you do anything with it?' he asked his sister.

'Christ, Joe, I don't think there's anyone who could do anything with that. We'll just have to try to tidy it up the best we can.'

Tidying it up the best they could, involved hauling me to the nearest old lady, style-and-set hairdressers. They begged a really rather fed up-looking hairdresser to do her best to fix it. She was clearly about to head home for the day, so they offered her a generous tip.

She did the best she could, but fashioned what could only be described as a crew cut out of it all. The result certainly provoked a reaction, but not one I might have hoped for.

'Look at you! Just look at you, cutting all your hair off like that. Oh, Heidi, when it broke your poor mammy's heart to lose her hair to the cancer and you're after hacking your own hair off,' Granny had wept and I had felt worse than I thought was possible.

Perhaps unexpectedly, Ciara had a cruel reaction. 'Did you have nits or something? Because I'll have to get Daddy to boil wash every towel and sheet in that horrible hovel of yours before I come and visit again,' she sneered.

When I had curled up on my bed and sobbed, no longer buoyed by the thought my actions might actually make my life a little easier, Kathleen had come and sat beside me, tenderly resting her hand on my shoulder.

'You know we all just need to be brave now, Heidi, don't you? And we all have to work together to get through this. I know it's very, very sore on you. And it's not one bit fair, but try to remember there are other people hurting, too. Yes, you lost your mammy and that's awful, sweetheart. But Joe lost his partner. He loved your mother very much and he'd hoped to spend the rest of his life with her. He's hurting too and he doesn't always get it right. But he does try. If we all try, it will come good. I promise.'

That was the first time I almost told her. The words were on the tip of my tongue. She was being kind. She was listening, at least. She was saying it was hard for us all. But she didn't know the truth. She didn't know that after my mother had died Joe had started to do those things to me. Maybe if I told her, she'd talk to him just like she was talking to me. She would tell him to stop. Tell him that he had to try harder, too.

I wanted so much to tell her, but I was eleven. I couldn't find the words. I couldn't say why it felt wrong, or how I knew it wasn't natural, or how I just wanted it all to stop. So I curled up in a tighter ball and shrugged her hand away. I didn't speak. Didn't interact. And after a while she stood up and, without saying a word, left.

I think she had already made up her mind about me.

Chapter Thirty-One

Heidi

Now

'I heard about your doll; I'm very sorry. You must be very upset about it,' Ciara says. 'I know how much she meant to you.'

I feel my cheeks burn. The room is silent. Kathleen is staring down at the table. She looks as if she has aged ten years overnight. I've come downstairs with Lily to find them all, apart from Stella, sat around the table drinking tea. Alex can't quite meet my eye and I know without having to ask that they have been talking about me. I notice Kathleen looking at the dressing on my hand. God only knows what they have been saying, but I feel my paranoia grow.

Ciara sounds genuine in her sympathy, but she has always been one to manipulate a room.

'It's okay,' I lie. 'I'm over it. It's only a doll, right?'

'Oh, but she was your special doll, from your mum.'

Her tone is so subtle that not everyone would pick up that

she is goading me. I try to ignore her. I don't have the patience for her games right now.

'Has there been any news?' I ask, eager to change the subject.

Kathleen answers, 'Not yet. Marie phoned earlier, said she was trying to get some information from that DC King woman. I just don't like it one bit. This is cruel. To take him away from us like this. It's cruel and unnecessary. You think they could at least keep us informed. I've had people calling, texting, asking what's happening and what am I supposed to tell them? That he has unexpected marks on his body?' She bursts into tears, her shoulders shuddering. 'It's mortifying.'

'It's just procedure,' I say. 'We have to keep telling ourselves that. I'm sure none of us has anything to hide.'

'I'm sure Mum will call as soon as she has any more news,' Ciara adds. 'But maybe I'll text her again to be sure.'

Kathleen nods as Ciara starts to tap a message to Marie on her phone. There's a moment's silence that does nothing to quiet my growing paranoia.

'I think I'd like to stay here tonight,' Kathleen says, breaking the silence. 'In case there's any word. I mean, it's getting on a bit and I don't want to be anywhere else if he comes home.'

'I'd say they probably won't release his remains until the morning now,' Alex says.

Kathleen and Ciara both glare at him as if the thought has only just struck them for the first time.

'I'm just saying, we've had no word at all. It's almost eight now and if they did release him, sure it would be the best part of two hours down the road from Belfast. The roads are icing up, too. Might be better for everyone if we just settled ourselves to the notion it will be the morning.'

'Well, we'll be staying here anyway,' Ciara pipes up. 'And if Kathleen wants to stay then she should stay.'

'But where will she sleep?' I ask. 'We'll be in my old room. You and Stella are in the spare room.'

'Sure, there's Joe's room,' Kathleen says.

I look around, waiting for someone else to say that there's something a little weird about that. His room, where he died. Where all his belongings still are. His bed, which he died in.

No one speaks. 'Is that not a little . . .' I start.

'It's not a little anything,' Ciara snaps before turning to Kathleen. 'I'll get you some fresh linen and towels. I can ask Stella to pick up some of your things from Pauline on her way back here.'

'That would be brilliant. I can call Pauline and let her know she'll call in. It will really mean a lot to me to be here,' Kathleen says, blinking back tears.

I look at her and think of the vibrant young woman she used to be.

'Of course it will,' Ciara says, rubbing her hand. 'This was your brother's home.'

There's no doubt this dig is entirely in my direction.

I bite my tongue again. Now is not the time to say I want space. I can't in good conscience force them to leave, or tell them they should all go until we have news from Belfast. And I certainly can't make a solid case for Kathleen not sleeping in Joe's room, other than the thought of it makes my skin crawl more than a little. If she's happy enough to do so, if it doesn't make her feel uncomfortable, who am I to argue?

Kathleen stands up, wipes away her tears on the sleeves of her cardigan. 'I think I'll go and get the room ready. Maybe even have a sleep.'

'I'll help you make up the bed,' Ciara says, getting to her feet.

I'm about to ask Alex if he finds it all as strange as I do, when the doorbell rings.

'I'll get it,' he says and leaves me holding the baby and feeling an impending sense of doom.

I hear an unfamiliar voice, solemn, formal. Alex says, 'I think you'd better come in.' He calls to Ciara and Kathleen, and me, that DI Bradley is at the door with two of his colleagues and he would like to speak to us.

Chapter Thirty-Two

Heidi

Now

We expected a phone call. We expected the funeral directors. We didn't expect DI Bradley to show up at the door. I'm not naive enough to think that a senior police officer calls out to a home at night without good reason or simply to pass on 'good' news.

DI Bradley follows Alex into the living room, asks if it's okay to sit down. I follow them in. The woman in the room is DC Eve King who came out earlier. I don't recognise the third colleague, but watch as he awkwardly sits down on one of the dining chairs we have moved into the room. He's at least six foot four and looks as if he is made of right angles, his legs too long and gangly. I stare at his feet, which seem inordinately big.

DI Bradley introduces the big-footed man as DC Mark Black, who in turn takes out a notebook and pen, his large hands dwarfing the pencil in them. None of us speak, and we are joined by Kathleen and Ciara.

'Is Ms Brown here?' DI Bradley asks.

'Stella's running a few errands. She'll be back in about an hour or so,' Ciara says.

'Okay,' DI Bradley nods as if he is giving himself time to think.

I wish he'd just spit it out. I can't breathe with fear.

'I'm afraid I have some distressing news for you, and in light of this we will need to speak to each of you on an individual basis. We can speak to you all here, or if you would prefer, we can talk at the station.'

I see Ciara glance to Kathleen. There is panic on her face. Ciara never usually shows anything but cold coolness in her expression. That she is rattled makes me feel worse. I press my fingernails into the palm of my hand, hoping the sharpness will stop me from spiralling into a panic.

'What is it, Officer?' Kathleen asks, her voice thin and reedy. She is twisting her hands together, pulling the skin tight against her bones.

'We have the preliminary results from the postmortem examination that took place this afternoon on Mr Joe McKee. These are, as I stated, preliminary results and we are awaiting further findings.' He cleared his throat and continued. 'It would appear from examination there is evidence to support the hypothesis that Mr McKee's death may not have been natural or indeed accidental.'

Kathleen blinks. 'What? Sorry? I don't . . . Can you speak in plain English?'

'What do you mean, not natural or accidental?' Ciara asks, cutting across her aunt.

I just sit and try to take in how this has all shifted again. How Joe has become the victim for once.

'There are early indications that Mr McKee, your father, died as a result of asphyxiation, most likely suffocation. There are

133

further injuries on his body, which the pathologist believes are of a non-accidental nature.'

Ciara's mouth hangs open. Her eyes are fixed uncomfortably on me before she staggers to her feet and gasps that she needs air.

DC Black is quick to stand, too, indicating to Kathleen that she should remain seated as he guides Ciara by the arm out into the hall, where the cold night air is whistling through the still open front door.

I hear muttering. Kathleen is blessing herself and whispering what I think are the prayers of the rosary. It's hard to tell through the buzzing in my ears. Lily starts to fuss and Alex tries his hand at settling her, but I can see he is thrown, too.

'What indications?' I ask. 'He looked very peaceful when Alex found him.'

And he had. When Alex had called us up, Joe had been lying in his bed as if he was merely asleep. One hand was under the covers and the other arm curled across his chest. He was flat on his back, his mouth just slightly open as if he were about to snore. His head turned just a fraction to the left. The bed was tidy. The room was tidy. I can still see it now.

'The pathologist will provide more information in due course,' DI Bradley said. 'Suffice to say, the pathologist is a very experienced professional. I believe there may be some unexplained bruising, to the torso and one of his hands. Some internal markings also.'

'But couldn't whatever marks you found just be down to the surgery, or bruising afterwards, or him bumping into something or falling or any number of things?' I note there is more than a hint of hysteria in my voice and yet I seem powerless to quell it.

I think of how Ciara stared at me. Does she think I did it? Did she think I was capable of killing someone? Maybe I need some air, too. Am I allowed to leave the room? Will DI Bradley have to escort me?

'As I've said, the state pathologist is a very experienced professional. We expect that further results will corroborate his hypothesis.'

Big words with a big impact. I see Kathleen look up from her prayers. Her brow furrows. She looks at me and I wonder, is she thinking I'm responsible? Has Ciara been whispering in her ear? Am I being judged for the messed-up teenager I was?

'We fully appreciate this must be a terrible shock,' DI Bradley says.

It seems such a bizarre thing to say. So completely understated.

'A terrible shock? You're telling us one of us might be a killer and the best you can say is that "this must be a terrible shock".'

I feel Alex's arm on mine, steadying me. He is trying to ground me. I shake it off. I don't want to be grounded. I'm scared. I'm scared that someone in this room might be a murderer and I'm terrified that most of the people in this room seem to think that the murderer is me.

'What happens now?' Alex asks. 'Are we all under arrest? How does this work?'

Under arrest? No. That can't be . . .

DI Bradley shakes his head. 'No. We are still gathering evidence, which is why we need to speak to you all. There isn't sufficient evidence to arrest anyone at this time. You may, if you wish, have a solicitor present while we talk, but I want to make it clear that we are examining all possibilities and no one person is under direct suspicion at this time. What we do need to do is have forensics come in and look around the house, in particular Mr McKee's bedroom, where we believe he died. Can I ask, has anyone been in that room since this morning?'

'We've all been in it,' Kathleen says. 'The girls tidied and stripped the bed. I've just put new bed sheets on. I was going to sleep there. Alex, you were in too, weren't you?'

He nods. 'I think so, earlier. Yes, I brought some laundry up, put it in his chest of drawers.'

'Okay,' DI Bradley says with a slight shake of his head. 'We'll still need SOCO to come in and look around, although the scene has been compromised. The bed linen? Has that been washed yet?'

Ciara comes back into the room, her face sheet-white, and answers, 'Yes. Washed and dried. It's still in the dryer, though.'

DI Bradley sucks in air through his teeth. 'That's unfortunate. We'll take it anyway, just in case. Detective Constable Black will be staying here with you until SOCO arrive. We'll appoint a family liaison officer. It might be less distressing for you all if you have somewhere else you can go while the team examine the house.'

'I'll be staying here, thank you,' Ciara says. 'I don't want you rifling through my father's belongings without a family member present.'

Kathleen has stopped praying and finally speaks. 'This has to be a mistake,' she says. 'I don't care how experienced your pathologist is, he or she is wrong. No one murdered my brother! That's ridiculous. It makes no sense. Who in here would be so brutal as to hurt a frail old man?'

Her voice is getting louder. She looks at me while she spits out her last few words and I have all the confirmation I need that I am very much in the frame for Joe's murder. In the eyes of his nearest and dearest, at least.

Chapter Thirty-Three

Heidi

Now

The clock in the hall ticks loudly and the old radiators rattle as the heating comes on. It's bitter cold outside now, I can hear the rain lash against the windows.

The police van has pulled up, officers are coming in, dressed in white suits, carrying cases and bags and lights, and people are asking questions. I can see curtains twitching across the street. A neighbour's car pulls up, but he doesn't go straight into his house, despite the cold. He stands and watches. I see him lift his phone. The word will spread quickly.

It's late now. After ten. I'm exhausted and I can feel my nerves jangling. I want to do just what DI Bradley suggested and go elsewhere while the police pull the house apart, looking for God knows what, but Ciara has stated her intention to stay, as has Kathleen, and there is no way I'm leaving them to it. I dread to think what they could say or do to point the police in my direction. I'm still hoping the pathologist, for all his experience, is wrong. Not that Joe didn't deserve to be murdered – but just that the thought of there being a killer in our midst is unsettling and exhausting.

I yawn. 'I'm really tired,' I say as Alex and I sit together in the living room.

We haven't spoken much since DI Bradley left. I don't think we know what to say to each other. We're in shock.

I rest my head against Alex's shoulder and feel that he is tense. Guilt washes over me for embroiling him in this mess. I feel him kiss my forehead. It's typical of him that he is trying to comfort me.

'Curl up here,' he says, wrapping his arm around me. 'Take a nap here on the sofa if you can. I'll not leave you.'

He has barely finished talking before I've started to drift off.

I jump awake to Marie's voice, loud and distressed, in the living room.

'It's a nightmare,' she says. 'A nightmare.'

Ciara walks into the room and flings herself at her mother as if she is still a child and the pair sob loudly, dramatically.

'I didn't hurt him. I didn't do anything,' she sobs, her shoulders heaving up and down.

Marie pats her back, kisses the top of her head the way Alex had kissed me. They rock together, keening and sobbing, and Marie whispers over and over again that of course she knows that Ciara did nothing. Sure, Ciara doesn't have a bad bone in her body. She would never . . .

'I wanted to make it right between us,' Ciara cries. 'I thought we would have time. I thought he would've . . .' She descends into floods of tears again.

It feels as if they are putting on a show for the police's benefit. There had been no obvious indication before now that Ciara had wanted to make anything right with her father. Like me, she was tolerating him out of a sense of duty. This display does nothing to reassure me that a narrative that will ultimately point the finger of blame in my direction is being played out in front of me.

I can't bear to listen to them or watch their spectacle unfold any more, so I go to the kitchen, where I'm surprised to find Kathleen alone, her mug in her hand. No police officer is near.

'That big tall fellah has gone to make a phone call,' she says. 'I'm surprised he left me alone. If you're making a fresh cup of tea, I'll have one. This has gone cold.' She gestures to the murky beige liquid in the cup in front of her.

I hadn't been planning on making a cup of tea at all, but I fill the kettle and switch it on anyway.

'I just keep running everything over and over in my head all the time. Trying to make sense of it,' she says, her voice cracking as she struggles to keep her emotions in check. 'I can't help but wonder what they found . . . what they saw . . .' Her sentence drifts off.

I don't answer her. I simply make her tea and stir in a sugar before sitting it in front of her.

'I should've come home earlier,' she says. 'I should have, as soon as we knew he was sick. Sooner even.'

'Sure, we didn't know how sick he was. Not until the operation.'

That operation had changed everything. When his treatment had turned from curative to palliative. When we knew we were in the end game, we had a limited time to say all we needed to say and do all we needed to do. She came as quickly as she could after that.

We sit in silence for a bit, our thoughts doing enough talking for us.

'Things are very strained between you and Ciara, aren't they?' Kathleen asks.

I shrug. I don't know what she wants me to do. I can't deny it.

'It's been a very stressful time for everyone. You know things have always been challenging between us. Between all of us.'

She nods. 'I thought once you two girls grew up, you'd see some sort of common ground. It can't have been easy for Joe, dealing with his illness and the two of you at each other's throats.'

I'm annoyed. We were hardly at each other's throats. Yes, the tension was palpable, but we just did what we had to do while ignoring each other as much as humanly possible. There'd been no screaming, roaring rows.

I'm not sure how to answer. 'I'm not sure what you mean,' I stutter.

Kathleen moves awkwardly in her seat. 'Ciara says you've been cold with her, and I've seen it myself. Telling us all you couldn't wait to sell the house? And that was before he even . . .' She doesn't finish the sentence, can't bring herself to say that he has died. 'Look, I understand that this is a stressful time but, you know, given everything, it's not a good look for you.'

'Given everything? What exactly are you implying?' I say, feeling heat rise in my face. My heart rate starts to increase.

'I'm not implying anything,' she answers.

'Yes, it's true there's been no love lost between us, but that's not all down to me, Kathleen. You know that. You were there, remember? I tried to be a friend. As a child I tried, but she drew a very straight, very deep line in the sand and she's never wavered from that. And now? Well, now I'm big enough and ugly enough to choose not to pander to people who clearly don't give two damns about me.

'But that doesn't mean I've done anything wrong. I've been protecting my feelings. I've been protecting my family. I've not set out to hurt anyone. Not your precious niece and certainly not Joe. Though, God knows, there's little love lost there, either. But that doesn't mean I *killed* him, for the love of God!' I whisper the world 'killed', afraid to say it out loud.

'You are a cruel person, Heidi Lewis,' she says bitterly. 'I'm not saying he was perfect. I know his flaws, but he did the best he could for you when no one else wanted to. You never showed him any love. Any respect, even. Is it any wonder Ciara thinks you're responsible for what happened?'

'She can think what she wants, Kathleen,' I snap. 'It doesn't make it true.'

There's so much that I want to say. I want to tell her I showed him more love and respect than he ever deserved. That I had hurt myself by not breaking contact with him. That I had kept his sordid secrets because I was too ashamed of myself to admit them to anyone. I know I could shatter her illusions with a sentence or two – but what good would it do now? As far as I could see she had made up her mind, just like Ciara, and anything I could say would only be dismissed as the lies of a bitter woman.

'There's no need to get upset,' Kathleen says.

I look at her incredulously. She's just confirmed my suspicions that Ciara is pointing the finger of blame at me, and I'm not supposed to get upset?

'There's every reason to get upset,' I tell her. 'I see what's going on here. I know Ciara isn't the only person who thinks I'm to blame. Because of course I'd be to blame. Poor Heidi. Unhinged and mad. Sure, it was only a matter of time before I did something really bad, wasn't it?' I mock.

Kathleen has the good grace to blush, but I see how her body language changes, too. She tenses, pulls herself away from me a little. Does she think I'm not done? Does she think I've more people to despatch from this earth? More people who have wronged me? Because I'm sure she knows she wronged me, too.

Each of the McKees is as bad as each other and I won't be the fall guy for their twisted ways any more.

'I'm not saying that at all,' Kathleen says meekly.

'But you're thinking it,' I say, my voice low. 'It's written all over your face.'

I'm about to say more, when DC Black comes back into the room. As quick as anything, Kathleen is on her feet making him a cup of tea, even though he says he's had more than enough for one day.

I think we've all had more than enough – of everything – for one day. I've had more than enough for a lifetime.

Chapter Thirty-Four

Heidi

Then

Even as a teenager Ciara McKee could be unspeakably cruel. She was spectacularly lacking in any form of empathy.

She wore her hatred for me as blatantly as she wore her heavy goth make-up and her thick-soled boots. She was as wicked as any evil step-sister could be. I started to dread her visits.

It soon became not good enough that I simply stayed out of her way when she came over. She would come and find me, seemingly with the express purpose of making me feel as bad about myself as possible.

I spent my prepubescent years dreading every second weekend, knowing what was coming. The fact that I dreaded it even more than the weekends she didn't visit – the weekends when it was just Joe and me in the house – said a lot.

Is it any wonder my young mind started to struggle with notions of love and boundaries and what constituted abuse, given I was so desperate for attention and for affection?

When I was roughly eleven and Ciara would have been sixteen, I remember her perching on the end of my bed as I tried to read. I had taken to keeping my head in a book, escaping to more peaceful worlds as much as possible.

I wanted Ciara to leave me alone but I was too afraid to tell her to get lost, so I just did my best to ignore her.

'Do you know what I'd do if nobody wanted me the way no one wants you?' she said, a fraction too loudly for me to ignore.

I made the mistake of looking up and catching her gaze for the briefest of moments.

I didn't ask her to tell me, though. I stayed quiet. I'd learned that staying quiet generally made things go away quicker. I had already become adept at managing harmful situations. Or so I thought.

'I'd kill myself,' she said, as if she was talking to no one, then she turned to look at me. 'Don't you think that would be an idea? I mean, you must miss your mum a lot, and you could be back with her? I know some people say it's a sin, but how could it be? You'd just be going to be with your mum.'

She stared at me for a moment while I stared back. I didn't know what to say. How to react.

'That's what I'd do anyway,' she added before getting up and walking out of the room, leaving me, an eleven-year-old child, wondering if she had a point.

Chapter Thirty-Five

Ciara

Now

'We can do this in the morning, if you're getting too tired.' Detective Constable Eve King sits opposite me. She looks younger than me. Prettier too. Petite and able to carry off one of those pixie haircuts I'd love to have but that wouldn't suit my taller, more rounded frame.

She has a gentle way about her, a face that shows sympathy. I have to remind myself why she is here and why she wants to talk to me in the first place.

'I think I'd rather get this over and done with for now,' I say.

'And you're sure you don't want to have any legal representation?'

'There's no need. I've not done anything wrong.' I wonder if I sound too defensive.

'Okay,' DC King says. 'You can ask for legal representation at any time, and I'll remind you that you are not under any direct suspicion at this time. However, we will be making a note of everything you say and if things change, this information could be used in any court proceedings.'

I nod, wonder how long it will take. I'm so tired by now I think I could lie in bed while the SOCOs searched around me and not be bothered.

'When was the last time you spoke with your father?' she asks, DC Black at her side, pen poised.

'I'm not sure. Maybe it was around eight thirty. Nine perhaps. I brought him a cup of tea.'

'And did you stay with him for any length of time?'

'Not really. Five minutes maybe.'

'And what did you do when you were there?'

I shift in my seat. I don't want to tell her what I did when I was there. Things had become heated. Tension that had been simmering had boiled over. There's no way she would understand. There's no way in which telling her the truth would work in my favour.

I edit the facts in my head before I speak. 'I sat with him, on the chair by his bed, for a bit while he drank some of his tea. We talked about how he was feeling and then he said he was tired and was going to sleep, so I left.'

'And how did he say he was feeling?'

'Still quite sore from his operation, lethargic too.'

'And his frame of mind? How did that seem to you?'

Should I answer 'needy as be-damned'? Would that start a whole other series of questions coming my way?

'Well, he knew he was dying. You know, of cancer. He'd been quite low about that. And that he didn't feel he was rallying from his operation the way he should.'

'Had he expressed any thoughts of wanting to end his life?' She is looking at me directly in the eyes.

I shake my head. 'No. He wanted to hang on for as long as he could. He's . . . he was . . . a stubborn old goat.'

She pauses. 'I know in some circumstances like this, people who are terminally ill want to have some say in when they die. It's understandable really, especially if they worry they may be facing a lot of pain as their illness progresses. Sometimes they may ask someone to assist them in ending their life . . .'

So, the police think this might have been some sort of mercy killing? That someone had helped him go gentle into that good night? If only they knew the truth about my father, they wouldn't be so generous about anyone's motives.

I shook my head. 'He didn't want to die yet. If you're asking me if I performed some sort of mercy killing, you're on the wrong track altogether,' I said.

'I'm not saying that's what happened, of course,' DC King says. 'Although it would be understandable if someone wants to help someone end their life rather than see them suffer. Could he have asked any of the others?'

'I can't speak for what happened between my father and anyone else. But I'll state again, it's my firm belief that he didn't want to die.'

Detective Constable King nods, pushes a stray lock of her hair behind her ear and readjusts herself on her seat before looking back at me.

'After you left your father in his room that time, you didn't go back to see him at all?'

I shake my head again. 'No. I went downstairs. Watched a little TV with Stella and Auntie Kathleen. Stella went out to run some errands and Kathleen and I sat and chatted in the living room.'

She nods and DC Black scribbles furiously on his A4 pad of paper.

'Did you notice anyone else go to see your father?'

'I don't know,' I say. 'We were all in and out all the time.'

'Had you told the others he was going to sleep?'

Had I? I didn't remember.

'I don't know. We were all so tired and stressed. Things had been tense.'

She raises one perfectly arched eyebrow. DC Black stops writing for just a moment and looks up, too.

'How's that?' she says.

I'm getting tired now. Out of my depth. I've had enough.

'There's a complicated family dynamic here,' I say, trying to choose my words very carefully. 'And of course, knowing my father was dying was hard on us all.'

'What do you mean by complicated family dynamic?' she asks.

'Aren't all families complicated?' I say. 'It's been a long day and a long evening.' I can feel my lip start to tremble and I'm embarrassed to find that I'm on the brink of tears.

'Take your time,' DC King soothes and I roughly brush away a tear that has shamed me by running down my face.

'Look, Heidi is the daughter of the woman he left my mother for. He raised Heidi after her mother died. I was still just a teenager. Things were difficult. Heidi and I never saw eye to eye and we still don't. She was a very troubled child well into her teenage years. You know, mental health problems and the like.

'My father did his best to do right by her – at the expense of his relationship with me at times – but she never seemed to view him with anything other than utter disdain. But that doesn't mean she'd have done anything . . .' I said, knowing full well that it meant she was more than capable of it all the same.

'Of course it doesn't,' DC King says. 'How did she appear on the night of your father's death?'

'Tense,' I say. 'But we all were. We were all walking on eggshells. Just the night before she had told us she wanted to sell this house as soon as possible. It goes to her, you see. It was her

148

mother's and although my father was allowed to live here until he died, or formed a new family, it was always going to go to Heidi.

'It seemed very distasteful to have that conversation with him dying upstairs, but that's Heidi, you see. Cold at times. And she has just become a mother and by all accounts the house she's living in now isn't big enough for a growing family . . .'

'I imagine that conversation made you angry?' DC King asked.

'Well yes, of course it did. It was callous. But my anger was with Heidi and certainly not with my father. I mean, there's no telling what she's capable of . . . not that I'm saying it was her, of course,' I say, even though I want the blame to be shifted squarely onto her shoulders. It might just teach her to be more sensitive to other people and their feelings.

Chapter Thirty-Six

Heidi

Now

I've escaped the house for a while and am pushing Lily in her pram along the quay and back again, even though it is freezing and my face has started to go numb with the cold.

I needed to get away from the house. It's been just over two days since the police dropped the bombshell on us and we've spent hours talking to different officers. Going through the same details over and over again. They've been professional with us, nice even. But I can sense DI Bradley getting frustrated. They're no closer to finding any answers. None of us are, but I can't help but feel that they are all looking in my direction.

They've kept asking me about my relationship with him. How had we got along? Had there been tension between us? They say things must be stressful for me, with a small baby and now losing my father. I don't correct them that I have never considered him my father, in any sense of the word.

They've asked me repeatedly about the house. Did I really

have plans to sell it as soon as possible? They've asked about my mental health, any medication I'm on. But I'm not on medication just now. I've not been on medication for seven or eight years. I've been coping on my own. Doing well. And when I was sick, I directed all my self-loathing towards myself and only myself. I've never hurt anyone. I wouldn't.

They've asked if Joe had wanted me to help him die. If I thought someone might have helped him to end his life. I snort. While there was breath in his body, Joe McKee would have wanted to suck up whatever attention and sympathy he could muster. He wouldn't have willingly skipped out on his grand finale.

Alex has gone to work today to 'finish some urgent paper-work' and he couldn't wait to leave the house this morning. He'll be back as soon as he can, he says, but I have a feeling I won't see him for hours and as he's my only ally in the house, being without him there is too difficult.

After another round of questioning this morning, I'd called him and told him how I felt as if the walls were closing in on me. He said I was being paranoid. But I can hear something in his voice. Worry, or suspicion, maybe.

People stop talking when I walk into the room. I know what that means. I know who they are talking about.

I'm afraid to kick off. Afraid to fight my corner. Afraid to show any sort of strong emotion in case it feeds the narrative that I'm unhinged. What had been a stressful situation to begin with had now become almost unbearable.

So I'd rather face the cold than go home, even though it's threatening to rain and I should have worn a heavier coat. Keeping moving helps, you see. I focus on what I see, smell and hear. Keep mindful of the exact moment I'm in and ignore the bigger picture because I fear it will overwhelm me if I let it.

When my hands are so cold they start to turn blue, I push

Lily's pram into a nearby coffee shop and order a large latte. I catch my reflection in the window. I look old and haggard. Unkempt, with the dressing still on my hand. My other hand bruised and grazed from my run-in with the peeler. Dark circles under my eyes. No make-up, not that it could perform the miracle I need it to if I'm to look more human.

'Can I get you anything else?' the waitress asks as she puts the coffee down in front of me.

I shake my head, lift the cup, immediately using the heat from it to warm my hands. I could almost cry from this small feeling of physical comfort.

I just have to get through the next few days and weeks, I tell myself. I just have to believe in myself. I know I didn't hurt anyone. I know I'm innocent. I have to believe that will be enough to get me through this.

I feel a heaviness in the pit of my stomach. I look at my coffee. I don't think I've the stomach to drink it any more. My sense of freedom is slipping away.

Suddenly, I have to leave the café, even though I've just arrived. It feels, like so much in life, just too small. Much, much too claustrophobic. The scarf around my neck feels too tight. My coat too hot. The chatter of people around me too noisy. I feel as if they are looking at me. Talking about me. And us. Gossiping. The thing with living in Derry is that while it's a city, it still retains that small-town mentality. Everyone knows everyone else's business. Ironic really, given that no one stepped in when my life was falling apart after my mother died.

But they will all be talking. The rumour mill will be in full flow. Someone will have heard something and passed it on, and the Chinese whispers will have spread. *He's not home yet. Something must be up. Did someone hurt him? I always thought that girl of his looked like a bad sort! Do you remember the time . . .*

I push the pram out of the shop, out onto the quay again,

without making eye contact with anyone. I hear their voices anyway, as I walk as fast as I can, the rain thumping down now – thick, icy drops. I try to focus on my senses. What I see, smell and hear again. But it's all too much.

I want to scream at everyone to just shut up. I keep my head down trying to block out the noise, but it just seems to be getting louder and louder. It comes as a huge shock to me then when I look up and see that save for a few cars driving past, the street is empty.

I pause as tears roll down my cheeks, mixing with the raindrops. I pause and focus on the real noises around me. Try to slow my breathing.

Then my phone rings.

Chapter Thirty-Seven

Ciara

Now

'I never thought I'd have him back under this roof,' Mum says.

The coroner has agreed to release Joe's remains to her. He is satisfied there is no further physical evidence to be gathered from his body, and that we can go ahead and lay him to rest.

Well, I say we. There was no way they were letting his remains come back to his home at Aberfoyle Crescent and certainly not to any of us 'suspects'.

My mother, on the other hand, with the help of a canny solicitor, has come to an arrangement that her home would be suitable for him to be brought back to.

My mother is beside herself with emotion that he will be back in what was our family home. It does nothing to make me believe she doesn't still love him. That she never stopped loving him.

We can't all escape the overall feeling that everything is off-kilter, though. Yes, we will be able to bury him, and that will provide a small amount of relief, but a cloud hangs over us all. Nothing is really resolved. They will be watching us all intently as we grieve. Looking for clues. For some reason, they don't seem to be picking up on my hints about Heidi. As usual she seems to be able to win people around with her little-girl-lost act. But I'm not buying it and I'll make sure no one else does, either.

'Can we keep the house private, Mum?' I ask. It will be bad enough to have the police hovering.

'Lots of people will want to say their goodbyes to your father,' she says.

It's virtually unheard of for houses to remain closed to visitors during a wake. She's right, of course people will want to traipse in and out, pay their respects, offer a quick prayer by the coffin side and then sit with us and drink their tea while eating curling sandwiches.

'Lots more will want to gawk,' I say. 'People are talking, Mum. They know something is up. Don't you think they'll all just want a nosy at us? They'll be trying to figure out whodunnit.'

The expression sounds more flippant than I intended and my mother baulks.

'There's no need to be so crass. Your father is dead, Ciara. Murdered, if the police are right.'

She says the word 'murdered' in a whisper. None of us can really believe we are even saying these words or thinking this way.

'Well, that's more reason not to have all and sundry walking in through the door, then. There'll be people who didn't even know him or care about him wanting in. They can gawk at the funeral if they want, but give us this at least.'

'He deserved a better send-off than this . . .'

Mum looks bereft. I've never understood how she remained so fond of him for all these years. I remain convinced that if he had asked her if they could try again she would have jumped at the very thought. Her continued loyalty to him is something that I have to admit I struggle to understand. Then again, she doesn't know everything. That angers me. Her unyielding loyalty to him.

'What he doesn't deserve is people wanting to make him nothing more than a news story and what I don't need is people eyeing me up, trying to work out if I'm responsible for putting him in the ground in the first place!'

My voice is high-pitched. Screechier than normal. I can see Mum recoil further and further as the volume of my voice increases.

'Ciara, please,' she says, her voice small, lacking in its usual authoritative tone. 'Please just stop. I don't want to have this conversation.'

'Don't you?' I ask her. 'Don't you want to have this conversation instead of dancing around it all? We're all walking on eggshells. You've not even asked me if I did it, Mum. Don't you want to know if it was me? If I was the one who put the pillow over his head and pressed down until he stopped breathing?'

I feel the sharp sting of her hand across my cheek before I even register what is happening. My mother has never once, in all her life, lifted her hand to me. She never smacked me as a child. Even as a teenager when I was a little bitch and probably deserved a good slap, she would let me rage until I was spent, and then we would sit down and talk together.

The shock of feeling her strike me winds me. I gasp, stare at her, while I bring my own hand to my injured cheek, feel the heat of it rise.

I can see my mother's gaze, steely and strong. She doesn't look shocked that she hit me. She certainly doesn't look sorry.

'Ciara McKee, I never want to hear you talk that like again, do you understand?'

I stare and she steps closer to me, dropping her voice lower. It's more menacing than her screaming at me could ever be.

'I said, do you understand?'

I nod, willing the tears that sprung to my eyes to stay where they are and not to betray me by falling.

'I don't need to ask you if you did it because I know you, Ciara. You are my child and I know you could never have done something like that. You're not capable of it, and even if you are too stubborn to admit it, I know you loved your father just as he loved you. Now, I want you to pull yourself together and help us all get through the next two days. We'll do it your way. Closed house. Now let that be an end to this stupid conversation.'

She turned on her heel and walked away before I could say anything else. Before I could tell her that she was wrong. I did not love my father. It wasn't something I was simply too stubborn to admit. I hated him.

And I did have bad bones in my body – a badness I'd maybe inherited from him. Or maybe, just maybe, it was more that I had a sense of justice. You couldn't mess up people's lives without any consequences. That was not how the world worked. Everyone had to learn that lesson, no matter how painful.

'You're awful pale-looking,' Kathleen says.

We are sheltered together on the back porch of my mother's house. I'm sucking on my e-cig but it's still not quite hitting the mark. I remind myself it's better than nothing.

Kathleen has 'tapped' a sneaky cigarette from Pauline, who swore she didn't smoke but always has a box in her bag 'for emergencies'. My aunt is clearly not an experienced smoker – she splutters and coughs as she tries to inhale the warm smoke.

'Out of practice,' she says when she's got her breath back. 'But it's either this or a double vodka.'

I am shocked. With her new sensible appearance, her conservative take on life and the rosary beads she had pulled from her bag and insisted were to be placed in my father's hands when the coffin was opened, I didn't see her as the double-vodka type. I don't even see her as the single-vodka type, if I am honest.

Her hand is shaking ever so slightly as she lifts the lit cigarette to her lips one more time and inhales again, exhaling more naturally this time.

'It's all too much at times, isn't it?' she asks, looking out at the small patch of lawn that makes up my mother's garden.

'It is,' I agree, asking for a drag of her 'proper' cigarette, enjoying the hit of the warm smoke at the back of my throat. 'I'm nervous. Of seeing him again, you know. Is that silly?'

'Is that what has you so shaken up?'

I nod. I'll not tell her about the set-to I've just have with my mother, even though the sting of her hand still burns at my cheek.

'Among other things,' I say wryly.

'Do you think they have any evidence?' Kathleen asks. 'I mean, you see these shows now on the TV and they always catch the killer. There'll be a hair, or a fingerprint, or a drop of blood or something . . .'

I shake my head. 'I don't know. I'm trying not to think about it much. I'm still hoping they'll come back and say they made a mistake.'

'Do you think they will?' Her eyebrows raise. 'I thought it was all pretty conclusive at this stage. They wouldn't release his body if there was any question.'

Her expression sags again as she speaks. Almost as if she allowed hope to flicker in for the briefest of seconds before the reality of where we are sets back in.

I suck on my e-cig before sending a billow of fragrant steam into the air.

'I don't get the impression they are minded to drop the investigation any time soon,' I say.

She sniffs at the air, drops the half-smoked cigarette to the ground and grinds it out with the heel of her shoe.

'What if they can't pin it on anyone? What do you think they'll do? Will it be worse if we don't ever really know what happened?'

She looks sad. Lost. Dad was her only sibling. She has him on some out-of-reach pedestal and while I'd love to knock it out from under him and tell her the truth, not even I would be that cruel.

'I don't know,' I say with a shrug.

I can't think straight any more. I'm exhausted with thinking. I'm exhausted by it all.

My mother's voice from the kitchen, announcing that she needs us to discuss a floral tribute, disturbs us. I take one last drag from Kathleen's cigarette before handing it back to her.

'I suppose we should get on with this,' I tell her.

She has already ground out THE HALF SMOKED CIGARETTE

VERY BAD EDITING

Chapter Thirty-Eight

Heidi

Now

I'm back at Aberfoyle Crescent, picking through a house that has been picked through by the police a number of times now. There is dust from where fingerprints have been taken. Things have been placed back on the chest of drawers, or on shelves but just not quite in the right order. Kathleen wanted me to pick up some things for the wake. A framed picture of Joe at the library, one of his silk hankies to place in the pocket of the suit jacket he is to be laid out in. His prayer book, so that she can help Father Brennan choose some of Joe's favourite readings from the Bible or prayers for the funeral service.

I've been looking for the book for twenty minutes now, in all the usual spots, but it can't be found. I don't actually recall the last time I saw it, but then it had become such a part of him, I'd almost stopped noticing it at all.

'I'm really sorry,' I tell her over the phone. 'But I haven't seen it and I'm not sure where else to look. Unless maybe the police put it somewhere?'

'Why would they do that?' she asks, an accusing tone in her voice.

'I don't know,' I answer. All I know is that I can't find it and I don't want to be here for any longer than I need to be.

I hear Kathleen have a muffled conversation with someone in the background before her voice comes back on the line.

'Ciara seems to think she saw you with it, but sure, maybe she's mistaken? These things happen.'

There's a tone in her voice that lets me know she doesn't quite believe me.

I have pulled open every drawer in his room and in the living room. Opened every cupboard and wardrobe looking for it. As the clock moves closer and closer to the time Joe's remains will be brought back to Marie's house, Kathleen is becoming more frantic. I'm tempted to tell her it's okay to use whatever prayers she sees fit. It's not like Joe will be able to hear them anyway.

'I didn't see his prayer book,' I tell her truthfully. 'I've not seen it days, come to think of it. 'I'm not sure what Ciara saw me with, but it wasn't that.'

Kathleen sighs. 'Why is nothing going right?' she says, and I'm not sure for a moment or two if she expects an answer. 'Look, I think maybe just get here to Marie's. Joe's remains will be back soon and we really do need to give a united front. Things are bad enough as it is.'

Her negativity weighs heavy on my mind as I drive to Marie's. Not even picking Alex up from work and having him sit beside me can calm my nerves. I notice that I'm gripping the steering wheel tightly. The rhythmic swiping of the windscreen wipers, battling the sleety rain, gives me something to try to concentrate on, to time my breathing with. Neither Alex nor I talk.

I've never been in Marie's house before, but I can't imagine, despite what she has said, that I'll be made to feel welcome there. And up until now I didn't think it possible that I could feel any less welcome than I already have over the last few days.

Marie lives in a terraced house in Lower Creggan. Her home is clearly her pride and joy, the small front garden beautifully manicured and tended. Flower beds and garden ornaments guide us along the concrete path to her front door, which Alex knocks on while Lily and I shiver behind him.

The door opens and Marie is standing dressed all in black, face solemn. 'Alex,' she nods at him before looking at me. 'Heidi,' she says, offering me a half-hearted kiss on the cheek. 'Come in,' she says as Kathleen calls out, 'We're through in the living room.'

We follow her through a small hall into her lounge, where I notice a row of sympathy cards lined up on her mantlepiece, declaring how very sorry people are for her loss. It strikes me as more than a little odd, given how long ago their marriage ended, but I realise that saying anything to that effect wouldn't be received well. So I keep quiet and let Marie continue acting the part of the grieving ex-wife with aplomb.

'Here, let me help you with your things,' Kathleen says, taking the changing bag from me and trying to help me out of my coat, even though I'm more than able to take it off myself.

Marie adds, 'Ciara has just nipped out to the shop but she'll be here soon. As will Father Brennan. Joe should be home in about an hour.'

She looks fidgety, on edge. Her nervous energy adds to my own.

'I've cleared the box room upstairs for him,' she says. 'Ciara asked that the house be closed, so I figured we wouldn't need that much room.'

'Thank you for doing this for him,' I say, because it feels like the right thing to do.

'Why wouldn't I do it? It should be from his own home, but I'll do my best for him. And I suppose this was his home for a time, and most of that time it was a happy home.'

Her tone is sharp, her comments pointed. I want to turn and leave, but that would only give them something else to think badly of me about.

'Of course,' I mumble and turn my attention to my still-sleeping daughter, taking her out of her car seat and slipping her out of her snowsuit.

It feels too warm in Marie's living room. I can't have Lily overheating. It's bad enough that I can feel the first prickles of sweat on the back of my own neck.

The doorbell rings, a sharp, shrill noise that, given that we are all on our nerves at the moment, makes us jump. Marie takes a deep breath as if settling herself and goes to answer the door. I hear her tone, markedly more welcoming than she was with me.

'Come in, Father,' she says. 'You're very good to come, and this not even your parish.'

'Sure, he'll be buried from his own church, even if he couldn't be waked from his own home. How're you all holding up?'

Father Brennan speaks in hushed tones. A soft Donegal lilt that I sometimes swear they train priests in at the seminary in Maynooth.

'As best as can be expected,' Marie replies, although to me she appears to be in her element as chief mourner. 'Sure, you go on in to the living room and I'll bring through some tea.'

He walks into the room, nodding, as always, to me and then lifting one of his long, pointy fingers and trying to tickle a still-sleeping Lily under the chin.

'A blessing in these dark times,' he mutters.

I resist the urge to slap his hand away.

Father Brennan is a small man, whose shoulders always seem

to slump and whose head always seems to be nodding in some perpetual motion, so it looks, at least, like he is always listening to you. Joe had a great deal of time for him. I did not. Something about him gave me the creeps – perhaps it was the way he regarded me up and down every time he saw me.

He sits down and doesn't even try to make small talk, something for which I am eternally grateful. He speaks, of course, when Kathleen comes into the room, asking her how she is. Telling her it's an awful business altogether and that he is here for her should she ever need his counsel.

She thanks him for his time, sits down and straightens her skirt, and we fall into silence while waiting for Marie to arrive with the tea.

'Maybe I should offer to help,' I say to no one in particular.

'I'm sure she has it under control,' Kathleen says.

I interpret that as a clear message that I'm not wanted in Marie McKee's kitchen. The front door opens again and I hear Ciara shout her hellos as she comes in. Once she takes her seat in the living room I will feel truly outnumbered.

I try to remind myself to breathe.

Ciara comes in, closely followed by her mother.

'Did you really not find that prayer book?' Ciara asks as if I'd not looked hard enough, or had hidden it just to be difficult.

'I looked high and low and couldn't see it,' I say. 'I've not seen it in days.'

Marie sighs deeply. 'That's a shame, you know.'

'I could have sworn I saw you with it. The day he died?' Ciara's tone is accusatory.

I shake my head. 'No, you have to be mistaken. I did see his diary, when I was with you, but you took it from me, remember?'

'Oh yes,' she says, 'because you were prying in it. I remember now.'

I blush. I want to say something back to her but I'm aware we have an audience and none of that audience would naturally fall on my side.

Father Brennan's head turns between the two us, as if he's watching a tennis match and it's Ciara's turn to serve.

He interjects, 'Sure, never worry,' clearing his throat. 'I knew Joe well. We can still make his requiem Mass a fitting one. I know these must be very difficult times. Very difficult, indeed,' he says with a shake of his head. 'But we do owe it to Joe to try to remain civil to each other and I must say, to you all now, that if anyone feels they wish to chat to me, privately, the sanctity of the confessional is as good a place as anywhere to get something off your chest.

'We know that something very disturbing happened, perhaps, as it has been suggested, with some good intention behind it. A merciful release from the suffering that may have awaited Joe, but that suffering has to go somewhere. And it will eat at the heart of us all, not least the person responsible. God is good, He is forgiving, even of the most serious of sins. But you must repent.'

I don't dare speak. I am holding so much inside that I'm afraid to.

It seems I'm not the only one. We descend into silence, only disturbed by Lily waking and starting to fuss. She needs her nappy changed and I lift her bag.

'Where can I change this little one?' I ask Marie, grateful for the reprieve.

Ciara is on her feet. 'I can take her and change her for you,' she says. 'You can sit here and talk to Father Brennan about the Mass, since you knew my father better than anyone. I'm sure this wee dote won't mind her auntie Ciara changing her. Won't you not?' she says, cooing at my daughter as if she has been a permanent fixture in her life.

165

She seems terribly eager to get out from under the glare of Father Brennan's eyes.

I want to tell her to leave my baby alone. Not to touch her. But I'm aware I'm already walking on eggshells and causing an even bigger scene could be disastrous.

'Ah now,' Ciara soothes as Lily wriggles in her arms. 'There's no need for that! I'll just get you a fresh nappy on,' she adds, reaching for the baby bag.

I don't want her taking it – it has my phone, my purse, other random items from my life inside.

'I'll get you a nappy and wipes,' I say, trying to take the bag from her.

'Now, Heidi, I'm sure I can figure out what is what myself,' Ciara says, turning and walking upstairs with my baby and my worldly belongings.

I am frozen to the spot, unsure of how to react to this ambush but aware that four sets of eyes are looking at me and waiting for my reaction, including Alex, who I need to believe in more than anything. I try to settle myself, turn and nod towards Father Brennan and Marie before taking a seat beside them.

Father Brennan clears his throat, a guttural sound that has a hint of phlegm about it. I feel mildly queasy.

'I know how difficult this must be,' Father Brennan says. 'But, Heidi, maybe you might know what his favourite readings were, or maybe his favourite hymns. I've a soloist from the choir who is available to do some singing if you want?'

I try to focus on what he is saying but I'm distracted listening for the sound of crying from upstairs.

'Heidi . . .' I hear Marie speak my name.

'Sorry . . . I, no. I can't think. He always, I suppose, he liked that hymn 'Be Not Afraid'. He used to sing that, after my mother died. I remember that.'

As soon as I say it I want to take it back. I don't want any memories from then. From that time after she was gone and things just became worse.

'That's a grand one,' Father Brennan says and Marie nods.

'But don't feel you have to use it,' I say as I hear a squeal from my baby echo through the hall. 'I mean, Marie, maybe you would know more.'

Lily is quiet again. I'm still incredibly uncomfortable. I feel as if all my nerve endings are fizzing.

'Father, you'll know, no offence, I'm not a big churchgoer, so I'm fine with whatever you choose,' I say.

I wonder, could I make my excuses and escape for some fresh air? I don't care that the sleet has now turned to snow. I just need to breathe.

I make to stand up.

'Now, have you thought about the Prayers of the Faithful at all?' he says, stopping me. 'Would you want to say them, or are there any friends or relations who might? I know some people even like to write them themselves, within reason, though. This is a Mass, after all.'

I shake my head. I don't want to say them or write them. I'd be happy to drop him off at the cemetery gates and be done with the whole thing.

'I can sort that out, Father,' Marie says, her voice solemn.

'Now, can I check family names? You know I'll be wanting to mention you all in the homily – and I'd hate to leave anyone out. So there's yourself, Heidi and Ciara, of course. Marie, you were his wife.'

'They were divorced,' I say. 'More than twenty years ago. He was with my mother, until she died. Natalie. Her name was Natalie.'

I'm shocked to feel tears spring to my eyes at the mention of her name. Then my stomach lurches. He won't be buried in the same plot as her? Oh Christ, I don't want him there. I don't want him near her. I feel a panic build in me. I should've said to the undertakers. But surely Ciara wouldn't want to give any legitimacy at all to Joe's relationship with my mother? She wouldn't want them buried together. But I should check anyway. To be sure.

I hear a wail from Lily again and I have to close my eyes and force myself to sit on my hands not to run directly to her and pull her from Ciara's arms.

Marie pales, looks at me like I'm quite mad. I hear Marie say something, which I can't catch because there's a buzzing in my ears, and I blink to try to bring myself back into focus.

'Sorry?' I ask. 'What was that?'

I see Father Brennan has turned a funny shade of puce.

'I don't know how you don't know this, Heidi. But Joe and I were never divorced. We were separated yes, but legally and in the eyes of the Church, we were still very much married.'

Chapter Thirty-Nine

Heidi

Now

Still married? After all these years? I don't understand. My brain doesn't process what Marie is saying.

'I suppose we just never got round to it, and there didn't seem so much of a reason after . . .' Her voice trails off.

I know what she means to say. That there didn't seem to be much of reason after my mother died. Marie's replacement was gone – no longer a threat.

Joe didn't ever have another serious relationship after that. There was no one who wanted to usurp her role as Joe's wife and clearly she was happy to retain the title.

'The notion of divorce never really rested easy with Joe,' she says and I truly wonder if I am going mad.

This man who left his wife, his daughter, and inveigled his way into my family, into my mother's bed – wasn't really comfortable with the idea of divorce? He'd a funny way of showing it.

'Yes, well, he was a religious man, a good man,' Father Brennan says, and I can no longer sit and listen to these platitudes or resist the urge to run to my daughter.

I get up without speaking, because I don't trust myself not to say something that will be used against me in the future.

I am furious like I have never been furious before. I can feel the anger surge in me as if it is running through my very veins. I'm angry not only on my behalf, but also on behalf of my mother – who loved him. Who trusted him. Who sat down and wrote in her will that this man she had known just over a year could stay in the house she owned until he remarried or passed away. This man who had no intention of ever remarrying. Or unmarrying anyone.

I wonder, did my mother, my beautiful, trusting, kind-hearted mother know that he had never divorced Marie? That he found the idea of divorce uncomfortable. That he was a hypocrite of the highest order – knelt at the altar rails every morning and prayed while he betrayed, lied to and hurt everyone he came into contact with. How could Marie be so calm? How could she be so forgiving of him? After all he had done?

Maybe she liked that she always had some sort of a connection to him – one more than sharing a child together, which was clearly not enough for her – but to be his wife? To have had, all these years, one up on the woman he left her for? My hands are curled into fists and I know I'm stomping up the stairs to find my daughter in this unfamiliar house, and I know I have to calm down before I reach Lily because she will feel the tension radiating off me in massive waves.

I reach an open door at the top of the stairs where Ciara is cooing at my daughter and for a second I feel myself relax, but then I notice the small, navy leather-bound book at her side. Joe's prayer book, tatty and well thumbed. Prayer cards and Mass cards poking out. A thick elastic band holding it all together.

'Where . . .' I start as her eyes dart to mine. 'Where was that?'

'Like you don't know, Heidi. I don't know what games you're playing or why you'd pick now of all times to play them, but this is hard enough without you making it harder.'

Confused, I look at her. She is angry. I see that. I see the same anger that I'm feeling in my veins reflected in her. I see the almost imperceptible shake of her hands, hear the slight but definite tremor in her voice.

'I don't know what you mean,' I say, struggling to control the tremor in my own voice.

'It was here, Heidi. In your bag. In that bloody baby bag. Right there, where I couldn't miss it when I went to change Lily.'

'No,' I shake my head. 'It wasn't. I didn't have it. I haven't seen it for days.'

Lily starts to whimper again. Clearly, she can feel the tension growing anyway, even if I'm not holding her. This room feels like all the air is being sucked out of it. Ciara stands up and I'm a scared child again, looking up at her and trying to understand her, but not being able to break through the walls she has thrown up.

'You're mad!' she spits. 'Fucking mad! Just like your mother before you. She had to wreck things and here you are messing with our heads now. Making accusations. Hiding things. Jesus Christ, Heidi! How far will you go? How far have you gone? You complete fucking loony bin. Why the police haven't carted you off long before now is beyond me. It's beyond anyone.'

Before I know it, before I even have the chance to think about it, my hand is raised and moving, and I have to use every ounce of strength in me to stop myself.

'Fuck you,' I hiss, my hand tingling with the unspent force of a slap directly across her face.

Ciara just glares at me. Anger radiating from her.

'I'll take this with me,' she says in short staccato beats, lifting the prayer book from the bed. 'And thanks for giving me one more thing to tell the police about,' she adds, sidestepping me and leaving the room, closing the door softly behind her.

My breath comes rushing out of my body as I crumple onto the bed beside my daughter and try to soothe her, and at the same time try to soothe myself.

Chapter Forty

Heidi

Then

I was given my first mobile phone for my fifteenth birthday. My grandparents, who I knew had very little, had saved up and bought me a Nokia. They might as well have given me a million pounds.

I felt spoiled. And so grown up as I plugged it in for the first time and charged it before spending half an hour tapping in the details of the few friends I had from school, as well as my grandparents' landline number.

It rarely rang, of course, because calls cost so much money we were almost afraid to use the phones. Text messages were a little less expensive, so I exchanged those with my friends. Silly little things about homework, or who we had a crush on, or to arrange to meet at the bus depot on Foyle Street before wandering around the shops.

This phone, basic as it was compared to the phones that exist now, was a lifeline. It meant that when I went home I was no longer confined to long nights with just Joe for company. I would escape to my room, close the door and engage with my friends. I'd asked Joe if we could get a computer, maybe even get the Internet at home. He'd refused. Said I could go to the library and use theirs. But the thought of spending more time under his eye was more than I could take.

At least, at that stage, his night-time visits had stopped. Not that it meant he treated me any better. In fact, there were times when he just seemed even angrier at me. Fed up with me. I suppose I didn't serve him any purpose any more. I was just a drain on his resources at that time.

God, it was so messed up. Because, of course, I was glad the abuse wasn't happening any more. But I was fifteen years old and craved the affection of a father figure. I tried to make him like me. I cringe now when I think of it. Weep for the poor child I was.

I never told my friends. I would die if they knew. When they talked about their first boyfriends, their clumsy first experiences of kissing and more, I stayed quiet. I had no interest in finding a boyfriend. I had no interest in kissing anyone, never mind having sex. It baffled me that some of them seemed to enjoy it so much.

I was midway through a text chat with one of my friends about how she had let her boyfriend touch her boobs, under her clothes, when a new message buzzed its way into my inbox.

For a moment I allowed this small feeling of smugness to wash over me. I was, sort of, popular. My phone was buzzing. With a sense of great anticipation I opened the new message to see it was from a number I didn't recognise.

You're nothing but a mad little bitch. Everyone hates you.

I recoiled from the phone as if it had actually burned me, tossing it to the end of my bed. Then I scrabbled to reach it again, to look at the number, which I wrote down on a piece of paper. I figured I'd ask around at school to see if anyone knew who the number belonged to, but then I realised they'd all ask questions. They'd all want to know why I needed to know and I'd be too embarrassed, too scared that they would tell me the message was the truth, to show it to them.

I read it over and over again. My heart thumping. Was that why bad things happened to me? Because I was mad? Because I deserved to be punished? I covered my ears to try to drown out the voices in my head, which was about as successful as you would expect, and I curled myself into a ball on my bed and wondered if Ciara had been right all along. I should just kill myself and be done with it.

Chapter Forty-One

Heidi

Now

Alex walks into the bedroom moments after I hear Ciara stomp downstairs. I'm scarlet with rage and embarrassment. What will she be saying now to everyone? To Father Brennan?

'Erm . . . what's going on? Ciara's very upset,' he asks me. 'She says you raised your hand to hit her.'

There's a look of disappointment about him. It actually emboldens me. Angers me further. That he isn't automatically on my side. Why is no one ever automatically on my side?

I'm ashamed that I raised my hand, but I'm not sorry. What she had said had been vile.

'I didn't actually hit her!' I protest. 'She deserved a slap across the face but I stopped myself.'

'Jesus Christ, Heidi! It's her father's wake. She's down there bawling and giving out in front of everyone. What will they think of you? Is it not bad enough that our every move is being watched anyway?'

'They can watch all they want, Alex,' I spit back at him. 'Something fucked up is going on in all this and I've had enough of trying to keep the waters smooth. She accused me of stealing Joe's prayer book – of hiding it in Lily's changing bag so they couldn't see it to choose stuff for the funeral.

'She called my mother mad. And me, too. She says I'm crazy. I'm not the crazy one or the one keeping secrets, Alex. Marie's just told me that she and Joe never even got divorced! After mum died, they just didn't bother. How on earth am I supposed to react to that? Just sigh and accept it as not as messed up as it really is?

'And I'm sure they are setting me up for this. They want everyone to think it was me. That I killed him. Everyone is looking at me as if I did it. Ciara more or less said it outright, that she believes it was me.'

He sits down, his head in his hands. His long fingers brushing through his hair before he straightens himself and takes a deep breath.

'You can't hit someone over a prayer book, no matter how much you might want to. She's grieving too, you know. Emotions are running high, but you have got to at least keep them in check. And, God, I know the news about the divorce must be a shock, but this is all so messed up. All of it. I don't think anything would surprise me any more. And they can't pin it on you if you didn't do it,' he says. 'I'll not let that happen.'

I take his hand. 'I don't see how you can stop it, Alex. I'm not stupid. I know all the signs are pointing at me. This is how it goes, you know. Every time I think I have a chance at happiness . . .'

I feel a tear slide down my cheek, which I brush away. It hurts; my skin is still so raw from all the tears I've cried over the last few days. I know I'm falling apart. Physically and mentally. And there's nothing that can be done to fix it.

I look at him. He looks as wretched as I do. I'm wracked with guilt for putting him through all this. He did not sign up for any of this. This exceeds the 'better or worse' clause of our marriage by miles.

'There is so much going on here. I know it. Whispers and the doll . . . and the prayer book . . . and Ciara. She's poison but she plays the game well. The police don't even seem to have glanced in her direction.'

'They're watching us all, Heidi. Don't you see that? We're all going through this. I know you're overwhelmed and they've told me, you know, how things can get tough for you when you feel under pressure. Are you sure you're not just reading into things that aren't there?'

I look up at him. The look on his face is one I'm familiar with from other people. That mollifying look – the 'there, there' glance. The expression that says, 'I think she might be losing it.' Seeing it on Alex's face – the one person in this world who I thought I could trust to be 100 per cent on my side – is devastating.

I shake my head slowly. 'Why can't you see what she is trying to do? Why can't you see how she is setting me up for all this? You don't know her like I do, Alex. You don't know how cruel, how dangerous she can be. She hates me! She has always hated me. And she's planting seeds, and whispering in ears, and before I know it, I'll be the one in jail. They all want it to be me. No one will come to my defence.'

'It won't come to that, Heidi. Sure, we're several days in now and even the police say they are no further forwards. The coroner has released his body. It will all settle down.'

'Not until they have pinned the blame on someone, it won't,' I say, wiping my face again, wincing at the pain of my raw skin.

'We can leave,' he says, hoping I'll agree. 'We can leave them to their wake and their funeral. We don't have to be a part of this.'

I pause and look at him, seriously considering it for a moment, but I realise it wouldn't solve anything.

'We can't do that,' I say, shaking my head. 'If they suspect me now, won't that just be giving them, and everyone else, reason to suspect me even more?'

'I don't care,' he hisses. 'I really don't care any more what they think of you or us or any of it. This whole thing, everything, is so toxic. It's eating at us. I can't sleep and I know you're not sleeping, either. I don't want to be near them and I certainly don't want them anywhere near Lily. She doesn't deserve to be caught up in all this.'

'People will talk. People outside of here.'

'Maybe it's time they talked,' he says, and I'm suddenly just so tired.

I feel as if I'm hanging on to my sanity by a thread and little else.

'What do you mean?' I ask him.

There's something in his expression that I can't quite read. He looks at me, opens his mouth to speak but stops.

'Alex, what do you mean?' I ask him.

'Nothing,' he shrugs. 'Nothing.'

He pauses, looks to Lily and then back to me. 'We'll wait until he's brought home and then can we just get away from here for a bit? I think I need us to get away from here for a while.'

He looks defeated, and maybe that's because in that moment we are defeated. I realise I'm shaking and I long for him to wrap his arms around me but I don't want to ask him to. I want him to know instinctively that is what I need. If he hugs me, I tell myself, I'll know we'll be okay. Us two, our little family unit. We'll at least make it through this and no amount of lies will change that.

'I love you,' I whisper.

He sighs, shakes his head as if he's having a conversation with himself that isn't going the way he hoped, and reaches out and gives my hand a squeeze. It's not a hug but it will have to do for now.

'I love you too, but I worry about you, Heidi,' he says. 'I'm worried about you now.'

I nod. I'm worried about me, too. We're disturbed by the sound of the doorbell downstairs. I stand up and peek out of the window to see a hearse pulled up, a small group of nosy neighbours and an unmarked police car not far behind. Out of it steps DC King and DI Bradley, both wearing serious expressions on their faces.

My chest tightens.

Chapter Forty-Two

Heidi

Then

The messages kept coming. Mostly late at night. Mostly at the weekend. I tried calling the number back a couple of times, but it just rang out until an automated, factory-set voicemail message told me the person I was calling was not available just now.

Is it true your mammy didn't really die of cancer? That she killed herself to get away from you?

If I was as ugly as you are, I'd never show myself outside the front door another read.

Your friends are only being nice to you because they feel sorry for you. You're like their care in the community project!

Nobody wants you.

You are so disgusting. Your friends just hang out with you so it makes them look prettier.

Kill yourself!

Put your head in the oven!

Ugly bitch!

And so it went on. I wanted to block the number but at the same time I was drawn to the messages. Wondered what would be said next. I believed they'd eventually leave a clue as to who was behind them.

I started looking at my friends differently. I started looking at everyone differently. I couldn't even be in the same space as Ciara, just in case she was behind the messages. And there was every chance that she was. My hatred for myself grew until I couldn't stand to look in the mirror any more. I stopped taking care of myself. I started finding release in dragging my finger-nails as hard and as deep as possible along the top of my thighs, over and over again until I drew blood.

If I thought the sight of blood would disgust or deter me, I was wrong. It felt good. There was a euphoria in being in control of my own pain for once. This was my choice.

Only when the wounds started to heal again, the vivid red scars marking my skin, would my self-loathing creep back in.

The reason my mystery texter was having such an effect on me was because whoever it was was only telling the truth. They were only repeating the same things to me that my own mind had been saying to me for years. The voices in my head were now everywhere.

Chapter Forty-Three

Ciara

Now

I start to shake as soon as Mum tells me the undertakers have arrived. I'm already feeling a little jittery. My altercation with Heidi was far from pleasant.

She almost hit me. She was just a hair's breadth away from slapping me across the face. I seem to be bringing that out in people today, I think, my face still tingling from where my mother had slapped me. I'm wishing Stella was here as I hear my mother call to me that 'it's time'. She should have been back from the shops by now. I'm not sure I can do this without her.

I can hear the tremor in my mother's voice and it unsettles me. My mother usually stays calm. Even when he left, she kept her cool, despite the fact I knew her heart was shredded. I stand on wobbly legs and grab my coat to stand outside while the undertakers bring my father in. I see Heidi and Alex come down the stairs. Both of them look pale and shaken. I've no space to think about them more than that. I don't care how they feel. I have way too many of my own feelings to deal with right now.

My mother and Kathleen are huddled together at the bottom of the path. I walk towards them, fat flakes of snow falling at my feet. I see our neighbours, the people I grew up beside, stand out as a mark of respect. I'm touched they are here for us. For him. Especially after he turned his back on them as well as Mum and I when he left. He was too good to be seen around here after that. But still they come out of their houses and stand solemnly as his coffin is carried into the house.

I look to them, see them whisper between each other. Are they talking about us? It strikes me that maybe they aren't standing out as a mark of respect after all, but more for a chance to get a good look. Are they trying to figure out who the guilty party is? How much do they know about it all?

They are staring and whispering and I am shaking more and more. I've not even dared to lift my head yet to see the coffin. The coffin that carries my father. The coffin that carries the man who broke my heart over and over and over again. It's true that there is the finest of lines between love and hate.

Slowly, blinking against the falling snow, I lift my head and it is there. This wooden box. Not much for an entire life. Not much for a man who seemed larger than life in so many ways. His body is inside. I try not to think about the fact that his heart has stopped beating, his lungs have stopped breathing. I try to think about how he has been carved up and put back together again.

And still the neighbours are whispering, and Alex and Heidi are clinging on to each other as they walk down the path. The sound of Kathleen crying, now more of a wail than a sob, pierces the air. I want to put my hands over my ears and run. I want someone to hold on to.

Then I see them, those police officers, DI Bradley and DC King, standing a respectful distance from us, but they are there all the same. Watching, no doubt. Reading for signs that might give away what happened. Do they think we're all in it together? Do they think, as Father Brennan suggested, that we gave him a merciful death? That we're all covering for each other?

Would I mark myself out as more of a suspect if I told them that I didn't think he deserved a merciful death?

Or do they suspect that there are darker secrets among us that we've not told anyone yet?

I want to hurry him inside. Away from the spectacle. Not out of any respect for him, but because none of those people really give a ha'penny damn about him, about us, or about what has really gone on in our family.

I don't cry, not until I see Stella. She is walking down the street and when I catch her gaze, she is mouthing that she is so sorry and she speeds up her step to get beside me. The warmth of her hand as she takes mine has the effect of opening the dam of emotions I've been doing my level best to keep locked up.

Everything in my life is crumbling. Except for Stella and what we have. At least, I hope . . . God, I hope she is still with me. Still believes in me.

She keeps me together. She makes me want to be a better person. A good person. A lovable person. But she'd be ashamed of me if she knew what I'd said to Heidi upstairs. She'd be ashamed of me if she knew how I'd challenged my mother.

So when I cry, I'm crying for me and the bitter, harmful woman I know lurks inside, for Stella and her naive trust in me that I am a good person. I'm not. I never had the chance to be. He made sure of that.

'It will be okay,' she whispers into my hair as she pulls me into an embrace as his coffin is carried past me. 'I promise you,

185

it will be okay. I'm here for you. I will be here for you. No matter what. You've got me.'

As I truly allow myself to believe what she is saying, I vow that I'm going to try to find it in me to tell her the truth. The horrible, shameful truth.

Chapter Forty-Four

Heidi

Now

I'd woken in the early hours, our house dark and silent, and had listened to Lily's soft breathing from her cot beside our bed. Alex's parents were forever telling us we should have her in her own room by now, but I can't bear to be apart from her. She's not even six months old. Still tiny. She'll be in her own room soon enough, and for long enough.

For now, I need to know she is safe and secure. I need to feel the security that having her close to me brings me, too. The coming day will be hard and I need to remind myself there is good in the world. It's two days since Joe was brought back to Marie's house. Two days of mourning. Of stilted conversations. Of awkwardness. Of walking on eggshells. I'm exhausted to my very soul by it all. Exhausted by the paranoia and trying to fend off the negative thoughts that swoop in on a regular basis, making me want to hide.

I want it to be over. I want to be back to my life, my family. This child who means so much to me.

The golden rule, of course, is never to wake a sleeping baby, but when I had woken, I'd needed to hold her. I'd crept out of bed and lifted her, warm and soft, her breath sweet with milk, and had placed her in the bed beside me. She'd fussed – 'fissled' as my mother used to call it – but didn't wake, and I allowed myself the luxury of holding her, stroking the soft skin of her cheeks, kissing her tiny fingers and marvelling how I had any part in making something so pure and so innocent. I'd drifted off at some stage, only waking now, Alex standing at the bottom of the bed in the half-light of the room, panicking about where Lily is.

'She's here, Alex,' I say, shuffling over a little so that he can see where she is, lying safe and sound beside me.

'In the bed? Jesus, Heidi. Why is she in the bed? And you were sleeping! You could've rolled over . . .'

'I didn't, Alex. She's fine. I was awake most of the time. I just needed a hug.'

'But what if? Heidi, we agreed no co-sleeping. You know how scared I am that she'll overheat or get smothered.'

He seems really panicked, even though I'm showing him evidence of a perfectly healthy baby beside me.

'She didn't, though. She's safe. Look, she had no duvet over her and plenty of room to stretch. She was fine, Alex. I can be trusted to keep her safe, you know.'

I'm not sure where the tone in my voice has come from, but as soon as the words are out I know that they say more than I thought. They're accusatory. Defensive. I feel on edge, my hackles already rising before I've even got out of bed.

He sits at my feet and reaches up and lifts Lily, waking her from her sleep and prompting a wail of hunger in return.

'You know I'd die if anything ever happened to her,' he says. 'We can't take risks, Heidi. Not with Lily. She's not one of your dolls!'

He kisses the top of her head, holds her close to him as if I've just held her dangling out of the window, or committed some other such heinous crime against her.

'Of course I know she's not one of my dolls,' I snap back at him. 'Christ, Alex, I just needed to be close to her.'

Can't he see how hard all this is for me? I feel tears spring to my eyes. This whole episode is a nightmare. When I do manage to sleep, my dreams are filled with terrible images from my past, and visions of police officers hauling me away from my family, never to see them again.

'I'm sorry,' Alex says, not entirely convincingly. 'We're all on edge. I'm on edge. Of course I know you wouldn't hurt Lily. That was stupid and cruel of me to compare her to a doll,' he says.

He hands her to me and I see it as a gesture that he trusts me, that his panic from earlier has passed.

'Will we get this day over and done with?' he asks. 'The undertakers are coming at nine thirty. We need to get up and ready and go round to Marie's.'

I nod. In a matter of hours, Joe McKee will be in the ground. One half of this ordeal will be over. We will just have the police to face then. Just the police . . . ha! If I say it fast enough maybe it won't sound so scary.

'Grand,' he says, pulling on a pair of tracksuit bottoms and a T-shirt. 'I'll go and get started on breakfast. Why don't you jump in the shower? I'll have something ready for you when you're done.'

Although I'm hungry, I'm not sure I can eat. My stomach is unsettled. Nervous.

'I'll probably just have a piece of toast or something,' I tell him. 'Don't go to any trouble for me.'

He kisses the top of my head and takes Lily from me again, stops for a moment to look at me; really look at me.

'Nothing is too much trouble for you, Heidi. One day, you might believe that.'

Chapter Forty-Five

Heidi

Now

The spectacle of Joe McKee's funeral has begun. Prayers to a God I most certainly don't believe in around the coffin. Standing outside, aware that the coffin is being closed and that there are no further chances to see his face again.

Marie has now reached peak grieving-widow mode. All that's missing is a black mantilla and she would give Jackie Kennedy a run for her money. She sniffs, dabs her eyes. She'll travel in the funeral cars with Ciara, Stella and Kathleen. Alex and I will make our own way in our car. We are sidelined already. No doubt that will give a message of its own to the gawkers and the grief voyeurs. DI Bradley and DC King are here again. Of course. Maintaining a respectful distance but watching all the same.

I'm sure I also saw a press photographer outside as we arrived. This will be news. Maybe not today, but soon. When the police solve their mystery, or when Ciara can manage to persuade them it was me all along. The cold-hearted, ungrateful wench of a step-child. My not crying won't help me look any less guilty, but I won't cry for him. I won't pretend. They can look at my stony-set face and draw their own conclusions. I'm past caring. Or so I tell myself.

There's a scuffling of shoes, people moving backwards as the door to the house opens and the undertakers guide Joe's coffin over the threshold. Some of the male neighbours, a work colleague and Alex step forwards and hoist the coffin onto their shoulders. They'll walk to the end of the street and then they will put the coffin in the hearse and some of us will continue to follow on foot. A procession of grief, dressed in black, heads bowed against the January wind and sleet. Family, friends, colleagues. Neighbours. People who feel a sense of duty to be there.

Alex has gone back to fetch our car. He'll meet me in the church grounds. Never have I been so glad that I have Lily with me in her pram. I won't have to link arms with any of them and walk together, serious of face. I hate it.

I hate how people look.

I remember that from when Mammy died. The people who looked. Who saw me, in my black coat, with my shiny patent shoes, black tights and black dress. Ribbons, black of course, in my hair. My hand limply in Granny's as she linked on to Grandad.

'It would break your heart,' I heard people mutter after. 'Parents having to bury their child and then that wee girl left.'

'Joe will look after her. God love him,' someone muttered back.

We reach the church, St Eugene's Cathedral near the centre of town, and Alex is beside me, Lily now in his arms, as we file down the aisle after the coffin. I listen to readings and prayers and hymns are sung. Father Brennan tells us the gates of heaven will be open wide to welcome Joe McKee back into the Lord's house, and that while we might be sad, there will be rejoicing in heaven as a man of faith, of strong heart, of generosity, comes home.

I fidget in my seat. The priest talks of how Joe is reunited with those who went before him. His parents. His cousin, Paul. His aunt, Alice. I brace myself for hearing my mother's name – knowing each time I hear it, it gives me comfort to know she's remembered, but at the same time hurts because I still miss her so.

I close my eyes and breathe deeply.

'And all those who have gone before him in faith to rest with the Father,' Father Brennan says, skipping over my mother's name. Erasing her from his narrative.

I open my eyes, look around me. Ciara and Marie both have their heads bowed in prayer. Kathleen is clutching a wrinkled tissue in her hands and looking straight ahead. I wonder can they feel my eyes on them. I wonder which of them told Father Brennan not to say her name.

Alex rests his hand on my knee, as if calming me. Is it an act of comfort, or is he afraid I'll make a scene, right here, in the church in front of everyone? When everyone is starting to think I've lost the run of myself anyway. No, I'll keep my peace. Grit my teeth and get through the day. Focus on being home in my own space later, away from it all.

Before I know it, we're filing out again, in convoy behind the coffin, heading towards the City Cemetery. I realise I didn't speak to Ciara, or any of them, after all, about the plot he will be buried in, but I assure myself it will be fine. They didn't acknowledge my mother's life at all during the Mass, so surely none of them would be so crass as to think he deserved to lie with her now.

So my stomach lurches as we approach the cemetery and the

hearse does not turn down towards the new plots but instead turns left and travels up the hill to the older graves. To where my mother has been lying for the past twenty years.

'They're making a mistake,' I say to Alex.

'I think they know what they're doing,' he replies, his car following slowly, trying to gain a purchase on the icy ground.

But I can see it. I can see that my mother's grave has been disturbed. A large mound of brown soil covered with a green plastic cover rests beside it. Before I know it, before I've had time to make a conscious decision to do so, I have unfastened my seat belt and am reaching for the door handle.

'Heidi!' Alex's voice is loud and clear, the car is still moving, but slowly. I can still jump out.

I open the door, feel his hand on my arm trying to hold me back, but I shake him off. No. This is a step too far. He can't go there. He can't. No.

Alex slams the brakes on in the car and I lurch a little but not enough that I lose my balance. I am out of the car and I am half walking, half running up the remainder of the hill towards the funeral car they are all in. All eyes are on me. I can sense that, can hear things around me. Whispers.

My heart is pumping hard and I can feel a cool sweat break out on my forehead, even though it is bitterly cold. I want to scream. I want to claw at Ciara. To ask her what on earth she is thinking. To ask her why. Why would she do that? She's not a stupid woman, she would know how much pain it would cause me.

The funeral car stops and the door opens just as I reach it. Ciara steps out, her face set thick with concern and a hint of fear.

'What is it, Heidi? Are you okay?'

'You can't bury him here, in my mother's grave!' I shout and any eyes that weren't already on me are suddenly focused in my direction. 'You can't do this. I can't believe you're doing this. Make them stop. Now!'

I watch as tears form and start to fall from Ciara's eyes, how she takes a step back as if she is afraid of me. I'm aware of Stella getting out of the car and trying to direct her away.

'But . . . it's what he wanted. His final wishes. You were okay with that . . .' Ciara says, crumpling. 'It's breaking my mother's heart but it's what he wanted. When we talked about it, you said we were okay to follow his final wishes. You agreed.'

I was okay with it? When did I say that? My head is swimming and I can hear the thumping of my heart so loudly I fear it will burst through my eardrums. The edges of the conversation I had with her are fuzzy. I'd been feeding Lily and was still reeling from the heated conversation with Alex.

Maybe I'm losing my grip on reality. I can feel it slipping away. I can feel the physical sensation of it falling from my hands as if it is my skin peeling from my bones. I feel it and it is the thing of nightmares, and I want it to stop. I need it to stop.

I feel a hand on my arm, strong. It's Alex.

'Heidi, please. Come away. Don't make a scene. Not now. This is hard enough.'

He is whispering, but his voice is urgent. Embarrassment radiates from him as he tries to encourage me back to the car. I'm almost catatonic with a mixture of rage and fear, and I want to push him away. I want to run to my mother's grave and do everything I can to stop them from going anywhere near it, and yet the sight of her open grave hits me with such a punch in the stomach that I fear I might throw up.

I can't take my eyes from it, but I don't want to see. I'm scared. I'm like that child again, nine years old and not understanding why they were putting my mammy in a hole in the ground. That wasn't heaven, either. They said she was going to heaven. Not to a cold, wet hole in the ground. I had stood there, aged nine, shaking so badly with fear while people wept and wailed around me, desperate to tell them they were making a mistake but trying to be a good girl, just like Granny had asked me.

When the first shovelful of soil was dropped onto the top of her coffin, I had been so scared that I had, to my eternal shame, wet myself. Soaked through those black tights bought just for the occasion. The pee running into my shiny patent shoes. I was scared and humiliated.

And now, her grave open, the thought of where she is, how she is, that he will be placed on top of her remains – it makes me want to do whatever it takes to stop them.

But Alex is pulling me backwards. Using all of his strength. And still everyone stares. And still Ciara is weeping on Stella's shoulder and Kathleen is glaring at me while Marie just looks lost.

And none of them, not one of them, has the right to be more upset than me.

Chapter Forty-Six

Heidi

Now

'Don't tell me how to react,' I bark at Alex. I have my head in my hands and I am rocking back and forth. It's the only way I seem to be able to try to settle the noise in my head.

He has driven out of the cemetery, leaving the rest of the mourners to witness the burial I can't even bear to think about, and we are driving back towards Marie's.

'I'm not telling you how to react, Heidi, but remember, everyone is watching us all at the moment. Looking for any signs that any one of us has something to hide, or isn't the full shilling.'

'But I can't let this go. Was I supposed to say nothing? When I'm faced with my mother's open grave and that . . . that . . . monster being settled in with her? Everything about this was designed to hurt me, to wind me up. To make me lose my temper. But that? That was the final insult. That was cruel, Alex. Just cruel.'

My heart is still thumping as hard as it did in the graveyard. I'm trying not to shout. The last thing I want to do is wake Lily and disturb her from her sleep, but I can hear the volume increasing in my voice anyway. I'm so angry and growing angrier.

He pulls the car over to the side of the road. He puts the handbrake on and releases his seat belt, turning in his seat to face me.

'Heidi,' he begins and his face is grey with worry.

I can see that I'm scaring him. That he thinks I'm as crazy as Ciara would have everyone believe.

'I can't even imagine what seeing your mother's grave open like that must have felt like, but I can't help but think . . . Is there something more to this? Is there something you're not telling me?'

He must think I did it, I think. He must think my descent into apparent madness is the result of my guilt over Joe's death. It makes sense now. I see it there on his face. That's why he's been so off with me since it happened. He's scared of me, what I'm capable of. He thinks . . . he thinks I could hold a pillow over a man's head and hold it down until the life went out of him. He thinks I could do that to a frail, sick, terminally ill man and if I could do that, what else must I be capable of that he's not even allowing himself to consider? Is that why he reacted the way he did to Lily sleeping in bed beside me? Jesus Christ, did he think I would kill my own child?

'I didn't kill him. I'm not a killer!' I say. 'If that's what you're thinking.'

'Jesus Christ, Heidi, of course I'm not thinking that.'

But he doesn't sound convinced and I feel sick. If I don't have Alex on my side, then I have no one on my side. The hunt for the evil witch continues and I am the number one suspect. They might as well burn me at the stake now, or prepare me for the ducking stool. If I float I die, if I sink I'm innocent. Maybe that's what it will take.

'Heidi.' Alex's voice cuts through my thoughts. 'Are you listening to me?'

I nod, even though I haven't been listening to him. I don't want to listen to him any more. I want to be seven years old again, before we met Joe, before Mammy got sick, before everything . . . all the pain. Before it all went wrong.

'So? Is there something else?' He is looking directly at me, his eyes boring into me.

'Why can't it just be the case that you believe, or you see, how completely unreasonable they are all being? That you see what they are doing. They're messing with my head and they know they can . . . they know I'm vulnerable . . .'

I realise I've possibly said too much. Will he think I'm just vulnerable because I'm bereaved? Will he probe deeper?

'How are you vulnerable, Heidi?' he asks, his voice soft, his face serious.

He's still looking at me directly, searching my face for clues. There is something in his expression, the furrowing of his brow, the sadness in his hazel eyes – a sadness that can't be ignored. That is as real as any I have seen.

'Tell me, please. You can tell me.'

I can't breathe. I can't hold his gaze for any longer. I have to look away. I realise that my hands are gripping the sides of my seat tightly. I feel that tightness, the nausea, in the pit of my stomach. Despite the freezing cold weather, the persistent deluge of sleet-filled rain on the windscreen, I feel a deep heat rise in me. Shame. Pain. Memories that I have tried to keep stuffed somewhere in the darkest recesses of my mind flood my head. It's almost a physical impact, the way these flashing images hit me. And the physical sensations as if I'm back there.

As if it is happening right now. But I'm bigger now, you see, I'm bigger and stronger and I have somewhere to run.

I unclip my seat belt and without really thinking, I am opening the car door and climbing out. I am climbing out and running, and I can hear Alex behind me. I can hear him call my name, but I know he can't follow. He can't leave Lily in the car and I'm being clever. I'm heading for alleyways and pathways where his car can't go. I need to get away. That's all I can think – that I need to get away.

My skin is crawling. It feels like a separate entity to me, with a mind of its own, burning, and I swear if I could tear it off, I absolutely would. I would tear it off and leave it to bleed on the snow-covered ground.

Alex's voice fades into the background, the sting of hailstones hitting my face and hands giving me something to focus on as I just keep running.

Chapter Forty-Seven

Ciara

Now

I am emotionally numb. My heart is beating and I can feel the thrum of it in my chest. I am aware of my inhalation and exhalation. I'm aware that there is a hair clip digging into the right side of my head, pulling my hair too tight. I'm aware that my feet are freezing. That black court shoes were not the best choice for a day as cold as this. I can feel, physically, all that is going on around me.

But I am numb. I cannot feel right now. I cannot grieve. I cannot be angry. I cannot sympathise with my mother and Kathleen and their horror at the scene at my father's graveside. I cannot deal with the people asking questions. I cannot cry. I cannot allow myself to feel at all because if I do, I fear I will become so very angry that I will never be able to put that anger back in its box and put it away.

It will become who I am.

I know Heidi isn't acting rationally. I know that Heidi is

damaged. But I never thought in a million years that she would make such a scene at a graveside. Her anger, her fear was so visceral, so raw that I was scared of what she might do. If it hadn't been for Alex hauling her back into the car, I dread to think how far she may have gone.

The looks on the faces of our fellow mourners as she screeched and screamed like a banshee will stay with me forever. The horror. As if people didn't have enough to talk about. To gossip about.

Although I imagine from now Heidi will become the focus of their gossip. They will be watching her. We will all be watching her.

DI Bradley had come to speak to me at the graveside after all the other mourners had left. I'd wanted some time with my father, you see, now that he was underground. Now that I knew I would never see his face again. I'd wanted to tell him I was sorry. Sorry that I wasn't stronger. Sorry that I ever allowed myself to be caught up in his horrible life again. I wanted to tell him not to expect fresh flowers to be placed on his grave. I would not be standing there and weeping. He was gone and I was happy about that.

The other mourners had wandered off, tongues wagging, no doubt. My mother and Kathleen had taken shelter in the car, both of them borderline hysterical. I had been whispering my final thoughts to my father on the wind, when I heard footsteps approach. I looked up to see DI Bradley, his hands plunged deep in the pockets of his long black coat, his collar turned up to protect him from the elements, standing a short distance away.

'I don't mean to disturb you,' he said. 'I can wait until you're done.'

I looked down at the hastily covered over grave in front of me. It had been covered with a wooden lid for now, which was decked in the wreaths people had sent to offer their sympathy. The mound of dirt, turning into claggy muck in the sleet and hail, would be pushed in on top of him later. The black marble headstone, bearing Natalie's name, declaring her a beloved daughter, mother and partner in gold letters, would soon bear Joe's name, too. In that space at the bottom. It was as if it had always been waiting for him.

I blinked and shook my head. 'It's okay,' I said. 'I have nothing more to say to him. Not today, anyway.'

'This must be very hard for you all,' DI Bradley said.

I knew that his words were not just those of a police officer interested in catching the bad guy. They were the words of someone who sees the human tragedy playing out in front of him for what it is. A shitshow of a mess that is destroying everyone.

'It's not easy,' I told him with a shrug.

'Heidi was very upset.'

'She was,' I said. 'She didn't want him buried here. I didn't realise. Maybe I should've.'

I didn't want him thinking poorly of me. Thinking that what Heidi had said was true and that I could legitimately be that cruel without so much as a second thought.

'We've looked into her history. Her mental health history,' he said. 'She has had a rough time. But she has been stable for quite some time.'

'She has, I think. As I've told you before, we never actually spent a lot of time in each other's company. Very little, in fact. Especially in recent years.'

'But she was responsible for the majority of care your father received, especially as his health deteriorated.'

I blushed. There was a judgement in his statement. How awful was I that I didn't do my bit.

'You know, my relationship with my father could best be

described as complicated. We didn't have the time to work on it.' I looked back to the gravestone. I'm not sure having all the time in the world would have made an ounce of difference. 'Things were complicated. Things are complicated. I have to live with that. But it doesn't mean I did anything to hurt him.'

'No, of course it doesn't,' DI Bradley said. 'I didn't mean to imply anything. This isn't an official visit. I'm just offering my sympathies.'

I nodded. 'Thank you.'

'We will get to the bottom of this, you know,' he said, shaking my hand and walking away.

I didn't know whether to take it as a threat or a promise. Or both.

I let the conversation run through my head all the way to Mum's house, wishing we could just go home to our own place. But it's expected we'll go to Mum's, to join the other mourners for tea and sandwiches for the wake. She'll be so cross if we don't.

Stella just holds my hand. She doesn't ask questions. And when we arrive, she doesn't question me when I say I need some space. I climb the stairs and sit in my old bedroom – a room my mother long ago transformed into a 'sewing room'. She has an upcycled Parker Knoll chair by the window and I sit here doing my best to hang on to the numbness that has come over me.

Heidi hasn't shown her face. It's a good thing. If she does, I don't think anything in the world will be able to stop the rage from bursting out of me.

Chapter Forty-Eight

Heidi

Now

I find myself with the two people in the world I have always felt safe and secure with.

My grandparents live in a small, always overheated, flat in sheltered accommodation close to the city centre. They've lived there for more than ten years now and even though I wish they had somewhere with a little garden to potter about in, or somewhere just further away from the sometimes anti-social activity of the city centre, they seem happy.

They've done their best to make the one-bed flat their own; crammed as many of their possessions onto shelves or into cupboards so that there is still an air of the house I used to visit as a child about the place. Pride of place on the wall of their living room is a large framed photograph of my mother and me.

Professionally taken, in the early nineties, it looks dated. A heavy wooden frame. Soft blurring around our faces. My mother's hair, teased and backcombed. Her lip gloss a shiny pale pink – I can still remember the sweet smell of that gloss and how it would leave sticky marks on my cheeks when she kissed me. I'm there, all of three years old, hair much curlier than it is now, tied in two pigtails with pale blue ribbon, and a pretty, flouncy, completely over-the-top party dress. We are looking not at the camera but at each other, and we are both grinning.

I wish I could say I remember the day it was taken, but I don't. Still, every time I see that picture in my grandparents' flat, part of me feels like that day says everything that needs to be said about my relationship with my mother.

I'm looking at it now, sitting on a small brown two-seater sofa, while my grandparents, perched either side of me in their armchairs, look between me and each other, waiting for me to speak. My granny has wrapped me in a blanket after roughly towel-drying my hair. She gave me her housecoat to wear while she hung my coat, dress and tights around the various radiators in the flat, adding to the stuffy, humid feel of the place.

I'm wearing a pair of my grandad's thick woollen socks and I think my teeth have finally stopped chattering.

They know Joe's funeral was this morning, but neither of them are in good enough health that they could attend. My grandfather is now entirely immobile. His days are spent being hoisted by carers from his adapted bed to his hospital-issue bed and back again. He is a prisoner in his own house and, increasingly, a prisoner in his own mind. There are days when he doesn't so much as utter a word, Granny tells me. Other days he gets agitated wondering when 'his Natalie' will come to visit.

Today, he is staring at me through cloudy eyes, his jaw slack. He is trying to place me. To remember who I am and what I am to him, and I'm reminded once more of just how cruel life can be.

Granny does her best to be positive, but she is broken. She has been broken since the day my mother died. I do as much as I can to help them, but over the last few weeks that has been very little. Still, they never make me feel guilty. I think they carry their own guilt at not being able to take care of me after Mammy died. We, all of us, are weighed down by guilt.

When I arrived at their door I was barely coherent. My grandmother didn't ask questions. She just pulled me in through the door and set about making me feel better, looking after me as if I was still that scrappy little girl who had clung to her legs on the day my mother was buried. I don't know how I'm going to tell her about Mammy's grave. I don't know how she will react. I decide just to blurt it out.

'Granny,' I start. 'I'm really sorry, but I have some bad news. They put him in Mammy's grave with her.'

I start to cry and I can't even bring myself to look at my grandmother's face. I hear a sharp intake of breath and a whispered 'Jesus, Mary and St Joseph' and that tells me what I need to know.

I lift my head. 'I don't know how it happened. I know you were both to be buried with her. I don't know if Ciara did it to spite us all, but she says she didn't and I'm just so sorry . . .' I crumple.

'Hush, pet.'

My grandmother's voice is soft. I feel the gentle pat of her hand on my knee.

'I don't want you getting upset over it. I suppose he'd every right to be buried with her.'

She is trying to soothe me, but I can't help but notice the defeated tone in her voice. Her hands are shaking just ever so slightly, enough to give it away that she is struggling. As if her life isn't hard enough already.

I know that I will never, ever tell her just why he had no

right to ever be near to my mother again. Why he should never, even in death, be allowed near another person again. It would kill her.

If she knew – God, if she knew what had happened it would destroy her altogether. She deserves to believe she did the best she could for me all those years ago when I was left in his care.

For the first time ever, I'm grateful for my grandfather's dementia. None of this can touch him now. But my poor granny.

She wraps her arms around me. Everything about her embrace screams comfort and security. The familiar smell of her talcum powder, the softness of her jumper. The feel of her skin, warm and soft. I let her rock me and I revel in the kisses she places on my head, and how she tells me that everything will be okay over and over again.

'You poor pet,' she soothes. 'You've not had it easy, but you have to focus on the good things now. On Alex and that wee baby of yours. Don't be fretting on behalf of your grandad or me. We've been through enough battles to know we'll win the war as long as we have each other.'

Her words should soothe me completely, of course, but all I can think is just how awful all this is. I'm not going to let them get away with this. Ciara is not going to get away with this. I've had enough.

Chapter Forty-Nine

Heidi

Now

Guilt, or a sense of duty, or a sense of not wanting to make things worse with Alex, brings me back to Marie's house. I've been AWOL for two hours, enough time for the small number of mourners who came back to the house to have had their fill of tea and sandwiches and gone home.

I've seen our car outside, so I know Alex is there. He will be angry with me. I know that. Angry and worried. I've seen the missed calls on my phone, but I couldn't bring myself to call him back. What I need to say to him can't be said over the phone.

I'm sure I hear Alex's voice from the living room, so I pop my head around the door. Two sets of eyes, neither of them belonging to my husband, stare back at me.

'Are you feeling better?' a woman with a mass of messy red curls and too much make-up on her face asks me.

I don't know who she is. I nod and thank her for her concern.

I hear Alex again, realise his voice is coming from the kitchen, so I walk that way.

'I don't know why she would say that,' I hear Ciara say.

Her voice is thick with emotion. I press myself close to the wall to listen, even though there is no way they would be able to see me from where I am anyway.

'I know this is really distressing,' I hear Kathleen speak. 'But try not to let it, or her, annoy you. The poor girl hasn't had it easy. Losing her mum so early. And whether we like it or not, Joe was the only father she ever knew, so here she is without the pair of them and with a new baby to deal with, too. She might be finding it very hard to cope.'

I hear Ciara sniff. 'But she's not the only one who's had it tough. It's almost as if she's trying to make out I have some sort of vendetta against her. That I'm trying to make her life hard. And I swear to you all, I'm not.

'She wants everyone to think I did it, I know that. She wants everyone to think I was capable of killing my own father. I think she's losing the run of herself and is determined to drive us all mad in the process.'

I bristle. I've done no such thing. I've not tried to heap blame on her at all. If anything, she has been setting me up for a fall. I'm disgusted, angry at the tone in her voice. If I didn't know categorically that she was lying then I might even be convinced myself. If there was an Oscar for best performance at a family funeral, I was sure she would be a contender. I roll my eyes, anger making me immune to her sniffs and sobs.

But then I hear it. An unmistakably male voice. Alex.

'I know,' he says. 'I'm really starting to worry about her,' he continues. 'Only for her granny calling me to say she was okay, I'd have had the police searching for her. I think I need to get her some professional help. Especially given her history.'

My stomach tightens. I haven't told Alex of my mental health history, which means someone else has. Someone who never really understood it in the first place.

'That might be a good idea.' Marie's voice this time, firm and decisive. 'And I wouldn't wait too long. I really don't think she's herself and you know, you'd want her to be right in the head if she's at home with Lily.'

'She wouldn't hurt Lily,' Alex says, but his voice doesn't sound as confident as I would like.

'Not normally, no, and I've no doubt she's a great mammy and she loves that baby with all her heart. But she's been very erratic lately. Not herself. If it were me, and Lily was my baby, I'm not sure I'd want to take the chance. I know I couldn't live with myself if something awful happened.'

There's a pause. I start to wonder if she's done, but then I hear her speak again.

'You know about the fire, don't you?'

Chapter Fifty

Heidi

Then

It was Christmas and I was back at Aberfoyle Crescent. I didn't want to be there, having escaped for the last three months to university in Dublin.

I hadn't come home at any time in those three months, not even for a weekend. My newly made friends, especially those also from Derry who went home at least once a month and certainly for the Halloween festival, couldn't really understand my insistence on staying in Dublin.

Our student digs could become quiet at the weekends and on a student income heading out partying wasn't always within my budget. Not that I was a party girl anyway. Still, I preferred it to travelling up north and spending time with Joe.

If I could've stayed there over Christmas I would have, but I knew I had to go home, if for no other reason than I wanted to see my grandparents. That was the hard part of staying away.

A bit of distance had maybe mellowed me. That and I was

eighteen and could see a life free from reliance on Joe open up in front of me. My phantom text-message stalker had given up after about eighteen months of messages. They tapered off at the end. Just like everything. The abuse had become a thing of the past. The nasty messages.

Yes, I still carried my scars – physical and emotional – from what I'd been through. I still had times when it all felt too much, when I'd wake screaming, a nightmare having put me back in my room, scared and defenceless and still a child. There were times when I still had to score at my skin. But slowly, I believed, I was healing. I believed that I could heal. I even started to think that maybe one day I would be able to find a partner. To take a chance on finding love. To consider being physical with someone. To believe that I deserved to be loved and cherished properly.

It was hardly surprising that my nerves were in flitters by the time I got back to the house. I refused, even at that point, to call it home.

Joe was in a jovial mood. He had made a half-hearted attempt to put up some Christmas decorations and there were a handful of presents underneath the tree.

'I want us to have a nice Christmas,' he said. 'Do you think we could manage that?'

There was something in the way he spoke that led me to believe that he thought I was the problem. I was the trouble-maker. He took no responsibility for his own actions. The hell he had put me through.

But I didn't want to let him drag me down, not then. Not yet.

'I've invited Ciara over for dinner on Christmas Eve,' he said. 'You're both adults now. Maybe we could start moving on. I've asked Marie too, and your grandparents.'

I could think of nothing that would be more awkward, but

I consoled myself that at least Granny and Grandad would be there.

'I'll do all the cooking,' he said. 'You just have to show up. Do you think you could do that?' he said. 'I've missed you, Heidi. I just want things to be better between us.'

He looked so earnest. His eyes were sad. I could almost convince myself that he was feeling sorry for what he'd done. But maybe he was just feeling lonely. People may have talked to him on the streets. He may have been able to hold court at the library, but when he closed the door to this house, the house that should never have been his, he was all alone.

Still, I agreed because I was tired of the constant warring, too. I even spent some of my money on presents. Silly little things. A brooch for Marie. An ornament which, in hindsight, was ugly as sin for my grandparents. A hand-made notebook wrapped in delicate tissue paper for Ciara. I wrapped them, along with a bottle of red wine for Joe, and added them to the pile under the tree.

Christmas Eve arrived and Joe was true to his word. He busied himself in the kitchen, shooing me away every time I popped my head around the door. Instead, I did what I could to make his sorry excuse for a Christmas tree look a little less haggard, and when that was done I set six place settings in the small dining room. I showered and dressed and even put on a little make-up. I was nervous, but also excited. It would be lovely to have my grandparents here.

Marie was first to arrive, in a fug of Chanel No. 5, impeccably made up and carrying a bottle of Moët & Chandon. Eighteen-year-old me was impressed. Real champagne! It felt decadent and grown up.

'You look lovely, Heidi,' she said, hugging me so tightly that I got a lungful of her perfume mixed with her hairspray. 'It's lovely to see you. Is Joe in the kitchen?'

I took her coat and soon heard peals of laughter as they chatted. I liked Marie. I always had. Unlike Ciara, she hadn't taken her hurt about Joe leaving out on me. She'd always been kind when we met, looking at me with sympathetic eyes. Sometimes I wondered how someone who appeared as kind as she did raised a daughter as cruel as Ciara. Then I'd remember, of course, who Ciara's father was.

My grandparents arrived next, dressed in their Sunday best. I helped Grandad through the door and to the living room. He was looking well. Feeling great, he said. He'd left his wheel-chair at home and was managing with his walker. My heart was aglow with love for them. Granny even agreed to take a small glass of sherry while Grandad remained a traditionalist with a bottle of beer I poured into a glass for him. Marie and Joe joined us and we were making polite conversation when the doorbell rang again.

Ciara had arrived. Very much in the party spirit. I could smell wine on her breath and her eyes were glazed. Still she grinned.

'So, where is it?' she asked, looking directly at Joe.

He shrugged. 'Where's what, sweetheart?'

She rolled her eyes in a dramatic fashion. 'The fatted calf? Surely it should be on the spit by now? Celebrating the prod-igal daughter's return from Dublin.'

'Ciara.' Marie's voice was low and stern. She was firing off a warning shot.

Ciara pressed her index finger to her lips and shushed. 'I know, I know,' she said. 'We have to be good. Keep quiet. Don't say what we all want to say.'

I shifted uncomfortably in my seat.

'Right,' Ciara said, 'where can a girl get a drink around here?'

'Ciara, you're twenty-three years old and acting like a brat,' Joe hissed, which was exactly the wrong way to try to endear Ciara to him.

'Oh, Daddy, you've noticed me! I didn't realise you remembered I existed,' she said, mouth turned down melodramatically. 'Kudos to you for remembering my age! I am impressed.'

'Ciara, please,' Marie said, her voice more urgent this time.

My grandparents were both staring into their drinks, trying to avoid the scene in front of them.

'Oh, Mum, why are you always on his side? Do you think he'll leave you if you aren't nice to him? Oops! That's right – he already did, didn't he? For some slut he'd only known a couple of months.'

I heard my grandmother gasp. My face blazed.

'And not only that, when she popped her clogs what, two years later, he stayed to raise her mad brat, too.'

'Ciara! That is enough!' Joe's voice was stern, angry.

My grandmother was crying. Grandad was shaking his head.

'Why? Why is it enough? Why is it always about her? Be kind to poor Heidi! She lost her mother. Be kind to Heidi, she's going through a tough time. Be kind to Heidi, she's not right in the head. She might hurt herself. Poor fucking Heidi.'

'ENOUGH!' Joe was shouting now.

Marie was crying. I was mortified.

'No!' Ciara shouted back. 'It's not enough. It's not even nearly enough.'

'Ciara,' I said, trying to keep my voice steady. 'Please. Why don't we all just try to calm down and have a nice evening. Your dad has gone to so much effort.'

'Well, that's nice of him. To go to some effort, for once. And of course it would be for you. For your big homecoming.'

'We're all here,' I said. 'We're all invited.'

She sniffed. 'Oh, Heidi, you know nothing. You've never known anything. You're so wrapped up in yourself. No one gives a damn about what the rest of us have been through. Why haven't you just pissed off by now? You should've pissed off by now. God only knows, I told you often enough. All those messages I sent. You never took the hint, though, did you? How stupid are you?'

I stare at her, my eyes wide. I knew Ciara hated me. Of course I did. But to have sent all those messages. To have told me, repeatedly, to kill myself? She'd almost, almost pushed me to it. She'd messed me up just as much as her bastard father had done.

'I think we're done here for tonight,' Joe said.

'I'll take this one home,' Marie said, grabbing a reluctant Ciara. 'How could you be so cruel?' she hissed at her daughter.

'Being cruel was bred into me,' Ciara hissed back.

After everyone had gone home, when what was meant to be dinner was wrapped in tinfoil or decanted into the bin and Joe went to bed, I sat in the living room and stared at the tree I had decorated earlier. And I looked at the presents underneath.

Any sense of hope, or belief that the worst was over, left me. If Ciara wanted me to kill myself, I would. Or I'd at least make a big enough scene that everyone would know just how bad everything was.

I lifted the matches from the fireplace, struck one and watched it burn until it threatened to singe my skin. Then I threw it in the direction of the delicately wrapped notebook and all the other Christmas presents, and I watched until they caught fire one by one.

It was only when the flames started to lick across the carpet that something in me, a survival instinct of sorts, kicked in and I panicked.

I screamed for help, rushing to the kitchen, grabbing a pan full of water that was wholly inadequate and throwing it at the fire. The smoke alarms were pealing at this stage and I saw Joe, his face stricken, at the top of the stairs.

'What have you done this time, you stupid girl?'

Chapter Fifty-One

Heidi

Now

I can't let Marie tell Alex about what happened. I can't let her control that narrative. No doubt she will leave out how completely horrific Ciara was before it all happened. How she had stalked me and humiliated me. She will focus on the fire, the six weeks I spent in in-patient care afterwards. The months in therapy. How I had to miss out on the end of my first year at university and start all over again the following academic year.

I was the demon. Ciara, who had admitted sending all those messages, seemed to be absolved of her sins. She had been drunk. Hurting. And sure, it had been almost two years since the last message.

I got a half-hearted passive-aggressive apology delivered to me while I was lying semi-comatose in hospital trying to find the energy to do anything other than stare at four walls. Joe visited almost every day. It wasn't out of love for me, far from it. It was because the thought of me being in therapy, of spilling his sordid secrets, terrified him. I saw the fear on his face with each and every visit. I saw the silent pleading.

He needn't have worried. Despite the gentle probing of my therapist, there was no way I was going to spill my deepest, darkest secrets to anyone. I was still too mired in shame, back then.

But standing outside of the kitchen now, hearing how damaging just one side of the narrative can be, I was starting to think it was time they all heard the whole truth, after all.

But I know that if I lose it now, it will only fuel their narrative that I'm crazy.

Stella is the first to spot me. Her face colours, knowing they have been caught out. She isn't quite as obvious as to cough or make a dramatic change in conversation but she does say hello. Her smile is soft. Her eyes warm and welcoming. I like Stella. She seems to be a calming influence on Ciara and a nice person. It's strange in this moment that she feels like the one ally I have in all of this.

'Heidi,' she says. 'You're here. Are you feeling okay?'

'I wouldn't put it quite like that,' I say.

Alex is staring at me as if he has never seen me before, but he isn't speaking. I try not to focus on him, because if I do, if I see how disappointed in me he is, I might just break.

'It's been a tough few days,' Stella says and I nod.

The others in the room haven't spoken yet. I wonder if they've even taken a breath. Bar the ticking of the big kitchen clock on the wall and the shuffle of the chair I pull out to sit on, the room is silent.

'It has,' I say. 'And there have been a few unpleasant surprises.'

I glance at Ciara. She doesn't react. Not even a little. There is no trace of surprise, of hurt, of anger or even denial in her expression.

Kathleen is first to speak. 'I understand there has been a bit of a mix-up.'

I remind myself not to give in to my heightened emotions. 'Yes, you could say that.'

'Sweetheart,' she says and I dig my nails in deeper.

I am not Kathleen McKee's sweetheart and nor will I ever be.

'So much gets muddled at these times. We're all through ourselves with grief. I swear I don't know myself these days. I keep thinking I hear him or see him . . .'

She starts to cry, which causes a flurry of activity. Hugs from Ciara, a tissue from Marie. Stella announcing she will put the kettle on.

Alex moves. 'I think I hear Lily. I'll go and get her.'

Lily isn't crying. I know that. I spot the baby monitor on the counter – no echoing cries through it, no moving lights, but still I step back and let him pass me.

'I think maybe we have some things to sort out,' Ciara interjects. Her voice is soft, but the expression on her face is hard.

'I don't think this is the time or place,' I say. 'But yes, there are things to sort out. To finally deal with. There have been enough whispered conversations, don't you think?'

'I agree,' she says.

The tension is palpable. I can see her stiffen.

Marie speaks. 'I'm sorry if today was upsetting for you, Heidi. I'm guessing you feel there has been some sort of a mix-up regarding the grave.'

'I don't feel there was a mix-up. There *was* a mix-up. Factually. Joe was never meant to be buried with my mother.'

'Perhaps we can resolve this, when we're all feeling a little less emotional.' Marie says. 'There are bound to be things we can do if you find this very distressing. Perhaps we could have him moved to a new plot?'

Kathleen gasps. 'Oh God, that would be unbearable. Today was hard enough.'

'But it clearly means so much to Heidi and really, we must all think of Heidi, mustn't we?' Ciara says. 'Some things never change. There isn't a scene or a family occasion that Heidi can't make all about her, even a family funeral.'

She's waiting for me to bite. She is goading me. Everyone can see it and feel it, and I know that whatever I say or do next will have lasting consequences.

No good comes of speaking in a temper, though. She has painted me quite successfully as unhinged already. Displaying any sign that it could in fact be true would be a bad move. Especially now, when the police are more keen than ever to pin this on someone.

'I think it's best we just leave all this for today,' I say. 'Nothing good can come of it.'

With my face blazing, tears unshed and a deep sense of shame eating at me, I turn and walk to the door. When Alex arrives downstairs with Lily, I tell him we're leaving. He doesn't argue. He doesn't speak at all, in fact. He just follows me out of the door and to the car.

Chapter Fifty-Two

Ciara

Now

The white wine in my glass is tepid now. Almost undrinkable. I've been nursing it for the last forty-five minutes, too distracted by my thoughts to bring it to my mouth and sip from it. Added to that, I feel sick. Deep in my stomach there's gnawing nausea that just won't go away. I don't want to eat or drink.

I wish I could sleep, but even that seems to be eluding me at the moment. I've been half watching something on the TV. Some reality show about properties being fixed up for half of nothing and transformed from perfectly lovely homes to functional spaces with cool, clinical lines. Where so much as a stray cup would have the place looking completely disordered.

A sandal-wearing male designer is waffling on about natural light and feng shui, and all I can think is that he has little to be worrying about. If I had any strength left in my body at all, I would lift the remote and switch the TV off, or, better still, hurl it *at* the TV.

The anger from earlier has left me drained. Exhausted. Pinned to the sofa with grief.

Stella sits down beside me, lifts up my legs and places them across her lap before repositioning the throw over them. She looks tired. Older. We're all a bit broken by the last week or so.

'How are you?' she asks.

I know she expects an answer – a proper answer and not just a shrug of the shoulders, which I'm not sure I've the energy to deliver anyway.

'Tired,' I say, setting my wine glass on the floor. I know I won't drink any more from it.

'Today was rough,' she says.

'It was.'

Stella sighs, strokes my lower leg with her hand. 'Things with you and Heidi. Have they always been this bad?'

'Perhaps not this bad – but nobody had been murdered before,' I say.

I know I'm being glib. I see Stella flinch at my words and I don't want her to think badly of me. Or worse of me.

'Yes, they have always been bad. Always. It didn't start well. I was angry with her, and her mother, over Dad leaving. I felt he chose them over me and I hated them for it.' I stop, take a deep breath and look back up her. 'I know that sounds pathetic now, as a grown woman. But I was young then and he was my daddy. I never thought he would leave, but he did. And even when Natalie died, when I thought he might come back to us, he chose to stay on. He chose her over me, and I don't think I've ever forgiven them for that.'

There's a tightness in my chest.

'It was a long time ago,' Stella says softly.

'It was. And I know that the adult me should be able to rationalise it all. Adult me does, to an extent, but there's still this child in me who is so hurt by it all. And I've not always done the right thing, Stella. I've done bad things, you know. Things I'm not proud of. I can feel myself slipping back into those bad behaviours and it scares me. I should be better than this.'

Damn it, I feel the tightness in my chest rise up. A tingle in my nose, stinging in my eyes. I feel as if the floodgates, while not exactly opening, are about to crack a little.

'We've all done the wrong thing when we're hurting. Good people can do bad things for good reasons. And you're a good person. I know that more than anything,' Stella says, picking at invisible lint on the throw and looking downwards while she talks.

I shake my head. 'I'm not sure I am,' I say. 'I've been so vindictive towards Heidi.' My face blazes.

'It's understandable. She was your competition in a lot of ways. But it certainly doesn't seem that she was fond of your father, either.'

'That's what angered me most when he left – you know, back then. That she seemed to hate him so much when I would've given anything to have him back. It was easier to hate her than hate him, I suppose. I didn't want to see him as the enemy.'

'But that changed?' Stella says, probing gently. Her voice is calm and soft.

A tear falls and I wipe it away hastily, even though my arms are limp with exhaustion. I nod, just as I can feel my heart rate start to rise.

'What happened to change it?'

I close my eyes. Images, snapshots of a time long gone flicker in my mind. Things I wasn't sure for a long time were real. Things maybe I'm still not sure are real but I feel they are. Somewhere inside me I know they are. He called it love, but it wasn't love, after all. It was never love. I'm scared to say the words. Afraid of judgement, even though I know that it wasn't me, you see. I was never, ever the one at fault. I was a child.

I was only a child.

That bastard.

I was only a child, and he took so much from me and tried to convince me it was because he loved me just so very much. And then, despite all that 'love' he said he felt for me, and only me, he left. Shame washes over me. The shame borne out of all those confused, fucked-up feelings I experienced. The loyalty I showed him. How I begged him, this monster, to come back.

In a voice as small as I feel in that moment, my face blazing with shame, my voice choked with emotion and my stomach churning, the small sips of tepid wine threatening to rise from my stomach and splatter the floor, I speak. I close my eyes and say the words I've not said to a single person before.

'When I remembered what he did to me.'

Chapter Fifty-Three

Ciara

Then

I was a precocious child. I was led to believe from a young age that the sun, moon and stars shone directly out of my backside. I was the apple of my mother's eye but I was, undoubtedly, a daddy's girl. I hero-worshipped the very ground he walked on. There was no one in the world who mattered to me as much as him, often to the annoyance of my mother.

We were a team and I would often be at his side as his 'shadow', going with him to the library or for long walks in the countryside. I'd sit with him while he did odd jobs around the house. Ask him to explain them to me. I'd always manage to get an extra cuddle or three from him, whenever I could.

I would tell him, with all the innocence that comes with being a young child, that I would marry him when I grew up.

'But I'm already married to Mammy,' he would say with a laugh.

'Well,' I'd tell him, full of the confidence of a six-year-old

– the kind that leaves by the time teen years arrive and never comes back – 'you'll have to get Mammy a new person to marry, because I love you the mostest and we have to get married.'

I'd become quite distressed at the notion of ever living in a house where he wouldn't be. I was as obsessed with him as any child would be with their father.

He knew that, of course. And there were times, after, when I wondered had I loved him too much? Had I brought it on myself?

That's what he did to me. That's how he damaged me. That I would dare question it was my fault.

I was six the first time.

Six.

I cry still for the baby I was then and what happened to her.

He had come upstairs to read me a bedtime story. Mammy was downstairs. I could hear her singing to herself in the kitchen as he did things that I instinctively knew were wrong. I didn't understand it. I didn't like it. I was scared but he was my daddy. And he loved me 'most of anyone in the whole world'.

Afterwards, he told me I was his best girl. That he loved me to the moon and back, and that no other daddy and little girl ever loved each other as much we did. We couldn't tell anyone, he said, because they would only be jealous. He'd laughed when he added, 'Especially not Mammy! She'd be so jealous and we haven't found her a new person to marry yet, have we?' he'd winked.

I heard him whistling as he walked downstairs afterwards, heard him joining in singing with my mammy when he reached the kitchen. He sounded so happy. They sounded so happy. I just felt incredibly confused by it all.

Chapter Fifty-Four

Ciara

Now

Stella sleeps with her arm wrapped tightly around my middle. She is the big spoon to my little spoon and her embrace is reassuring, protective, pure.

She held me in her arms and rocked me while I cried and roared and spilled my darkest secrets out. She said all the right things. She cried too. For the child I was and for the woman I have become – one who is scared to trust, who is confused about love, who lashes out with a tongue so sharp it can cut. The woman who has been holding this secret shame inside for two decades.

All the time she said the words I needed to hear, over and over and over. This was not my fault. I was a child. I did nothing wrong. He, Joe McKee, the man who I was grieving for in the most fractured of ways, was a monster.

I talked about all my mixed feelings. My anger at his betrayal. The rising sense that something was very wrong. The misplaced love. The rejection. The pain and anger. The shame. There was so much shame. Shame that I had, despite everything, begged him to come back into my life. How sick was I?

We talked about help. About support. About counselling. She held my hair back when I did indeed empty what little had been sitting in my stomach down the toilet. And she sat me tenderly on the edge of the bath and gently washed away my tears and the grime of the day with a facecloth.

She put my toothpaste on my brush for me and I know that if my arms had been too tired to brush, she would have done that, too.

She helped my exhausted body, the one that had felt as if it was wrong and dirty all these years, into a bath and she gently, so very gently, soaped me and cleaned me. And when we were done, for the first time in years I felt truly clean.

My body numb, she helped me to dress, slipping on my knickers for me and pulling the oversized T-shirt I slept in over my head. Taking my brush from the dresser, she teased it through my hair, and then she pulled back the bed covers and helped me to lie down.

'No one will ever hurt you again,' she'd whispered as she had wrapped her arms around me.

And I had never felt so loved, or so protected before. I felt the shame that had held me down for almost my whole life start to ebb away.

The sun is shining on the front of the house at Aberfoyle Crescent. It's glinting off the windows, making the place look warm and welcoming. There's no sign at all, from the exterior, of the drama that has gone on behind those doors over the last week.

If walls could talk, I think wryly, they'd tell a very different story on the inside. Then again, it's definitely better that they can't.

I wish that I could turn back the clock and not come to see him, even though he was ill. It was selfish of him to pull me back into his drama again. He wanted to 'make amends', he said, and yet he'd never once talked about the past. That sordid past.

Maybe, if he had even said sorry, I could be less angry. But he hadn't. The whole thing was just his way of trying to control me all over again. And I had fallen for it, because a part of me, that damaged part of me that was still mired in shame and confusion, believed it might have helped, needed him to say sorry and that he loved me, and that he knew he had done very bad things.

But I'd expected too much of him, just like I always did.

He knew if I'd ignored his request I'd look like the evil, ungrateful daughter. In his arrogance he had been sure that I would never reveal his filthy secrets to anyone. Or maybe it wasn't arrogance at all. I had kept quiet for years, after all. I had not called out his sick actions. Maybe if I had . . .

I try not to think about that. I try to hold on to the sense of relief that I feel now he is gone. Now he is rotting in the ground.

I never have to fear hearing his voice, or seeing his face, or feeling his touch again.

But I do have to clear out his belongings from the house Heidi so desperately wants to get rid of. I try not to think about that too much, either. Why she wants to get rid of the house so quickly. Why she is so damaged.

Stella asked me this morning if I thought I should tell people the truth of what happened when I was younger. I shook my head. What good would it do people to know now? It can't be changed, I'd thought.

'But at least they, including your mum and Kathleen, might stop talking about him as if he is some saint. That must be hard for you,' she said as she buttered some toast for me – still intent on pampering me after the previous night's revelations.

'Causing them pain won't make any of this easier for me,' I'd said.

They can't confront him. They can't make him face justice.

But I suppose he faced justice the night he died. He had no doubt experienced fear and terror and pain. He had known what it was like to be helpless. To be weak and vulnerable.

Karma had come full circle, I suppose.

'Do you think you should tell the police?' she had probed gently.

I'd shrugged. 'Why? It's not like they can arrest him.'

'No,' she said. 'But it might help them understand why someone killed him.'

She'd looked away, stared out of the kitchen window. It dawned on me that my revelation had given me a very strong motive for wanting him dead.

'You don't think it was me, do you?' I'd asked.

'It would be understandable if it was,' she'd said in a quiet voice.

I took a deep breath and steadied myself to admit the one thing that I'd not been able to say out loud before.

'It wasn't me,' I said. 'But I wish it was. From the bottom of my heart, I wish it had been me.'

Stella turned to face me, her eyes brimming with unshed tears. 'I'm glad it wasn't,' she said slowly, deliberately, 'but I would've supported you if it was.'

I nodded, my face blazing again. I could not speak.

She sat down beside me and took my hand. 'Can I ask something else?'

I nodded once more.

'If he hurt you, do you think he could've hurt her, too?'

'Who? Heidi?'

I thought of how she hated him. How she always seemed to hate him. How I always thought it was because he was intrinsically linked in her mind to the death of her mother. I might've given it a passing thought in the past, but to be honest I'd done my best not to think about Heidi at all over the last ten years.

But I knew she had never left his side, even as she grew up. They had never become estranged. Not like me. She still visited him. She may not have loved him, or even liked him, but she felt a duty of care to him and she acted on that. Would she have done that if he had hurt her in the same way?

But then I think of how messed up I was. How confused I had been about what love meant, and care and family. I think of how many times I'd told her no one else wanted her. That she was alone. That she'd be better off dead. My face blazed at the memory. I had been such a vindictive bitch. Even when I was old enough to know better.

I had goaded her through her life, and even when I came back to see Joe at her behest, I had still been unable to resist goading her. Acting like a child. Breaking that stupid doll.

And all the time refusing to acknowledge that she could be hurt, too. That she might have endured some of what I had. Except he had left me, hadn't he? He stayed with Heidi. From the moment her mother had died when she was nine and a half, he had been a constant. He must have thought he had died and gone to heaven, I think, and my stomach tightens and turns and guilt and fear wash over me.

We'd both been guilty. My father and I, of destroying her.

I could no longer look at the breakfast I'd been eating. I could no longer think beyond Stella's words. Had I been so wrapped up in my own pain that I'd failed to see what was most likely going on under my nose? If I had spoken up all those years ago, could I have stopped him from hurting her?

I'd turned all the hate and hurt I felt for him towards her. And that, ultimately, makes me complicit in his crimes.

If she was pushed to put a pillow over his head and end his life, then I was as guilty as if I had handed her the pillow myself.

Chapter Fifty-Five

Ciara

Then

I told someone once. A school friend. Someone I thought I could really trust. Someone I was sure would understand.

I think I was maybe sixteen or seventeen. Going through one of my rebellious phases. Dying my hair (and my scalp) jet black with cheap home hair dye. Wearing too much eyeliner and lipstick much too dark for my complexion. Rolling my eyes and swearing when my mum asked where I was going and when I would be home.

Talking back. Stealing from her purse. Enough for a carryout from the offie. A three-litre bottle of the cheapest, most disgusting cider money could buy. I'd pool my resources with the people I regarded as friends, so we had enough to get pissed and have enough cheap cigarettes to smoke ourselves hoarse.

We weren't original in our rebellion. We joined the other underage drinkers up on Derry's historic walls, sitting on benches or on the cold cobbles and smoking and drinking into the wee hours. Being rowdy. Making what my mother would call a 'holy show' of ourselves.

There was always someone to 'get off' with, too – and that was part of the rebellion. Random, meaningless sex acts that fulfilled some sort of need, I suppose. That was before I admitted that boys were not my thing – before I realised that sex didn't always have to feel shameful, intrusive and wrong.

When we were suitably pissed, and sated from our teenage fumbling, we would have those big philosophical discussions that only really seem very important at two in the morning when the rest of the world has gone quiet. We'd say things we'd never say in the light of day. Things it seemed easier to say under the soft cover of the stars.

Jude. That was her name. Short for Judith. She was shorter than I was, but her presence was larger. Everyone wanted to be Jude's friend, and when you were in her company she had a way of making you feel like the most important person in the world.

Unlike me, she could apply her winged eyeliner perfectly and her blood-red lipstick never found its way onto her teeth. She could drink an entire bottle of cider without having the need to throw up, or find a quiet place to have a pee.

But as well as being, seemingly effortlessly, cool, she was also a good listener. She showed a maturity beyond her years and it's fair to say I hero-worshipped her. In hindsight, she was probably my first girl crush.

So I'd found myself worse for wear one night, having one of our deep and meaningful conversations sometime after 1 a.m., when I told her what I didn't dare tell anyone else.

I'm not sure what I expected. Perhaps a hug. Perhaps she would cry and tell me she was sorry something so awful happened to me. Perhaps she would offer to come with me to the police. Perhaps she would just understand.

Instead, I saw a look of disgust on her face. Maybe even disbelief. I can still see her now, dragging on her cigarette before dropping it and grinding it into the ground under one of her trendy ox-blood DM boots.

'That's really fucking serious, Ciara,' she'd said, shaking her head.

I waited to see what she would follow it up with.

She'd simply shaken her head and walked away. I was left not knowing what I'd done wrong. Wondering if she thought it was my fault. Feeling like I was dirty and horrible all over again.

Jude kept her distance after that. Slowly but surely I was sidelined from her group, from my 'tribe' of so-called friends who drank on the Walls. I was too damaged even for society's misfits.

I promised myself then that I'd never tell anyone again. And yet, I'd told Stella and the world hadn't ended. Now I owed it to Heidi to tell her, too.

Chapter Fifty-Six

Ciara

Now

I'm nervous standing here, outside the house at Aberfoyle Crescent, waiting for Heidi to arrive, to discuss what happens next.

Like her, I now just want to get this all over and done with. I want the past put in the past. So much makes sense now that didn't before.

I'm not sure how I'll look her in the face when she arrives. I can feel my palms sweating, despite the biting cold. I don't want to be back in this house at all. I can't imagine how Heidi has kept coming here, kept facing her trauma over and over again. If it wasn't for my mother and Kathleen badgering me to make sure they had access to Dad's things, I'd have been happy never to come here again.

The house is icy, unwelcoming. No one has put any heating on in here in days and the temperature hasn't taken its time to drop, cold and damp settling into the very fabric of the building.

The big clock in the hall still ticks loudly. I can just hear the low hum of the fridge, but aside from that the house is silent.

I can feel it, though, for the first time. The badness of this place that gave Stella the creeps. I'd assumed she'd felt my pain, but it was possible much worse had happened here.

I see a picture of Natalie, a slightly older version of the woman Heidi has become, smile down from the wall. I wonder if I should've given Natalie more of a chance. For the two years she'd been in my life I'd treated her with nothing but absolute disdain. I'd hated her, although all she ever did was be kind to me. She was soft-spoken, like Heidi. Meek. Unaware of her own beauty. She'd try to engage with me, even when she was ill. Even when it was clear she was dying. I turned my back on her every time.

She'd tell me she understood. It must be hard for me, she'd say. I remember her saying that, sitting in the armchair in the living room, little more than a bag of bones. Her face grey, her eyes sunken. I remember her hands, long bony fingers. Bruises on the back of her hand, livid blue-and-green. Specks of blood from cannula sites. Her fingernails were still painted the palest pink. A pink I'd have asked her about if I hadn't hated her so much. The faintest wisp of hair escaped from a pale lilac head-scarf.

What a bitch I'd been not to give her a chance, even when it was clear that she didn't have much time left.

The same chair still sits in the living room. I can almost conjure her image in it. I wish I could talk to her now. Apologise for how I'd been with her. Apologise for not protecting her daughter.

I'm so lost in my memories that I jump when I hear the key turn in the lock behind me. Heidi walks in, carrying a sleeping Lily in her car seat and that ever-present changing bag. She huffs and puffs as she puts the seat down and wriggles out

236

of her puffy jacket. Of course as soon as she puts the jacket down she shivers, wraps her mustard scarf around her neck more tightly. She looks unwell, the colour of the scarf draining her pale skin. There are dark rings under her eyes. I think of her mother again, or how alike they look, my stomach twisting.

'Well,' she says brusquely, 'you wanted me to meet you here and here I am.'

She looks nervous, fidgety. She clearly doesn't want to be here. I'm tempted to tell her she's not the only one.

I feel awkward now. Lumpen and heavy. Misplaced.

'I'm not sure what your plans are for the house,' I start.

'Estate agents will be out at the start of next week to value it and get it on the market,' she says, looking around as if she's seeing it for the first time. Looking anywhere as long as it isn't at me.

I swallow. 'We'll do our best to sort through his things. As quickly as we can. Get out of your hair. I know Kathleen wants some things. The police said they've all the stuff they need, so there's nothing stopping us from getting on with it.'

'Take whatever you want,' she interrupts, her voice cold. She delves into her jeans pocket and pulls out a sheet of paper, folded in two. 'Those are the only items I want from here – anything else is yours if you want it. Once you've had your pick, I'll get someone in to do a house clearance. Dump or sell all the other stuff. I'll sort through the junk in my old bedroom too, but there's little I want from there. Probably my dolls – you know, for Lily. Of course, someone smashed Scarlett.'

She looks at me for the first time that day. She is accusing me. Suddenly it's as if I'm fourteen again and this precocious nine-year-old with the awful haircut is looking up at me, looking so needy and pathetic and wrapped up in her own selfish world.

I blush purple. 'I'm so sorry,' I say, the words sticking in my throat. I am mortified. 'So very sorry. I was a bitch. I'm such a bitch. I was just angry and hurt and wanted to hit out at someone or something . . .'

'At me,' she says, glaring at me. 'You wanted to hit out at me. You've always wanted to hit out at me. For whatever I did to you. I thought we might be past it now, but the last few days . . . nothing has changed, has it? You've not changed. You've not matured. You're as spiteful and manipulative as you ever were. You're still all about playing mind games.'

'I broke the doll and I'm sorry for that. I really am. But I've not been playing any games. Not this time. Look,' I say, 'I just want to get this over with as much as you do. Can we just do that? There's been enough hurt.'

'Really? We've finally reached a limit? Good to know after all these years we've crossed that hallowed threshold. We just needed to blame missing prayer books on me, talk about me behind my back to my husband and have my mother's grave opened against my wishes.'

Her eyes are flashing with anger, her voice harsh. Lily is starting to stir in her chair, no doubt disturbed by the angry tone of her mother.

'Heidi, the prayer book was in your bag. I found it there. I didn't disregard your wishes. I didn't know them. Everything was so messed up. I've apologised for breaking your doll. If I could turn back time . . . And yes, I've talked about you behind your back, but I'm sure you've said a few choice words too, about me.'

She shakes her head. 'Why are you lying? Why do you keep lying? Why can't you just admit it was you who killed him and you've been doing everything in your power to point the finger of blame at me since?'

I see her body tense, her hands ball into fists. I fear she won't stop herself from lashing out this time.

Before I know it she is lunging at me, pushing me as hard

and fast as she can against the wall. My back hits the plaster-work first, my head second – a sickening thud, the force of which causes me to bite into my tongue. I taste blood, feel my legs buckle. I try to centre myself, looking up to see her glaring at me, a fist raised, poised to come at me. I lift my hands, block her assault. Scream at her to stop.

She lashes out again, furiously. I can see she is crying.

'You're making everyone think I'm mad. You're turning my own husband against me. You have to stop! You have to stop!'

I can see years of pain on her face and I almost, almost, want to lower my hands and let her take out her rage on me. I deserve it. I could have saved her even if I didn't save myself.

'I'm sorry,' I blurt through my tears. 'I'm so sorry. I didn't mean to. I'm sorry. He hurt me too, Heidi, he hurt me too!'

Chapter Fifty-Seven

Heidi

Now

'He hurt me too.' Ciara's words cut through the noise. They cut through the thumping in my heart and the rush of blood through my veins. They cut through Lily's crying. They cut through my anger and pain.

I hear them and immediately I freeze. I register their meaning. I stop, drop the hand that was in mid-flight to my side. My anger seeping from me, through my feet, through the floor, leaving as quickly as it arrived.

'He hurt me too,' she'd said again. It is enough to change everything.

I look at her. At the expression on her face. For the first time, I see the same pain in her eyes that I see in my own every time I look in the mirror. Even when I think I'm happy. Even when I think I have it sussed and when I think I'm finally 'over it'. My eyes tell a different story.

Seeing Ciara now, the look on her face, I know she feels it, too. The pain, the betrayal, the hurt and the shame.

My arms are like lead weights. Ciara is crying now. Gulping lungfuls of air. Lily is still howling. It's only the sharpness of her cry that forces me to move, to turn from Ciara and focus on the tiny child who needs me. The innocent baby.

My girl.

My precious little girl.

I could never have allowed him to hurt her, you see.

When she was born, everything I'd thought I'd pushed to the back of my mind about Joe and what he'd done came back. And with it came such a primal sense of needing to protect my daughter, I vowed to distance myself even further from Joe McKee.

And then he became sick and it all seemed as though karma was finally catching up with him. But it trapped me. No one would understand if I walked away from a dying man, but I'd rather have died myself than tell people what I'd endured. They'd never understand. I doubted they would even believe me. Joe was regarded so highly, and I was always regarded as a strange one, a misfit, the girl who was a bit 'mad in the head'.

They'd never understand that it was more complicated than it ever appears in the movies. Mind games and manipulation. A destroyed sense of self. I had clung on to 'love' as twisted and as damaging as it was. I'd almost persuaded myself it had never happened. Until Lily was born. Until I woke up.

I'm aware of Ciara slumping to the floor behind me as I lift my baby and rock her to me. Hold her close and soothe her. Centre myself as she fusses. She's hungry. Her physical need reminds me I need to be present.

I lower myself to the floor and bring Lily to my chest. She quiets as she starts to feed.

'I'm sorry,' Ciara says. 'I'm sorry for everything. For what I said. Or didn't say. I'm right, aren't I? He hurt you.'

I nod, a teardrop plopping onto Lily's soft hair. It all seems so sad.

'If I'd spoken up, maybe, just maybe . . .'

I can't speak.

She shakes her head. 'I blocked it out,' she says. 'I didn't allow myself to think about it. I was so angry. It was so messed up. For years, I thought it was normal. He made me believe what we did, no . . . what he did to me . . . was normal.

'When you were ill . . .' Ciara blinks at me. 'Back when you were young, how you behaved, I should've known it was about more than your mother dying. But I swear I didn't. I don't think I wanted to see it. He told me I was his special girl, you see. His favourite.' Her voice cracks and she puts her hand to her mouth as if she might throw up.

'Oh God, I'm so, so sorry,' she says. 'I know you mightn't believe this, but it was only when I spoke to Stella last night and she said . . .' She pauses.

I can't speak.

'She asked me did I think he hurt you, too. I knew straight away he had. I felt it there and then. So much of what happened when we young just clicked into place.'

She is crying. Her fierce, cool, at times vicious exterior has been replaced with a vulnerability I've never seen in her before. Not when she was fourteen and screaming at me that she hated me. Not when she didn't realise I'd heard her beg her daddy to come back.

'I was so awful to you, Heidi. So awful. Even now, as a grown up. I don't deserve your forgiveness, but you must know I'm really sorry. More sorry than I can ever say.'

There is such desperation in her voice, it's heartbreaking.

'I'd have said something if I'd known. I think I would've said something.'

'I believe you,' I say, my body sagging but also knowing it was always more complicated than that. It was never as easy as just saying something. Just telling someone.

242

Ciara nods. We are both utterly exposed to each other for the first time.

'You've not told Alex, have you?' she eventually says.

I shake my head. 'I haven't told anyone. I was too ashamed and then I didn't want people, especially Alex, to look at me like I was damaged goods.'

'I know,' she says, because she really does know.

She knows exactly what this feeling is like.

'He told me no one else wanted me,' I tell her, feeling strange to say the words out loud for the first time. 'I had no one. Everyone thought I wasn't right, you know? Too much trouble. He told me he was the only person who loved me and he was the only person who would take care of me. He told me bad things happened to children in care and that's where I would end up.'

Saying the words hurt. Bad things had been happening to me then anyway.

Ciara drops her head in her hands. 'I told you those things too. If I'd known . . . Oh God, I made it so awful for you. I know it's no excuse, but I was hurting so much. It was so fucked up. He told me I was his special girl,' she sniffs. 'That what he did, what he made me do, was how people showed each other how much they loved each other.'

'God, when I think about it now, I was so stupid. So naive,' I say.

Ciara pushes her hair back from her face, shakes her head. 'We were children, Heidi. We weren't stupid. We were scared, vulnerable children. And the only way I knew how to communicate with people was to hurt them,' she says, wiping her eyes, then nose, with the back of her sleeve.

She pulls her knees to her chest and she looks, for all intents and purposes, like the truculent fourteen-year-old again I remember from all those years ago.

I realise we've both been trapped in time – stuck in an awful place of shame and hurt for so long that we never got the chance to grow up normally.

'I don't blame you,' she says eventually, and I blink back at her. 'I think you were brave. I'm jealous, almost.'

She must register the confusion on my face.

'For what you did,' she says. 'I'm not angry. I wish I'd had the nerve to do it myself.'

I blink, tense. 'What I did?' I ask.

'To him. To Joe. You killed him. It was you, wasn't it?'

I stare at her. I can't find the words – this is all moving on to a place I was not prepared for.

'I mean, I get it now, I understand. God, anyone would understand,' she says, her voice growing in confidence. 'And I'll help you in whatever way I can. We can tell the police, together, both of us. We can tell them how sick he was, and I mean in the head. What he did. How he manipulated us. What he took from us. They'll understand. If we both tell them. They'll have to take it all into consideration. Trauma and all that.'

I shake my head again. She really thinks I was the one to suffocate the life out of Joe.

'But, Ciara. I didn't do it. It wasn't me,' I say.

She blinks at me. 'You can trust me,' she says, more urgency in her voice. 'I'm on your side now. I understand.' She sniffs. 'The pressure you must have been under. Being in this house. Being around him all that time. No one – no one in the world would blame you. I don't think you have to be scared,' she says. 'Once the police know what he put you through, what he put us through . . .'

She's repeating herself. Rambling. Becoming manic. Breaking just as I had broken.

'Ciara, I didn't do it,' I repeat. 'I had nothing to do with it,' I mutter, but she just shakes her head.

'I think it would be better to go to the police before they come to you. To tell them before they find their evidence, you know. Don't they say that these things are always better for you if you come forward yourself? I'll go with you. We can go now, once you're finished feeding Lily.'

Her voice has risen an octave or two, become quicker. Her eyes are more manic. She is caught up in her own storm and she isn't listening to anything I say.

'Or I could just call them now, you know. I'm sure that DI Bradley would come over if I asked him.'

My chest tightens. Lily wriggles, responding to my body tensing. I lift her up onto my shoulder as Ciara tries to pull herself to her feet, moving towards the phone on the table.

She's not listening to me. She's convinced, no matter what I say, that I did it. And I know, despite her apologies and her tears, that she is very good at making people believe her.

Maybe all this, all these tears and confessions, have just been an act as well. I wouldn't put it past her. It's just a way of manipulating me further – of making me take the fall for her. The most disgusting of all her attempts to hurt me.

Could she be covering up for her own actions? She had the same reasons to hate him as I did. And there's no denying that she hates me, too. That doesn't just disappear in the course of one conversation, no matter the topic.

'Ciara, stop it! You're not listening. I didn't do it. I swear on Lily's life, I didn't do it. I wouldn't do anything that would risk me being taken away from her.'

'Lily will be fine.' Ciara brushes off my pleas. 'I bet you won't even serve time, once they know.'

She reaches for the phone and I scramble to my feet, my daughter still in my arms.

'Stop it!' I'm screaming now. 'You're not phoning the police. I won't let you.'

'Are you threatening me?' she asks. 'If you think you can intimidate me into taking the blame for something you've done, you can think again.'

She's twisting everything and I can't keep up. My head hurts.

'I'm not threatening you,' I plead, trying to reach out to her.

She shrugs and turns away from me, grabbing the phone with a shaking hand. 'All this could be over and done with if you'd just admit it. Have we not all suffered enough at this stage? I feel like we've suffered enough . . . And anyone can see you were distracted with everything. Not in your right mind.'

'Ciara!' I say firmly, my hand on her shoulder, spinning her round to face me. I know I'm in her face and I'm intimidating her now. 'You're not listening to me. I didn't do it. Why would it be me? You've as much of a motive as I have . . .'

She looks at me as if I've just come out with the most ludicrous statement of all time.

'Well, it was hardly me,' she says, turning the phone away from me again.

She's dialling the number. I can hear the phone ring at the other end and I snatch it from her quickly, throwing the phone as hard as I can to the floor so that it smashes.

'I won't take the fall for you. Or for anyone else,' I tell her.

She is glaring at me, her eyes dark, enraged. For the first time in days, anger is not my primary emotion – fear is.

Chapter Fifty-Eight

Ciara

Now

Heidi has knocked the phone out of my hand. It's in bits on the floor. I look at it, then look back to her. Why did she do that? And she thinks maybe I'm the one covering up for my actions.

She's actually suggesting I did it. That I killed my own father. She is delusional and dangerous.

'Why did you do that?' I ask, stepping towards her. 'Why would you be so stupid to do that? I only wanted to help!' I'm so angry now. Why won't she let me help her?

'You're not listening to me,' she says, but all I've done is listen.

Over the last few days that's all there has been to do. To listen to everyone gather round and talk about this man who was the 'salt of the earth'. How he 'deserved more than he got' and would be 'greeted at the gates of heaven by the faithfully departed'. Every single thing I've heard has made me want to throw up.

But I haven't. I've stayed because my mother needs me. And Kathleen, too. And here is Heidi and I'm offering to help her and she's acting like a woman possessed.

Why can't she see that all I want to do is help?

I get that she's scared. I get that she might not want to admit what she did. I get that she might even actually believe that it was me who did it . . .

'Why are you being so stupid? Why are you being so stubborn?' I'm shouting and she's hugging that baby to her in the way she used to hold that stupid, ugly doll of hers. 'I've said I'll help. I'll help make them believe.'

She shakes her head and my frustration grows stronger. I know that maybe I'm rambling a little bit, tripping over my words.

'Everyone has to know,' I say. 'And we have to tell them. You have to tell them.'

Heidi looks like a rabbit caught in the headlights. For every step I take towards her, she takes a step back. She is holding that baby of hers so tightly that Lily is starting to protest.

'Put the baby down,' I say, moving towards her.

'Ciara, back off,' Heidi says, taking another step backwards, straight into the wall.

'I'm only trying to help,' I tell her again. 'That's all I'm trying to do. If we can prove he hurt us, hurt both of us . . .' I want to cry, or shake her or find some way to get through to her and make her understand.

I can see panic in her eyes. She is rocking her baby almost too much.

'Give me the baby,' I say, reaching out for Lily.

All I want to do is make sure she is safe. Heidi is being too rough.

'Leave me alone,' she cries out.

And I know she is scared, but if she squeezes Lily any tighter . . .

'I just want to make sure she's safe,' I say. 'Please.'

Heidi is shaking her head. 'No. No. You want to hurt her and you want to take her from me. Everybody always takes everything away from me . . .'

She's becoming hysterical. Maybe if I call Alex. He might be able to talk some sense into her. He will be able to calm her down. She'll listen to him.

I step back, mutter to myself to remember to breathe. That I'm okay. I won't give in to the panic that is clawing at me, too. My mobile is in my bag, which is hanging at the bottom of the stairs. I know I put Alex's phone number in it on one of the evenings we were planning how to help Joe. Was it even on the night Joe died? It might have been. That night has become hazy now. I've barely slept since and my memories are blurring into one another.

'Okay,' I say, my hands shaking, reaching in and pulling out my phone. 'I know it's scary, but it doesn't have to be.'

'Who are you calling now?' Heidi asks. 'Don't call the police. I told you, it wasn't me. Don't call the police.'

I raise a hand to quiet her.

'Who are you calling?' she shouts at me.

The call is connecting on the other end. I can hear it ringing. Heidi is crossing the room to me. I will Alex to pick up, sag with relief when I hear his voice.

'Alex,' I say, fighting against Heidi's hand reaching out for the phone. 'You need to come home, to Joe's house. You need to come now.'

Heidi is shouting at me, Lily is wailing.

'What are you doing?' she's screaming.

Alex will be panicking. I hear him mutter 'What's going on?', but Heidi is almost on top of me now so I end the call and throw the phone back into my bag.

'What have you done?' Heidi wails. 'You can't do this.'

249

'He'll understand. Surely, he'll understand. He loves you. He'd do anything to protect you.'

'You don't get it,' Heidi says. 'Why don't you believe me? Why are you doing this, Ciara? Why are you doing your best to point this at me? You've done it all along. Making me think I'm losing it. Messing with things. And you're doing it now. You're trying to mess with my head to the extent that I will admit to something I didn't do. Do you think I'm mad? Do you really think I am mad enough that I would do this?'

'And why don't you see I'm trying to help?'

Lily is almost purple from the effort of screaming now and Heidi is only getting more and more wound up. If she's unstable there's no telling what she might do.

'Lily is getting upset,' I soothe. 'You have to calm down. Think of Lily. Look at her.'

She glances down at her distraught daughter and her face crumples.

'Oh my God, Lily. I'm sorry. I'm sorry.'

She looks at me, fear mixed with anger blazing in her eyes.

'Look what you've made me do. She's so upset. She's over-heated. What if something happens?'

She's shaking now. I can see the colour drain from her face.

'Heidi, you don't look so good. Give the baby to me. Give her to me.'

Heidi shakes her head, but it's enough to set her off balance and she looks at me, eyes wide.

'I'm going to faint . . .' she manages to mutter before she starts to drop to the ground.

I have just enough time to grab Lily from her before she lands like a sack of potatoes in the hall.

Lily is still wailing, Heidi is as white as a ghost and I'm shaking so hard that my teeth are chattering. I look around, grab my thick winter coat from the coat rack and lay it on the ground so I can place Lily on it. Then I kneel over Heidi, put my hand to her forehead. She's clammy and still. My panic is building, when her eyes slowly start to flicker open.

With one look at me she descends into tears, tries to sit up, and she is clearly still woozy.

'It's okay, just rest there a minute.'

'Lily?' she mutters.

'She's fine. Can you hear her? She's fine.'

Heidi curls into a foetal position and sobs. I tell her I'm going to grab a glass of water. I'm scared now but for a different reason. I'm seeing how truly vulnerable Heidi is. I kneel beside her, help to raise her head so she can sip the water.

'Take your time,' I tell her. 'Don't sit up until you're ready. You fainted.'

She nods and I lift Lily, try to comfort her. Poor little Lily who hasn't a notion what is going on around her. She wriggles and pushes against me at first. She looks at me with wide eyes as if she's trying to make sense of everything and then, as I do my best to soothe her, stroking the soft curls on her head, she quiets, grabs hold of my fingers, and I feel my heart contract.

Meanwhile, Heidi is pulling herself to sitting, the colour very slowly coming back to her cheeks.

'Please,' she says, 'give me my baby.'

She looks scared. Scared of me. Does she really think I would do anything to hurt Lily?

'I will,' I say. 'I just want to make sure you're well enough to hold her when I do. How do you feel?'

Heidi gives a small laugh, which quickly turns into tears.

'Awful,' she says. 'Nothing about any of this isn't awful. I knew you hated me,' she says, looking directly at me, 'but this much? To try to destroy me?'

'I don't want to destroy you. All I want to do is help,' I tell her and I realise that's the truth. Now anyway. I just want to get us both – all of us even – through this.

'You've made it worse,' she says, her voice sad.

She puts her hand to her forehead. No doubt she feels the cold film of sweat that has broken out.

'All these games,' she whispers. 'And now Alex.'

'Alex will want to help too. He loves you. I can see that. When he knows everything, he'll be able to help you.'

'He thinks I'm losing my mind,' she says. 'All these things, the last few days. The doll, the missing book, the grave. All those things have him thinking I'm not right. That I can't be trusted with Lily.'

Shame floods me again. The things I've done and said. But I'm not responsible for it all. Not for the prayer book. Not for the grave.

She starts to get up. 'I want to go now,' she says, reaching out for Lily. 'Give her to me.'

'You can't leave!' I say, holding Lily firm.

I won't allow her to just walk away. We're all living under a cloud and she is the person who has the power to stop it.

'Who are you to tell me what I can and can't do?' she says, stepping closer. 'Now please, hand my daughter over to me.'

Lily turns her head towards her mother's voice. I hold her firm.

'I'm not giving her to you when you're behaving like this.'

'I'm not behaving like anything. I just want to go because I don't feel safe around you. I don't feel safe in this house. I don't feel comfortable with your accusations. So please, give my daughter to me and let us both leave.'

I don't understand why she can't see that I simply cannot and will not let that happen.

I shake my head and it's me who is taking a step backwards now, taking her child further away from her.

'No,' I say firmly. 'At least wait until Alex is here and then maybe he can talk some sense into you.'

'Please! She's my baby.'

I can see the anguish on her face as she longs to hold her daughter. I don't want to be cruel.

'I'll give her to you,' I say, 'only if you stay. You have to promise me you'll stay.'

She shakes her head but I can see she is wavering. Her desire to have Lily back in her arms outweighs anything else.

She concedes. I hand Lily to her and then I make sure that the front door is locked and she can't leave even if she changes her mind. She has to realise that I'm doing this for her own good. It will be much worse for her if she doesn't come clean.

Chapter Fifty-Nine

Heidi

Then

The night Joe died, something felt out of sorts. There was a strange energy in the house, which at the time I put down to the growing tension that came from putting five people who didn't really like each other, together in a relatively small space under stressful conditions.

I had a headache, one that I couldn't shift. I'd taken some paracetamol, which is all I was allowed to take given that I was breastfeeding Lily, but what I really wanted was to take something more hardcore to knock me out for a few hours. Since that wasn't going to be possible, I wished instead for a cool cloth over my eyes. A lie-down in a darkened room. Preferably my own darkened room in my own house away from all of this.

Joe had been in bad form all day. Worse form than normal. Maudlin. Philosophical. Cranky. He didn't want to be left alone for any length of time and unfortunately for him no one, with the possible exception of Kathleen, seemed minded to want to spend any time with him.

He hadn't even tried to be pleasant when I'd arrived at around ten thirty that morning – griping that he'd had to wait for his breakfast and was hungry. It hadn't been my fault I'd been late. Lily had been fussy – teething, I think. She'd thrown up everywhere just as we were getting ready to leave the house and I'd not only had to change her clothes, but bathe her as well. Then it had been time for her feed and well, yes, maybe I had taken some time to myself. But I deserved it. I needed it. I didn't think, even in his weakened state, coming downstairs and making a slice of toast was beyond him.

Joe punished me for my tardiness by being extra demanding. He knew he could play on my guilt, that I was a soft touch, so he did. He rang that stupid bell so many times that I'd barely had five minutes to myself to run a vacuum round or grab a cup of tea or feed my baby in peace. I'd muttered that I wanted to shove that stupid bell where the sun doesn't shine at one stage, a feeling of being completely overwhelmed washing over me.

Alex had been at work, Ciara and Stella, too. None of them had the 'luxury' of maternity leave to keep them away from their respective jobs. Kathleen had popped in during the afternoon, but then said she had to leave again. Pauline was taking her out for a coffee. Pauline was worried about the strain she was under. I'd forced a smile, but I'm sure Kathleen knew it was far from genuine.

They'd all arrived en masse at teatime and of course I'd felt obliged to make something to eat for everyone – opting for the easy option of a spaghetti bolognese. Using a jar of sauce, of course, because I didn't have the time to whizz one up from scratch. I barely had the time to bless myself, never mind press garlic.

Kathleen had turned her nose up at my food, said she didn't

feel like she'd eaten a proper dinner unless it had potatoes in it. She'd set about preparing something for herself, and for Joe too, saying he had always been a plain eater and it was more important than ever that he ate well now.

She'd been lucky not to get a pot of spaghetti sauce tipped over her. I bit my lip. I wanted to tell her he was lucky to be getting anything. They all were. I definitely had better or nicer things that I could have been doing than looking after Joe McKee and feeding the five thousand.

I should have been spending time with my daughter – time I wouldn't get back once I was back in the workforce, helping to keep the inner workings of the local technical college ticking over. This should be time spent sitting on the floor with her, playing with her, marvelling at her tiny, perfectly formed fingers. Kissing her feet. Singing to her. Learning how to be a mother without having a mother to teach me.

It was no wonder I was on my last nerve by the time dinner was over. Angry and put out and tired. And my head still hurt. At least, I thought, at least Stella was courteous enough to stack the dishwasher while Alex took Lily for a walk to settle her. That left Kathleen, Ciara and I to discuss the way forward, which was not a comfortable conversation to have and one I could easily have done without after the day I'd had.

Still, we knew it was necessary, so I made us all a cup of tea and we sat around the kitchen table. We were just about to plan a rota of sorts, when Joe's damned bell rang again.

'I'll go if you want,' Stella said, popping her head around the kitchen door.

'That would be lovely,' I'd said, grateful to give my tired legs a break from running up and down the stairs.

She'd smiled, more in Ciara's direction than anything else, then had set off up the stairs, only to come back down again less than a minute later.

'He wants you, Heidi,' she said, her face a little flushed.

Both Ciara and Kathleen shifted uncomfortably in their seats. As if they were put out by it all. As if they wanted him to have asked for them instead. Neither of them knew that I'd be more than happy to let either of them take my place. Permanently.

I nodded, sighed and got to my feet, then trudged up the stairs.

Joe was sitting up in bed. His glasses perched at the end of his nose. He put down the pen he was holding and closed over the book he had been writing in, in slow, deliberate moves. He looked up, regarding me over the top of his glasses as if I were some sort of scientific specimen. Goose bumps, very much the unpleasant kind, prickled on my skin.

'Sit down,' he said.

It was an order, not a request. I knew his tone of voice well.

I pulled the chair from beside his bed just a little further away from him before doing what he'd asked.

He shook his head. 'I don't know why you always have to be so cold with me, Heidi,' he said sadly.

I didn't know what to say, so I stayed quiet. Fidgeting uncomfortably on the chair. I willed Lily to let out a cry so I would have an excuse to bolt. It shocked me how quickly he could make me feel as if he was in control again.

He sighed again. 'You're talking about me, aren't you? All of you. Downstairs.'

He sounded worried. But he always was a good actor, good at eliciting sympathy when he deserved none. I'd no doubt he was going to start laying down the law about what standard of care he expected. Joe McKee was nothing if not particular.

'Yes,' I said. 'We are. We're talking about how best to support you.'

He nodded slowly. 'And that's all?' he said, one bushy, over-grown grey eyebrow raised ever so slightly.

I wasn't sure if I imagined it or not, but thinking back, now I'm sure that it was a flash of worry that I saw on his face as he spoke. We'd never spoken of what had happened all those years ago. Joe had been a master of sweeping uncomfortable things under carpets and I'd been content to let all those secrets fester out of sight.

'What else would we be talking about?' I asked him, keeping my face as neutral as my voice.

'All sorts of things come up when someone is dying,' he said. 'Emotions. Unresolved issues.'

'Sure, what unresolved issues would we have, Joe?' I asked.

I knew I was goading him, but I wanted to know how far I could push him before he would crack. If, that was, he would crack at all.

'Well, I don't know, but I suppose what I'm saying is that there's no need to go upsetting yourself, or anyone else for that matter, by going over old ground.'

He made it sound like he was trying to do me a favour. Like he was trying to look after me. All that did was anger me more.

'What old ground would that be, Joe?' I asked as I struggled to retain my composure.

Would he actually have the balls to come out and say it? I wondered. Would he have the guts to say that he wanted to make sure his sick and sordid past didn't become the thing people remembered him for most of all?

He paused, blinked. 'Things weren't always easy,' he said. He swallowed, looked down then up and that time I knew what I saw. I knew I was looking at the face of a worried and scared old man. 'I did my best, you know. You were such a damaged child. With your mother's death. You were so difficult to manage at times, and I know you believed things to be true that maybe didn't happen like you remember them. Then of course the passage of time erodes memories, doesn't it? Fills in gaps in stories. Traumas mix together, don't they, so it's hard to remember what is real and what isn't. Especially when you were on so many medications.'

'So tell me, what was real? Those things that maybe didn't really happen? Or that my memory has embellished for me over the years? Why don't you tell me what of it really did happen? Just so I know.'

He shook his head. 'I don't think there's any need to drag things up,' he said. 'The past is the past and I hold no hard feelings . . .'

'*You*? You hold no hard feelings?' It was incredulous, what he was saying.

'None,' he said. 'You didn't know what you were saying. Your mind was in a very dark place. Everyone knew it. But you'll always be my special girl. You know I did so much for you, and I don't regret it for a second. I walked away from my own daughter for you, and your mother. To make sure you were taken care of. Even when it was tough. Even when you hated me, because I've always seen you as my daughter too, you know. All those years of providing for you. Caring for you. Loving you. They must count for something? Tell me they count for something.'

This man. This man who had terrified and traumatised me. He was now – weak, pathetic – trying to manipulate me again. Trying to make me think I was losing my mind again. Trying to tell me he'd done me a favour? Christ Almighty, I'd rather have been left to roam the streets on my own than endure what he did to me.

He reached out. His creepy bony hand, already showing signs of the weight he had lost during his illness. I saw his fingernails, just a little too long. I remembered his touch. How his nails would scrape at my skin. His clammy hands. His rank breath.

He had convinced himself, perhaps, of his own innocence,

but I knew what had happened. I had no doubts. None at all. As his hand moved closer to me, I flinched. I would not let him touch me. Never again. Not for any reason.

I batted his hand away, using more force than I anticipated. His arm, not as strong as it was, swung backwards, his hand bashing against the bedside locker. I can still hear the thud it made now when I think about it. He swore under his breath, but I didn't care. I stood up, scraping the chair back as I stood.

'Go to hell, Joe,' I said as calmly, but as menacingly, as I could, turning on my heel, ignoring his yelping about his injured hand or his attempts to call me back.

'Don't be like that, Heidi,' I hear him say as I closed the door and headed back down the stairs just in time to see Alex arrive back with Lily.

That was the last time I spoke to Joe McKee.

Chapter Sixty

Heidi

Now

My breath is catching in my chest. I feel as if someone has wrapped their arms around me and is squeezing too tight. Ciara is standing defiantly at the door. She won't listen to reason. She won't listen at all.

At least, I think, at least Alex shouldn't take long to get here. He only works fifteen minutes away. If the traffic isn't heavy, that is. And it shouldn't be. Although with the snow on the ground now, things could take longer than usual. I could be trapped here for longer. I start to spiral.

'I'm going upstairs,' I tell Ciara. I can't stand to be under her gaze for a moment longer.

'Where?' she asks.

'My room. I just want to settle Lily,' I lie. 'She's overdue her nap and she's upset and I want to make sure she's okay.'

Ciara looks as if she is weighing up her options. What does she think I'll do up there anyway?

'Okay,' she says with a degree of reluctance. 'Just for Lily.'

I nod. I won't thank her. She doesn't deserve any thanks for letting me leave her sight.

I climb the stairs, my legs still shaky from my fainting episode. I hold on tight to Lily, terrified to let her go. I don't want to let her go ever again. Ciara is pacing the hall, muttering to herself. Manic.

How will Alex feel when he knows what happened to me? Will Ciara be able to convince him that I'm responsible? Will she tell him I'm unhinged? Will she use the strange things that happened to prove it to him? Will she tell him all about how sick I was as a teenager? The scratching? The fire?

When he finds out how damaged I am, will he ever be able to trust me, to love me, again?

Or maybe that's been Ciara's intention all along. Maybe, despite our shared trauma, she hates me so much that she wants to see my life implode.

Chapter Sixty-One

Ciara

Then

On the night Joe died things had been tense in the house. Well, things were always tense in that house, but they were more tense that night. The great 'I'm going to sell this house as soon as he's gone' announcement of the night before had wound us all up.

I veered between not giving a damn what Heidi Lewis did with her godforsaken house and being so angry that she could look at it all so coldly.

I suppose I was angry because her coldness simply mirrored my own.

I wanted him dead. I hoped that he was right when he whined about maybe only having weeks and not the months the doctors said were possible. I couldn't stand the thought of spending months of my life in his presence. Spending months of my life in that poky bedroom, where the air was stale and there was little in the way of natural light no matter what the time of day.

I couldn't stand the thought of having to play nice. I didn't want to play nice. Seeing him had cemented that in my mind. I just wanted him to admit to what he'd done and say sorry. But it seemed that was too much to ask.

So that night, after we had eaten the begrudgingly prepared dinner Heidi had thrown together, sitting around the table in silence while Kathleen grilled a couple of pork chops for my father and had cut them up as if he were some feeble infant, my frustration had grown.

All this fussing around for a man who didn't deserve a moment of it.

It seemed like such a waste of everyone's energy.

He seemed like a waste of everyone's energy.

It was around nine when Kathleen presented me with a cup of tea and a plate holding three custard cream biscuits and asked me to bring my father up his supper. A man of plain tastes, custard creams were his favourite biscuit and Kathleen told us all that she'd gone and bought them especially. 'But good ones, mind, not those value pack ones that taste of nothing.'

I'd trudged up the stairs to find my father sitting on the edge of his bed, his feet in his slippers on the floor. He seemed to be lost in his thoughts.

'Kathleen asked me to bring you some supper,' I said in a voice that contained no trace of the warmth Kathleen had shown him.

'She's good to me,' he said, 'she always was.'

I crossed the room to put the cup and the plate on the bedside locker. I was just turning to leave, when he grabbed me by the wrist. For a man who was supposedly so weak he held a firm enough grasp on my wrist to make me wince.

'Ciara, love,' he said.

I felt my blood run cold just at the tone of his voice.

I tried to pull my hand away, but he held on tighter, pulling me closer.

'Ciara,' he said again. 'Can you help me? I need your help to get to the bathroom. My legs are feeling a bit weak.'

'I should get Alex to help you,' I said.

I didn't want to be anywhere near him, never mind take him to the bathroom.

'Sure you're here, you can help me, can't you?'

He looked up at me, the expression on his face painted as weak and vulnerable, but the grasp of his hand, the friction burn I felt starting on my wrist, told a different story.

I felt my own legs weaken, but I vowed to be strong. If he wanted help to get to the bathroom, I'd do it. He wouldn't upset me. That's what he wanted, I think, to set me on edge and upset me. To remind me that the balance of power would always fall on his side.

'Let's go then,' I said, stepping back.

He let go of my wrist, took my hand instead. I closed my eyes for just a second, just enough to steady myself.

I helped him to stand and we walked, him holding on to my arm, towards the bathroom.

'You were always such a good girl, Ciara,' he said. 'Such a great daughter. We were so close once, weren't we?'

I didn't answer, and we reached the bathroom in silence.

'There you go,' I said, not wanting to get drawn into his discussion about good girls and how close we were.

He stopped and looked at me. The way he always did. The way that stripped away all my layers, emotional and physical.

'Will you wait there 'til I'm done?' he asked. 'I'm not sure I can walk back myself.'

'Yes,' I muttered. I'd say as little as I could to get through this ordeal as quickly as I could.

'Good girl,' he said again and I felt another layer slip away.

Good girl. He used to say that then, too.

I closed the bathroom door between us and did my best to

gulp some air, to try to steady my stomach. What I wanted to do was go back downstairs, or leave. But I knew they'd see it, all over my face. Shame leaves its mark.

I could feel my resolve to stay calm waver. Could feel heat prickling at the back of my neck, unshed tears stinging my eyes. I jumped when the bathroom door opened and he hobbled back out, grabbing on to my arm again. My whole body cringed, tensed with his touch.

When we got to his room, he sat on the side of the bed again. Took some deep breaths. He did look pale. Shaky. Unsure of himself. I revelled in that for a moment or two.

'Could you help me?' he asked, and I didn't know what he meant.

'Help me into bed,' he added. 'Like a good girl.'

There was something in the way he said it, something in the expression on his face that made me snap. I couldn't do this any more.

Chapter Sixty-Two

Heidi

Now

I can hear Ciara moving around downstairs. I can hear her talking to someone. The noise is too muffled to make out whether she is talking to herself or maybe on the phone. I should have taken her mobile and thrown it across the room, too.

I look at my watch. It's seventeen minutes since she spoke to Alex and he's not here yet. I start to wonder, did she really speak to him at all? She could've faked the call for all I know. This could all be another move in her game. She is smarter than I'd ever given her credit for.

She'd painted a very public picture of me being on the brink of a breakdown while she'd, for all intents and purposes, maintained her poise. Any outpouring of emotion she'd shown had been perfectly in keeping with a grieving daughter.

And she was his daughter, after all. His blood ran in her veins. His sick and twisted blood.

I put Lily, who is now sleeping, into the centre of the bed, placing pillows on either side of her so that she can't roll off, then kneel down and put my ear to the ground to see if I can make out exactly what Ciara is saying and to whom.

There is an urgency to her voice. A manic quality. I press my ear tighter against the well-worn carpet.

'It has to be her,' I hear her say. 'She's upstairs. Yes . . . I know . . . there's no proof, but it makes total sense, don't you see?'

The loud ringing of the doorbell makes me jump. It's Alex, or at least I hope it's Alex. Then again . . . What if he believes her too? What if they all believe her?

I stand up, glance back to Lily and, content that she is safe, I go to the bedroom door and pull it open. I tense when I hear Alex's voice at the bottom of the stairs.

'What is it, Ciara? Jesus, you look awful. Where's Heidi? Her car's outside. And Lily?' The panic in his voice is evident.

'Come in, come in,' I hear Ciara say. 'Let's get a cup of tea and talk.'

She sounds so calm. So *normal*.

'Ciara, you're scaring me,' Alex says. 'Where's my wife?'

From the top of the stairs I call out 'I'm here,' but there is no hiding the tremor in my voice. Alex looks up at me, his face a picture of complete confusion.

'Heidi, what's going on?' he asks as Ciara glares at me defiantly.

I open my mouth to speak, but Ciara cuts in. 'Heidi here has something to tell you. About what happened to Joe. About what she did, but don't worry, because she had a good reason and the police will understand. We just have to stand firm together.'

Alex does not break his gaze from me.

I'm shaking my head. 'That's not it at all,' I say, but I can see the fear on his face. The shock.

'What's she talking about?' he asks.

'I didn't do anything. You have to believe me,' I say. 'It wasn't me.'

'It was self-defence,' Ciara says, ignoring me. 'We can tell the police it was self-defence. We're going to tell them what he did, Alex. We're going to tell everyone.'

Alex looks between the two of us. I gingerly take a few steps down towards him.

'Alex, don't listen to her . . . She has it all wrong.'

I'm forcing myself to maintain eye contact with him, even though every fibre of my body is screaming at me to look away.

'Heidi . . .' She says my name, just my name.

His face crumples. I can see I am losing him.

'Why don't we all sit down?' Ciara says, and I follow her, limply, to the living room.

I glance back at Alex trailing dejectedly behind me, all colour drained from his face.

Clearing my throat, I speak. 'Alex, you must believe me that I love you and I never meant to keep anything from you. I just . . . I just couldn't bring myself to tell you the truth. I've never told anyone. I wouldn't have told anyone . . . but Ciara . . .'

'Don't say it,' he says, raising one hand, closing his eyes, shaking his head.

I half expect him to put his hands over his ears.

But I have to tell him anyway, because it just can't stay hidden any more.

'Joe hurt me,' I say, closing my eyes because I can't bear to see the look on Alex's face when my words register with him. 'He abused me,' I say, my voice as small as it was when I was nine years old and heard that squeak of the floorboard. 'He did things . . . And I didn't know what to do because if I told anyone, he told me . . . he told me no one would believe me, or I'd have to go into a home and that no one would ever want me because I was too old for a family.'

The words are pouring out. 'He hurt me and I swear, I didn't do anything to encourage it. I told him to stop. So many times I told him to stop but he didn't. He said . . . he said he couldn't help it. And it was only because he loved me so much.'

I am bent double, my head in my hands, my chest as tight as if someone was squeezing it just as someone had squeezed Joe's chest on the night he died.

I can't speak any more, not for the moment. All I can do is cry, shame clawing at me. I hear Alex cry too. Alex, who never cries. The only time I've ever seen him shed a tear was the day Lily was born. The first time he held her in his arms and he vowed to protect her.

Ciara cuts in, 'Anyone would understand. I understand. He was a monster, Alex. If he hurt Heidi and he hurt me, who else could he have hurt? He deserved to die. No one would blame Heidi for snapping – all that stress she was living under. I've told her I'll tell the police what he did to me, too. And I can prove it.'

Chapter Sixty-Three

Ciara

Then

'No!' I told Joe, loudly and firmly.

I didn't shout. I just made sure I was very clear. I would not help him into bed. I would not coddle and soothe. I would not show him the tenderness he had failed to show me. I stood far enough away from him that he could not take a hold of my wrist again. Not without standing up on the legs he had proclaimed were too wobbly.

'You can manage it yourself,' I added.

'I'm not well, Ciara,' he said. 'I was only looking for a bit of help.'

With considerable effort, some of it put on for effect, in my opinion, he shuffled his way back onto the bed and pulled his legs in under the covers. With shaking hands, he lifted the cup of tea I had left him and took a sip.

'Can I leave now?' I asked him, all set to walk out.

'Can we not talk first?' he asked. 'Don't you think we've

things to talk about? God knows I'm not going to be around for long. Can we not start to try to find a way to make peace with each other?'

'I think we've gone beyond that,' I told him.

He shook his head sadly. 'It will destroy you, you know, in the long run. If you let the bitterness eat away at you.'

He looked so absolutely sanctimonious I had to restrain myself from lashing out at him.

'But I'll pray you're able to find forgiveness in your heart towards me,' he said. 'For the hurt I caused you when I left. For how abandoned you must've felt.'

'Is that all we need to pray about?' I asked him, incredulous that he could think my anger was just down to him walking away.

'Forgiveness and peace of mind are the greatest things we can achieve in this life,' he said.

'I'll forgive you, Dad, if you admit it.'

I was lying of course. I'd never be able to forgive it.

I crossed my arms in front of myself. Adopted the bravado that had been mine when I was a teenage girl. I may have been shaking inside but outwardly I looked in control.

One unkempt, grey-streaked eyebrow rose. A look of genuine bewilderment – or a very good impression of it at least. 'I don't know what you mean,' he said.

He actually had the brass neck to deny it.

'Don't you?' I asked. 'I know it's been "our little secret" for a long time now, hasn't it? "Don't tell anyone, Ciara. They won't understand." Or how about "Mammy would only get cross" or the famous "This is how all daddies show their little girls they love them and I love you the most in the world."'

I saw whatever colour was left in his sad, sorry, sick face drain away. He swallowed hard. I think, actually think, that he figured

I'd either forgotten or would never have the nerve to bring it up again.

'I don't know what you're talking about,' he said, but the tremor in his voice, the slick of sweat breaking through on his forehead, let me know that I'd got to him.

'Do you really need me to spell it out? In detail? Because I can do that, if you want? God knows the details have never left me. I can even go downstairs right now and spell it all out in glorious, multicoloured, revolting detail to Kathleen, and Heidi and Alex and Stella. And maybe Father Brennan would like to know, if he isn't already keeping your secrets in the sanctity of the confessional. It's amazing what can be forgiven with a couple of Hail Marys these days, isn't it? Suffer the little children and all that nonsense. Or maybe I could tell Mammy. I don't actually know, standing here now, why I never told her before.'

'You'd break her,' he mumbled. 'You'd destroy her.'

'What? What was that?' I asked loudly, my confidence building as I saw him finally acknowledge what he'd done.

'She'd never recover from it. Look, Ciara, be angry with me all you want. Hate me. Tell me to go to hell and sure, I'll be going there soon anyway. But don't destroy your mother. Not now when there's nothing I can do to make it right.'

He looked pathetic. He looked scared and I revelled in it. He deserved to look scared. He wouldn't get any sympathy from me for it. But he was right that it would destroy my mother, who, despite her unending loyalty to my father, would have been the first person to drag him to the police if only she'd known.

But her heart had been so hurt. She had been so broken I hadn't wanted to break it further when he left. I'd known even then that she wouldn't be able to bear it.

I looked at him, at his wringing of his hands, his hoping for a way to escape from that room. But he couldn't. His legs were too weak. There was nowhere to run and this time I could set the rules.

'You can start to make it right,' I told him.

'How? Tell me how.'

I looked around the room, looking for inspiration. I saw the leather diary and pen on his bed.

'Write it down,' I told him.

'What? You can't be serious.'

'I'm very serious. Write it down. Confess to it. Write it on a page in that diary. Write that you are sorry. Write that you are twisted man. Tell them you hurt me.'

'But your mother . . .' he said, his face contorting with grief at the thought of having to 'out' himself.

'I won't show her. Unless I have to. That's up to you, you can be the one who decides whether I have to or not, but I want it there just in case. And I want, no I need, for you to admit it.'

I could feel my composure start to crumble. All I had wanted, for so long, for the past twenty years, more than anything, was for him to say sorry. For him to admit he had damaged me so badly that I didn't know what it was like to really care for someone, to love them in an un-abusive fashion. That I had wept buckets of tears for the girl who begged her abusive father to come back because that's what she equated with love.

'I can't do that, love,' he said, looking up at me. 'Don't make me!' he pleaded.

I brushed away a tear that was threatening to fall, only to find another followed it.

Still, I took another deep breath.

'You can, if you don't want me to march downstairs right now and tell them all,' I said as firmly as my voice would allow.

'Ciara,' he implored.

'You want to make it right? Then make it right,' I told him.

Then I watched as he put pen to paper, in the back of his leather-bound diary, and wrote the confession, and the apology, I had been waiting for all my life.

'If you ever loved me at all,' he said when he was done, 'you'll burn this diary when I'm gone. I've made mistakes, but no one else needs to be hurt by them.'

'I'll check, every day, that you've not destroyed those pages,' I told him. 'If I find you have, everyone will know. I don't care how ill you are. I don't care if you are taking your last breath. They will know.'

Defeated, he slumped back on his pillows and I left the room.

He was dead just two hours later.

Chapter Sixty-Four

Heidi

Now

Ciara springs from her seat and rushes from the room to fetch the 'proof' she claims to have. I look at Alex, who quickly turns his head from watching her leave to look at me. He looks so sad. So incredibly sad that I want to apologise to him for telling him. I want to apologise for putting the demons in his head. It was bad enough that they were in mine to begin with.

'Heidi . . .' he says and shakes his head.

He looks so sad. So disappointed in me.

'I didn't want you to see me as a victim,' I blurt out, voicing my worst fears publicly. 'I didn't want you to know how damaged I was. Maybe you wouldn't want to be with me. Maybe you wouldn't want to have a family with me. I was so messed up, for so long. But I can promise you, whatever happened to Joe, it wasn't anything to do with me. I'm safe to be around. Our daughter is safe with me.'

He has his head in his hands and I just want to get through

to him. If I don't have him on my side then I might as well have killed Joe because nothing else will matter.

I pull back just a little and reach for him, put my hand to his cheek.

'Let's get away from here. Now. Ciara's not right. She's been setting me up, Alex. I feel it. She's been making me out to be crazy, but I'm not. We can go to the police and tell them that she's been setting me up.'

I'm aware I'm speaking too fast, the words tumbling from my mouth. And I know that to Alex, who surely must be trying to take everything in, this will only serve to make him wonder if I'm mad, after all.

I can hear Ciara move about upstairs. I can hear her footsteps creak on the floorboards overhead. She's in Joe's room. I hear her swear.

'We don't have long. I'll run and get Lily and we can go,' I say, trying to work out how I can get to my daughter without alerting Ciara to my plans to leave.

'I can't do that,' he says, to my horror.

I blink at him, wondering if I heard him right.

'I can't run from this any more,' he says. 'I never should've tried. It only made things so much worse. I'm so sorry, Heidi. I'm so sorry for not telling you before now. It was me. I did it. I killed him.'

Chapter Sixty-Five

Alex

Then

I'd wished I still smoked. Or there had been someone in the house who I could have cadged a cigarette off. The only 'smoker' there was Ciara and she used those stupid e-cig things. It wasn't the same. Not at all.

Work had been full-on. I'd wondered if half of my colleagues had any competency at all, because none of them seemed to be able to manage when anything out of the ordinary happened.

That day, one of my more annoying colleagues, a graduate called Dean, had stood over me huffing and puffing. He's the kind of person who has all the academic skills needed to score him a first-class honours but none of the common sense required to function in the real world. He'd been feeling under pressure to get the intranet system he was working on for a local firm up and running. And he'd been quite happy to pass all that stress on to me.

By the time I'd arrived at Aberfoyle Crescent, to be met with an atmosphere so thick with tension you nearly needed an oxygen tank to breathe, I was already on my last nerve.

Heidi seemed quite close to being on hers, too. Ever since Joe had taken ill, she had been put upon to care for him. I'd watched as, with every visit, she became less and less happy.

She withdrew more and more from me and as much as I tried to reach her, there was something untouchable between us. A sadness of sorts.

I saw it on her face when I came back to the house on that night. She was fidgety. Uptight. Despite the cold weather, she went to stand outside. Said she needed air and I followed her. Wishing for that elusive cigarette. Maybe a glass of wine. Maybe a time when Heidi and I could just be a part of our own little family again without all this noise around us.

'You seem tense,' I said.

At least she smiled – that kind of twisted 'you don't say', but there was a warmth to it. I wrapped my arms around her and told her I loved her. I could feel the thunder of her heart against my chest and I wished I could take away all her stress – to see her happy again.

I figured it might help if I offered to do a little more to help with Joe, though there was something about him that made me feel uncomfortable. I put it down to his self-assuredness, his arrogance. I knew the type well.

There was something sly about him, too. He gave off bad vibes, although I could never quite put my finger on why. What I did know was that Joe McKee liked to be in control as much as he liked to be the centre of attention. I'd seen enough of him over the years to figure that out.

Still, I'd be polite and I'd do my bit because God knows Heidi didn't need any more stress. It was bad enough to have Ciara and Stella, not to mention Kathleen, hovering around. That was a whole other complicated dynamic right there. There was no denying the tension that existed between them and Heidi.

She told me that she felt she'd never been accepted by any of them. Watching them interact with each other I could see that was true.

Just after ten thirty, or thereabouts, I'd gone upstairs to get Lily, stopping to use the bathroom first. I was so tired, I could feel my eyes starting to droop. I splashed my face with cold water, pushed the bathroom window open wide and had allowed the fresh, ice-cold air to wash over me. I prayed that Lily would sleep through the night. Both Heidi and I needed the rest.

I had just closed the window when I heard a strange, strangulated cough from Joe's room, which was just next door.

I tapped on his bedroom door, quietly said his name in case he was sleeping, and opened it just a crack.

'Are you okay, Joe?' I asked, looking at the figure lying in the bed.

His bedside light was still on, an empty teacup on his locker, a notebook or diary and pen discarded on the bed. I could hear the faintest of rattles, so I moved closer.

'Joe?' I asked again, a little louder but not much.

He didn't move. His eyes didn't even flicker. I wasn't sure for a moment or two if he was breathing, and then there it was again – a sickening gargling sound, not quite a breath but maybe. He went still. I couldn't hear another breath. I started to panic a little, sat down on the edge of the bed and took his hand in mine, tried to feel for a pulse. I couldn't feel one, or maybe I could. But it was so weak, I just wasn't sure.

I reached over to grab his other hand, thinking maybe I'd get a better reading from his other wrist, but as I stepped closer my foot caught on something on the floor. I looked down and there was a book, what looked like a diary, and it was open. I don't know, I'll never know, what it was that made me look a little closer rather than just kick it under the bed, but I did and my stomach contracted.

I didn't read it all. I swear I didn't read it all. Not at first. Just words that were blurring together and then spinning. Snapshots. But enough, more than enough, to make me want to hurt Joe McKee more than I ever wanted to hurt anyone in my life.

Girls. Child. Sick. Hurt. Perverted. Illness. Abuse. Sorry.

The words became more important than the pulse I was supposed to be looking for. I stopped focusing on how frequently he was breathing. Any instinct I'd had to try to help or call for help slipped away. I reached for the book, turned it around. Focused on the words.

A confession of sorts. He needed to get it off his chest. He was sorry. He was a sick man. He had always been a sick man and he had tried to control it but he was weak.

He never meant to hurt anyone.

He just had a compulsion.

My stomach turned. 'Just a compulsion'? Just who had he hurt? Had he hurt my Heidi? Was that why she seemed broken when she was around him? It would explain so much. How vulnerable she could be. How it had taken her a long time to start a physical relationship with me. My poor Heidi. And who else? Ciara? Unknown girls. Young girls. Just how young?

My mind flitted to my daughter. My innocent, beautiful daughter. Had he ever been alone with her? Had he changed her? I almost couldn't breathe for thinking about it. I knew he had held her. I knew there were pictures of him, smiling at the camera. His creepy grin. And my child.

Something in me snapped as I closed his diary and looked at him there, the mouth slack, minute foamy bubbles forming on his lips.

I made a decision then, you see. I could've saved him, maybe. I could've called for help, but I didn't. I sat and watched as those short, gasping breaths drew further and further apart, the odd gurgle growing quieter. I sat and wished he was at least conscious so I could tell him what a bastard he was. I hoped he knew he was dying. That he felt the struggle for every one of those short, shallow breaths. I hoped he felt fear. I hoped he felt pain. I hoped he knew I was there beside him, but there was no way I was going to help him. I hoped he felt as powerless as his victims had. Joe McKee, man of the people. Disgusting paedophile.

I waited until he was silent. Until there was no hope for him. I let him die.

The enormity of my actions, or my lack of action, hit me quickly. I was shocked, horrified at myself. Yes, he deserved to die, but was I now just as bad as him? Was I now a killer?

I lifted the diary and slipped it into the drawer of his locker. I'd deal with it later. Once I figured out how to talk to Heidi about it all. If she told me what I was now sure was true, if she confirmed what he had done, I could maybe find some way to justify it to myself. To live with it.

Of course, when I went back to look at the diary the next day, it was gone. Funeral arrangements were being made and I got swept up in it all. I tried to find the right time to tell Heidi, but is there ever a right time?

Then the police said it was murder and the crushing reality of the situation swept over me. I vowed I'd tell them the truth and I tried, I really tried, to find the courage to tell them. But then when they said he had been suffocated, I'd almost been sick. If I spoke up then, told them no, that he'd taken ill, and I'd just not called for help, they'd have no reason to believe me. Especially as I'd said nothing before.

They mentioned unexplained injuries and bruising, further test results from the postmortem. Things I knew I hadn't done, but I'd gone too far then and I was too scared to speak up. Heidi was unravelling. I couldn't make her life harder. And yes, I was a coward, too. I was scared of prison. I was scared of losing Heidi and Lily. I was scared that all anyone would see me as from now until the day I died was a cold-blooded killer.

282

Chapter Sixty-Six

Ciara

Now

I'm digging around upstairs trying to find my father's diary, where I made him admit his crimes, when I hear Heidi call my name. She sounds almost hysterical, so I abandon my search and run down the stairs to find her pacing the living room.

Heidi is shaking her head. 'No,' she says. 'You're not making any sense, Alex. Why would you say that?'

'Say what?' I ask.

Alex looks at me, his face pale. 'I did it,' he says. 'It was me.'

I feel dizzy, then I look at him again. Alex. Gentle, quiet Alex. I'm supposed to believe he was a killer? It just doesn't ring true.

He speaks, tells me his story, and I try to absorb what he has said. He sat and watched Joe die. He could have, maybe, helped and he didn't.

'But you didn't kill him?' Heidi says. 'You didn't kill him. He was just sick and he passed away, and that means no one is guilty.'

'But I didn't get help,' Alex says and he looks wretched. 'I was so angry. I'd read those words and I was so enraged. I'd wanted to kill him. I was happy to watch him die. I never thought it would end up like this. All this hurt and pain and a murder investigation, and the further it went, the less I felt I could speak up.'

I'm stunned. It seems Alex, who I'd written off as wet and pathetic, had a backbone after all. He'd watched my father die. But at the same time, he didn't have enough of a backbone to speak up about what really happened and to save us all from the nightmare we've been going through over the last few days. The topic of every over-the-garden-fence conversation in Derry, police interviews, newspaper reports, existing together in a virtual ticking time-bomb of tension.

'I want to talk to the police now,' he says, nodding. 'This has all gone too far. I can't run from it any more, Heidi. None of us can. We have to be honest. We can't keep going on like this. None of us can,' and he glances in my direction.

Heidi looks as if she's trapped in the glare of oncoming headlights. Except the headlights are coming from all directions and no matter where she turns, where any of us turn, there is no way out of this. She is shaking her head.

'But you didn't do anything wrong, not really wrong. He was very ill. He was dying. We don't have to tell the police. There is no way they could ever know. We just keep it quiet. It might go away.'

She is pleading with him and she looks at me and I see desperation in her eyes.

Alex shakes his head, defeated. 'It would always haunt me. The guilt. It's already destroying me, Heidi. Whatever happens, I have to tell the police. I'll not be able to live with myself if I don't.'

Heidi is crying. Silent tears running in rivulets down her cheeks. They both look so broken and I think of the little baby upstairs, the baby who curled her hand around my fingers not that long ago. Who trusted me to rock her back and forth. Those big, innocent eyes that had looked at me with such trust. And I realise that no one is really guilty here at all. Except for Joe.

And Joe, now dead and buried, holds the key to all this.

'It was his diary that I was looking for,' I interject. 'The one Alex saw. It will help back up Alex's story, won't it? It's not where I left it, but it has to be here somewhere. We just have to keep looking.'

'Then we'll do just that, we'll keep looking,' Heidi says, squeezing Alex's hands tightly.

She stands up and starts sorting through the drawers in the sideboard in the living room – pulling out old paperwork and shuffling through it. My father was nothing if not fastidious about keeping his affairs in order and it soon becomes obvious there's no diary of any kind hidden in the back of a drawer or under mounds of old bank statements.

I look in the drawer of the console table in the hall. Again, there is nothing of note. It's neat and organised. A book of stamps. Some pens held together with an elastic band. A packet of envelopes and a small address book, in which Dad had painstakingly written the names of his friends and colleagues in block capitals and always in black ink.

We both go together into the bedroom. I double-check the wardrobe, as does Heidi.

'It was there,' she says, pointing to the far left corner of the wardrobe, which is now just an empty shelf. 'That is where you put it. Remember?'

'Yes, but I looked and it's definitely not there any more.'

She pulls aside the rail of pressed shirts and trousers and looks down at the floor of the wardrobe. 'They're all gone,' she says, looking up at me.

'All what?'

'All his diaries and notebooks. He kept them there, in shoe-boxes. A diary for every year. There were at least twenty of them here.'

'Would the police have taken them?' I ask. 'Those SOCO guys were quite thorough. It's the only logical explanation.'

It strikes me that Heidi was able to open the wardrobe door without using a key – a key I knew I had. I run my finger to the lock, noticing that it has been broken.

'Someone's been in here. They used force,' I tell her, pointing to the door.

'Would the police have busted a lock? They left everything else just as it was,' Heidi says.

I shrug. I only know what I see in front of me.

'And if they had the diaries, and he'd written his confession of sorts, wouldn't they have found it? DI Bradley seems very thorough.'

'I don't know, Heidi.'

I can hear a harsh, frustrated tone to my voice. I was just angry that it was gone. I wanted to have proof. I wanted to have his apology to look at. It was the only thing I wanted from that man.

She winces at my tone and I apologise. Sincerely. Explain that I'm stressed. She nods. She understands. She feels it too.

'I'll call DI Bradley,' I tell her. 'Ask him outright. Tell him where to look if he has the diary to see what Joe wrote.'

'You're okay about all of this – what he did – becoming public?' Heidi asks.

I see the worry, the fear in her eyes.

'I'm not okay with it,' I tell her truthfully, 'but it's the right thing to do. For me. For you and for Alex. We've nothing to be ashamed of, Heidi. We never asked to be abused.'

Her bottom lip is trembling and I watch tears spill over from her eyes and run down her cheeks.

I reach out my hand to her, a gesture that would have seemed insane just an hour ago, and to my surprise she reaches back.

'My phone's downstairs. Let's go phone DI Bradley and get this all sorted once and for all.'

'But what about all their evidence? Injuries and suffocation and whatever? Won't they say Alex is lying?'

She looks frightened. Vulnerable. I feel so very sorry for her. Her life has been lacking in any real security for so long.

I wish I could reassure her, but I can't. I can only give her hand a squeeze.

'We have to trust that the truth will be enough. Something else must've happened to make him take so ill.'

'Or someone else hurt him first,' Heidi says.

But I can't help but feel she is grasping at straws. I suppose I'd do the same if it was Stella in the frame.

Unable to speak, I just shrug at Heidi and lead her downstairs. The first step is to call DI Bradley, I think. Get him to come here.

We go back downstairs to fetch my phone. Alex is still in the living room, his head in his hands. He looks up at us expectantly, and sags again when Heidi shakes her head.

'Alex, we're going to call DI Bradley now. We're going to tell him everything,' I say as calmly as I can.

He nods and Heidi sits beside him and holds him to her as he cries.

I pick up the phone and call the number DI Bradley had given me.

This is all such a mess.

Chapter Sixty-Seven

Heidi

Now

I gave up believing in God a long time ago. Probably around the time my mother died. I couldn't understand how any god, who my teachers described to me as loving and caring, would take a mammy away from their only child. And if that is hard to get my head around, I sure as hell can't understand how any god would let what is going to happen next happen.

Nonetheless, sitting in the living room of my childhood home, holding hands with my husband and waiting for the police to arrive, I can't help but offer up a silent prayer.

Please, I beg, please just make this nightmare end. Alex is not a bad man. Alex doesn't have it in him to be a bad man. 'Please, God,' I beg, 'don't take someone else I love from me.'

Ciara is restless. She is pacing up and down the living room, chewing on her thumbnail. It's doing nothing to soothe my nerves. She's looking a little manic again. Then again, I'm feeling a little manic myself right now. She jumps with every noise.

Alex is silent, but he is wringing his hands. The only person daring to make a sound is Lily, who has started to fuss as if the tension is nipping at her, too.

I jump when I hear a car pull up, and again when I hear the car doors slam.

'It's DC King and DC Black,' Ciara says as if it could be anyone else. 'I'll let them in,' she says and I turn to Alex, tell him I love him and we'll get through this. That he did nothing wrong and they're bound to find that out in time. The coroner has made a mistake. Something was very wrong with Joe when he died and yes, Alex was there, but he didn't kill him. Not calling for help is not the same as killing someone.

He squeezes my hand back and tells me he loves me too, and that he's sorry.

That's all we have time for before the two police officers come into the room, followed by Ciara.

'Alex, Heidi,' DC King says, nodding her head in greeting.

'Do you mind if we sit down?' DC King asks.

'Not at all,' I say, and I can hear the tremor in my voice.

I can feel a panic attack threaten. This is worse than anything I could've imagined.

DC Black is the next to speak.

'You've asked us to come here because you say you have more information for us about what happened here on the night Joe died.'

Alex coughs, a little nervous splutter. 'Erm, I need a glass of water,' he says and Ciara says she'll fetch one. 'My mouth is very dry,' he explains. 'Really it's me who wanted to talk to you.'

'It's okay, Alex. Take your time,' DC King says.

I like her. She's friendly. A gentle soul. I don't know how long she'll stay friendly or gentle for, though.

'Should we maybe get a solicitor?' I ask Alex suddenly. I'm nervous about how this will go down.

Alex shakes his head. 'I've nothing to hide. Not any more.'

I can't help but think of all the things that have been hidden. If I'd told him before now, on my own terms, would I have had the strength to break contact with Joe altogether? Would this even have happened? Oh God, it hurts that this is my fault. I'll never forgive myself.

DC King speaks. 'If you think that a solicitor would help, then by all means we can arrange one or you can call a solicitor of your choosing. If you decide to proceed without one, you can request one at any stage, if what you're going to tell us is that serious,' she says. 'You may want to continue this conversation down at the station. Just so we make sure it's all recorded properly. We will have to caution you, which isn't to say we'll charge you without anything.' She pauses. 'Do you think it's that kind of information, Alex?' she asks.

I can't stop the tears from falling.

'I think it might be,' he says slowly. 'I know I should've told you this before. I was scared. I'm sorry. I was with Joe when he died. It was me.'

I see DC Black sit up and take notice. There's something about him that reminds me of an over-eager watchdog. DC King shows more subtlety in her responses.

'Okay,' she says softly before launching into an official caution.

Words I've heard a thousand times on the TV but never dreamed I would hear in real life:

'You do not have to say anything but it may harm your defence if you do not mention when questioned, something that you later rely on in court. Anything you do say may be given in evidence.'

'You're entitled to have a solicitor present. Do you have someone you use or would you like us to arrange one?'

Alex shrugs. We've never had use for a solicitor before, save for the conveyancing of our house, and that's hardly anywhere near the same level.

'I know a good solicitor,' Ciara chimes in, handing him his glass of water. She takes a deep breath, turns to the two police officers. 'You have to know this about my father,' she says. 'He was not a nice man. He was not a good man. He did things . . .' she pauses. 'We can prove he did things . . . He confessed, in his diary. I'm sure your SOCO team took it with them?'

'We can certainly check that,' DC Black says.

'What kind of things?' DC King asks.

I can't look at her in the eye. Ciara is, as always, stronger than I am.

'He abused us, Heidi and me. For years,' she says.

If DC King is shocked her face doesn't show it. 'Then it's a shame he was never brought before the courts,' she says, and while she's right, the message is clear. Vigilante justice is no justice at all.

'Yes,' Ciara says. 'It is a shame. A crying shame. It's a shame he wasn't hauled before the courts a very long time ago, but he was a very manipulative man. Clever. He had us all scared to speak. He was very controlling.'

'I didn't know about it,' Alex blurts. 'Until that night, I didn't know. I only saw it in the diary. Where he wrote it. Heidi hadn't told me.'

Guilt wraps its way around my heart and pulls tight. It's a physical pain unlike anything I've ever experienced before. This time, I am to blame.

'I think maybe this really is a conversation we'd best continue at the station, don't you, Mr Lewis?' DC King says.

Alex nods.

'Would you like to come with us, please?'

I know it's not a question, not really. Alex will be going with them. In the back of an unmarked car.

'No!' Ciara says, and I look up at her. 'This isn't really necessary, is it? It isn't right. Alex says when he went in to see my father he was barely breathing. Gargling. And then he stopped. Alex didn't call for help, but you said my father was suffocated. All the evidence pointed to that. It pointed to someone putting something over his head and smothering him.'

The two officers exchange looks.

'I didn't do that,' Alex says. 'I didn't hold anything over his face. I swear. He was taking very shallow breaths. I should've called for help, but I was so angry I didn't. I should've. I should've turned the evidence over to the police. I know he was very ill, but he should've faced some sort of justice. Proper justice.'

'We really should continue this at the station,' DC Black says as he starts to guide Alex out of the house, and I watch my husband being led towards a police car.

Chapter Sixty-Eight

Ciara

Now

Heidi looks broken. More broken than before. She stares at the doorway, as if expecting Alex to come back in at any time.

'I can't believe this is happening,' she says eventually, looking downwards.

'I'm sure the police will find out what really happened,' I tell her. 'They will be able to see that Alex is telling the truth. All this has to have a rational explanation.'

Although I'm not sure what it could be. The coroner can't have got it so wrong. I wonder, for a moment, if Alex has told us the truth, or is he covering up something else? My gut tells me he's genuine, though. His story rings true, as does his fear and his sadness.

'Let's focus on what we can do to help,' I tell her. 'Let's see if we can find Joe's diary. If we can find that, and get it to the police, it could help in some way.'

'Do you think Kathleen or Marie took the diaries? Or Stella?' Heidi says.

I shake my head. 'Stella definitely didn't. I'd know. Possibly Kathleen or Mum.'

'Do you think the police might have taken them?'

I shake my head again. 'If they did, they would have told us, or they would have found what he'd written by now. I'm sure of it.'

'But maybe we should call them. Just to check.'

She is agitated, wringing her hands together and scratching her arm so vigorously, I'm worried she might break the skin.

'I'll call them,' I tell her. 'And I'll call Mum and Kathleen, too.'

She blinks at me, her eyes wide with gratitude. 'Could you? Would you?'

Her vulnerability unnerves me a little. It saddens me. I know I've seen it before, when I was young and vulnerable myself. I nod and lift the phone.

As expected, the police confirm they didn't remove any paperwork from the house. Heidi's face falls as I tell her the news. I see the livid red marks on her arms from her scratching. I kneel in front of her and take her hands in mine to stop her from hurting herself.

'You have to stay strong now, okay? For Alex and for Lily. I'll call Mum and Kathleen now. I know this is scary but,' I glance down at her arms, 'hurting yourself isn't going to help.'

She looks down, startled as if she hasn't even realised she is doing it, and starts to rub her arms gently.

'You're right,' she says. 'You're right.'

I sit beside her while I make the calls.

Chapter Sixty-Nine

Ciara

Now

Kathleen agrees to come over. I asked her if she had the diaries and she went very quiet for a moment.

'Yes, I do. But why do you need them?'

'Oh, just some admin. Dad left some passwords, pin numbers, that kind of thing, in his diary. I need to access some stuff to close accounts, access his savings, et cetera.'

'I can look through them, see if I can find anything?' she said. 'I'll call you right back. I'm sorry for taking them. I just wanted to feel closer to him. It's a comfort to me seeing his handwriting.'

'I get that,' I told her, trying to keep my voice level. 'It's really only his latest diary I need to see. If you could even bring that. I'll give it straight back,' I lied.

I didn't tell her about Alex. I didn't tell her to look or not look at the back pages of the diary. I just piled on the traumatised daughter voice thick and heavy until she sighed and agreed.

'I won't be long,' she'd told me.

That had been half an hour ago and Heidi and I are now both getting impatient.

I feel as if I could cry when I see a taxi pull up outside and watch as Auntie Kathleen, looking so much older than her years, climbs out of the car and looks at the house, pausing for a moment before she spots me in the window. She doesn't smile. She looks serious.

'She's here,' I say as if Heidi hasn't been as fixated on the window and watching for her arrival as I have.

'It will help, won't it? What he wrote?' she asks me.

'I hope so,' I tell her, but the truth is I don't really know if it will or won't.

She gives me a weak, watery smile. I jump when I hear the doorbell ring, even though I have watched Kathleen walk up the path and reach her hand towards the door.

'Okay,' I say. 'Try to keep calm,' I tell Heidi. 'Remember, as far as she knows we only need this diary for admin reasons. We want her to keep believing that for now. We don't want to upset her.'

Heidi nods. Sniffs and sits on the armchair, cradling her arms around her. I go and answer the door, my face impassive.

'Thank you so much for coming, Auntie Kathleen. We're just trying to get everything organised, you know. Tie up all the loose ends.'

She nods. 'I'm not sure what the rush is, but I respect your choices. I suppose it would be nice to have it all wrapped up before I go back to England. I can't stay here forever.'

'I appreciate it. We appreciate it,' I say as I lead her into the living room, where she spots Heidi.

'Oh, I didn't realise she was here,' Kathleen says, reaching into her bag and pulling out this year's leather-bound diary, handing it to me.

'Nice to see you, Kathleen,' Heidi replies. 'Thanks for doing this.'

Kathleen sniffs and nods. She's clearly still angry with Heidi for the graveside scene. My anger over that has gone now. Now that I know what Heidi has been through. It has been replaced by my own sense of guilt.

But I don't have time for wallowing in self-pity now. I want to get this to DI Bradley as soon as possible. I flick through the pages, trying to find my father's hastily scrawled words.

'Are you looking for something?' Kathleen asks.

'Just the pin numbers and passwords,' I say, feeling my palms start to sweat.

I was sure he wrote in the back of the diary but there's nothing there. I examine it closely. See ragged edges close to the spine where pages have been torn out.

I look up at Kathleen.

She is looking around the room. I see her look intently at Heidi. It must be obvious that she has been crying. Her eyes aren't quite as red-rimmed as they were but they are still puffy. She still looks miserable.

I feel my heart start to thud a little faster as I flick through the diary again. I'm not sure why I do, it's obvious that pages have been torn out, but it doesn't make sense and I can feel myself starting to panic.

I catch Heidi's eyes and she reads the worry on my face. Her eyes widen.

'Can you not find what you're looking for?' Kathleen asks. 'That's what you wanted, isn't it? His diary?'

'Yes,' I say, distracted as I run my fingers along the rough edges of the paper. 'It was this diary I wanted, but . . .'

Kathleen sits down close to Heidi, who seems to be shrinking further and further into herself.

'The house feels strange without Joe in it, doesn't it?' she says. 'I wonder who will live here next.'

She sounds so jovial. So relaxed.

'Did anyone else have access to this diary?' I ask her.

'No, I don't think so,' she says. 'Why do you ask?'

I try to stop my voice from shaking. Someone has torn the pages out. That much is clear.

'There just seems to be something missing. Some of the info I needed.'

'Pin numbers and passwords? That kind of thing?' she asks and I see it.

I see she is trying to catch me out. I see that she knows exactly what I'm looking for. She's just waiting to see if I'll confront her about it.

'Yes,' I say, 'that sort of thing.'

Heidi is looking at me, her eyes pleading with me to solve this huge problem that is beyond my ability to solve.

'Ah, good. Because the way you're acting, I'd almost swear you were looking for something else.'

'What else could there be?' I ask her and I know we are playing a game. Just as I know she is not on my side.

She shrugs. 'Maybe something that should never be seen by anyone else,' she says, flicking an imaginary piece of fluff from her skirt before holding my gaze. 'Because if you're looking for those disgusting things he wrote, I've destroyed them. Burned the pages. They contained all sorts of things. Lots of private information, you know, things you wouldn't want falling into the wrong hands. Things you wouldn't want the whole world knowing.'

Chapter Seventy

Heidi

Now

Has Kathleen really just said what I think she said? She's destroyed Joe's confession? There's nothing to show the police? Nothing to help Alex? I feel as if I might be sick.

'What do you mean?' I hear Ciara ask as I try to fight the nausea in the pit of my stomach.

'What I mean,' Kathleen says, 'is that I have burned whatever it was my brother wrote about things he said he did in his past.'

'But why would you do that?' Ciara asks.

I can hear the disbelief, the pain, in her voice.

'It's all very simple,' Kathleen says.

She's trying to maintain a façade of cold indifference, but I see that she is trembling.

'I saw the things he had written. That "confession" of his. And there was no way I was risking anyone else reading that.'

I can't hide the horrified look on my face.

'No!' Ciara says, shaking her head. 'No, you can't have done that. You'd no right to do that!'

'Had I not?' Kathleen asks. 'Do you think I want everyone and his mother talking about my brother in that way? I don't care if he's dead, I won't have people saying he was some kind of pervert.'

'He was more than a pervert,' Ciara says. 'He was a monster. He hurt us. Me. Heidi. Abused us. Raped us!' The last two words are shouted.

Raped us. The words out loud have a powerful effect on me. Like a punch in the stomach but one that releases all the hurt and anger that has just about been contained over the years. My fists clench. Tears run freely down my face, but I don't care any more. I am not ashamed. I will not be ashamed any more.

And at that moment I see a flicker of something on Kathleen's face. I can't miss it. She's not that good at hiding her feelings. And it all slots into place.

'You already knew,' I say, my voice little more than a whisper.

'What?' Ciara says. 'No, she didn't.'

'She did,' I say.

Guilt is written all over Kathleen's face. People will ask questions. People will want to know how he managed to keep it a secret. Except he hadn't kept it a secret, after all. One person knew, and that person, rather than confronting him and stopping it all, moved away to England and left me, left us, to our fate.

'Didn't you, Kathleen? You knew, all those years ago. You knew and you did nothing to stop it. We were just children and you let him do that to us. You're as bad as he was.'

Kathleen colours. For the first time the swagger she had when she came into the house leaves her.

'I . . . I . . .'

'No,' Ciara says. 'That can't be true. 'She would've stopped it, wouldn't you?' She's addressing Kathleen now.

'I did stop it!' Kathleen says. 'Or I tried. I thought he did. I thought I'd got through to him. I told him . . . told him I knew what he was doing and I'd go to the police. Or worse, I'd get the boys onto him. They'd have sorted him out. He was terrified of that, terrified he'd get his knees done. Or a bullet to the back of the head. Said he'd stop. Said he'd never do it again.'

Ciara's face is rigid with shock. She sits down, head in her hands. She looks like she might be sick.

'And you took the word of a liar?' I ask, but I don't need her to answer. I know the answer. I know that the fear of a bullet to the head, or years in prison branded a nonce, weren't enough to stop him and his twisted 'compulsion'. 'Maybe if you'd stayed, eh? Maybe if you hadn't left and gone to England.'

'You can't blame me for it!' she says. 'That's not fair.'

'Not fair?' Ciara is shouting now. 'Not fair? Are you serious? You were the only person who had the power to make sure it never happened again and you abdicated your responsibility. So yes, we can blame you and it's perfectly fair. And more than that, you destroyed evidence that proved what he did! Jesus Christ, Kathleen. Coming in here and talking about fair. You've no idea what you've done.'

'I believed he would stop,' Kathleen says, crying now. 'He knew he had so much to lose. He knew he was doing the wrong thing. And he was my big brother, and I loved him. I needed to believe in him.'

'You left him in sole charge of a vulnerable female child!' Ciara shouts. 'You knew what he was capable of and you never thought to get Heidi out of there.'

'Well, neither did you! You knew as well, Ciara. You knew what he did to you!'

'I was a child myself!' Ciara shouts again, crossing the room and pointing her finger directly at Kathleen. Jabbing it towards her, pressing it against her collarbone.

301

I can see her hand curl into a fist. She is trembling with anger.

'You! You were the grown-up. You were the person with the power. But instead you cleared off. Lived your life without a thought of what might have been going on here. You could just pretend it had stopped because it was easier for you to do that than to face what your brother had done. You're disgusting,' she screams, and there is no other word for it, into her aunt's face.

I see a fleck of spittle shoot from her mouth, landing on Kathleen's face. Kathleen looks as if she, too, might throw up. She can't move. She is pressed back against the sofa and Ciara is looming over her. I want to reach out and take Ciara's hands, the way she stilled mine earlier.

I've seen her lose her temper before, but this? This is a whole new level of anger. I'm not quite sure what she would be capable of but I'm determined that Kathleen will not be coming out of this situation as a victim.

She could never be a victim. What she did – or didn't do – is unforgivable.

It was bad enough what he did. But to have someone who could've stopped it, who chose not to? That was a different level of cruelty. I wonder how many times she'd seen me flinch when he stood too close. How many times she'd heard me crying. I wonder what had crossed her mind all those times she had soothed me, told me I had to be brave. Was she making excuses for him? Had she been as complicit in all of this as he was?

'Ciara,' I say gently and she looks at me, and it's as if she is coming out of her trance. Is aware of her position, her anger. Knows how close she is to losing control.

She steps back and I see Kathleen sag with relief that the immediate threat to her has passed.

Ciara takes a deep breath. 'You stupid, selfish bitch! You let him get away with it then,' Ciara says, her tone measured but no less intimidating, 'and by burning his confession, you're letting him get away with it now. And you've taken away the evidence we need to help Alex!'

'What on earth has Alex got to do with any of this?' she asks, blinking at us.

'Alex had the balls to do what you didn't,' Ciara says and I crumple at the mention of his name.

My Alex. My husband. Sitting with the police now.

'Alex made sure he was punished for it. Alex made sure he was dead,' Ciara adds.

Kathleen blinks in my direction, taking in the expression on my face. She turns her gaze to Ciara.

'What are you talking about?' she asks and her voice is heavy with bewilderment.

'Alex, my Alex,' I say as evenly as I can. 'He told us this morning. He was with Joe when he died. He found him unwell and . . .' I can't say the rest. I can't bring myself to have someone, especially not Kathleen, judge Alex.

'And what?' Kathleen asks.

Ciara continues. 'He didn't call for help. He chose not to. He saw the diary and he was so upset, so angry, he let my father die.' Ciara's voice is devoid of emotion. She is not upset with Alex. She's not angry with him. 'He's with the police now. Making a statement about it all.'

'They took him away,' I blurt, thinking of his stricken face as he climbed into the back of the police car.

Kathleen is shaking her head. 'That's impossible,' she says.

'It's all too possible. Those two officers, King and Black or whatever their names are. They cautioned him and he left with him.'

Kathleen is still shaking her head. I want to rattle her. To

303

grab her by the shoulders and scream in her face that it's her fault, just like Ciara screamed in her face.

'No. Not that. I'm not talking about the police. I'm talking about Joe. It's impossible he was still alive when Alex went into the room.'

She looks stricken. Panicked for the first time in all of this. Her eyes dart between Ciara and me.

'He was dead. He was definitely dead when I left the room. I made sure of it,' she stutters.

Chapter Seventy-One

Ciara

Now

I can't quite believe what I'm hearing. Kathleen? Her words stop me in my tracks.

'What?' I exclaim, and I can see that Heidi's eyes are as wide as mine.

Kathleen is fidgeting, curling her hair behind her ear. Her legs jiggling up and down with nervous energy. She shakes her head periodically, as if trying to put together the pieces of a puzzle in her mind, and then stops.

'I . . . should've checked for a pulse. But he wasn't breathing. I know that. He was still and he'd stopped fighting me . . .'

I'm dazed by her words.

'I don't understand,' I tell her.

There is nothing about this that makes sense. Kathleen has grieved the loudest and hardest of all of us and now she's saying she was responsible all along? Were her tears borne out of guilt and not grief?

'I don't know how I can make this any clearer,' Kathleen says. 'I . . . I killed him.' She pauses, chokes back a sob then takes a deep breath to try to compose herself. 'I put a pillow over his face, a knee to his chest, and I held it down until he stopped moving.'

She is looking at neither of us as she speaks. It's as if she is replaying her actions in her head. I see her shudder.

'Did you know it takes longer than it usually does in the movies to kill someone that way? You have to . . . well, you have to try and put pressure on their chest, too. I can't stop thinking about it. How I had to do it. How I felt him struggle beneath me, but I was trying to make it easier for him. To make it quicker. I read about it . . .'

'You read about it?' I ask, stunned by her words. 'What do you mean? Do you mean you planned it? Jesus Christ, Kathleen!'

'No!' She blinks at me, eyes wide before she casts her gaze downwards again. 'Well, not really. I'd researched it but, you know, half-heartedly. It didn't mean anything. I didn't expect to . . . Well, I didn't think I'd ever do it. I just wanted to know how, in case things got really bad for him.'

'For him?' Heidi snorts. 'In case things got bad for him? What about the rest of us, Kathleen? Did you ever research how you could save us if things got really bad?'

Kathleen shakes her head. Brushes the tears from her eyes. What little trace of make-up she had been wearing has now been rubbed clear.

'He was my brother,' she says mournfully. 'You can't possibly understand. I'm not saying he was perfect. God knows he wasn't. God knows he did some things that were unforgivable, but he was still my big brother. I still loved him. You can think that's wrong all you want, if that's what makes you happy . . .'

'Nothing about this makes us happy,' I tell her. 'Nothing at all.'

I'm trying to take in everything that Kathleen is saying. To take in her twisted loyalty to Joe even though she knew what he was capable of. Even though she had moved hundreds of miles away, he still had this pull over her. She still felt compelled to come back to him in the end. She still loved him. She wanted to help him in her own way. In the end.

I think about my own relationship with him, how he retained that same pull over me, too. How he'd been able to summon me back into his life, too. That he had kept Heidi in his web all this time. Despite everything he'd done.

I find myself shaking. 'Nothing at all about this makes sense. You loved him, you say, but you were the one who killed him. You can try to dress it up as a mercy killing if you want, but you murdered him.'

She winces at the word. Rubs her temples. Perhaps all this is giving her a headache. God knows my own head is starting to thump right now.

'I never wanted him dead,' she says eventually, the word 'dead' almost a whisper. 'But I'd seen this before. This cancer. How it eats away at people. The death it gave my father.' She shakes her head as if trying to shake away the memory. 'You were so young at the time, Ciara, I doubt you even remember it. But it was horrific, and I didn't – God, I just didn't want to see Joe go through that. No matter what he'd done.

'Heidi, you must understand? Your poor mother. You saw what cancer did to her. How it ate away at her. No one deserves that. If Joe had been an animal he'd have been put to sleep and spared his misery.'

'He *was* an animal,' Heidi spits. 'And don't dare bring my mother into this. There's no comparison. She didn't deserve her pain. Joe deserved every bit of his. Every last twinge.'

I sit beside Heidi. Rest my hand on hers to try to keep her calm so that Kathleen can say her piece. I need to understand why she did this.

307

'No one deserves that pain,' Kathleen bites. 'I was trying to be compassionate. That was my intention. I didn't think all this would happen.' She gestures around the room. 'I didn't expect that the police would become involved. I thought – well, I thought I'd dealt with that side of things.'

'What do you mean?' I ask her. How on earth had she 'dealt with things'?

She takes a deep breath. 'Dr Sweeney,' she says.

I feel my breath catch in my throat. Dr Sweeney? Kind, old Dr Sweeney with the soft expression and the soothing voice? He had something to do with this? My head starts to spin. I close my eyes and breathe deeply, trying to steady myself, but I can hear Kathleen still talking.

'You mustn't think badly of him. He was trying to do the right thing. He's a good man.' There's a hint of warmth, of emotion in her voice again. She wipes away another tear. 'I'd spoken to him about how I didn't want Joe to suffer, you know. I thought if I just . . . you know . . . helped him on his way. It wouldn't be painless, but it wouldn't be as bad as what was ahead of him.

'Of course he told me that such things aren't legal and that he couldn't condone it or advise me on it. In fact, he urged me to be sensible. Told me palliative care had come on leaps and bounds since my father died, even since your mother died, Heidi.

'I didn't plan it, you know. But that night, Joe was in so much pain. He was scared. I suppose I got scared, too. Before I even knew it, I'd done it.' She glances at her hands as if she can't quite believe what they were capable of.

'When I called Dr Sweeney that night he knew as soon as he saw Joe that something had happened; that I'd done some-thing. He asked me, when you were all out of the room. He asked me to tell him what I'd done, so I did. But he understood what you can't seem to. That I was doing Joe a favour. That I

308

was saving him from pain in the long run. That my intentions were good. I pleaded with Dr Sweeney not to say anything and, well, we were friends a long time ago and he agreed. He was only trying to help . . .'

'Well, we have to tell the police this,' I say softly. 'You know that, don't you, Kathleen?'

She looks at me and blinks as if the thought hasn't even occurred to her. 'I don't think we do,' she says.

'Of course we do!' Heidi replies, casting my hand off from hers, pointing a finger at Kathleen. 'My husband is sitting in a police cell now for all we know. He has been beating himself up for causing Joe's death when he did no such thing. He did nothing wrong.'

'That's where you're wrong,' Kathleen says and there is a dark glint in her eyes. The softness, the grief, is gone. The change in her tone shocks me. 'If he'd just kept quiet. Don't you see? The police had nothing to go on. Apart from the postmortem findings. There was nothing there to link this to any one of us.

'It would've gone away in its own time, but no, Alex had to come forth with some big bleeding-heart confession and risk it all. I can't go to jail,' she says, her voice cracking. 'I won't go to jail. I was only trying to do the right thing!'

'If you're really interested in doing the right thing, you'll tell the police. You'll not let anyone else suffer because of your actions,' Heidi says.

'I've already told you, I'm not contacting the police. Not for you, or Alex, or anyone. My plan is to go back to England in a couple of days and I'm not going to change that.'

I can hardly believe what she's saying. How she is so cold. Maybe she is more like her brother than I ever thought before.

'You really think it's as easy as that?' I ask her. 'That we'll just let you go without telling the police? Come on, Kathleen. You're not a stupid woman!'

'Yes, I do think you're going to let me, because at the end of the day, it will just be your word against mine, won't it? And neither of you come across as particularly stable these days. Neither of you showed an ounce of compassion towards that man. You'd more reason to want him dead than I did. Everyone knew you both hated him.'

'We'll tell them what he did!' Heidi says. 'All of it. All the details.'

'Don't you think they'll wonder why you didn't tell anyone before now? Come on! Heidi, you were still visiting him and you want the police to believe he abused you? And as for you, Ciara, you didn't even tell your mother. So tell them if you want. It will just make you both look even more like liars.' She pauses. 'In fact, maybe you've been lying all along. You made that poor man write those words. Those horrible, horrible words.'

'How dare you!' Heidi shouts and she is on her feet, storming towards Kathleen, and I have to stand up, grab her and pull her back, even though I'd love to reach for her myself.

How dare Kathleen suggest we're lying!

'I'm just fighting my corner,' she says. 'Because out of all us, I'm the one person who deserves to go to jail least of all. I loved him.'

'So much so that you moved away years ago and never came back?' Heidi sniffs.

Kathleen shakes her head. 'I kept in touch. He knew where I was when he needed me. He knew I'd come to him when he was sick and I did. And when I did, I showed him compassion. I showed him I loved him. I showed him I forgave him.'

Her words are fast, tripping over one another. She's spiralling now. She must realise how ridiculous she's being. She must realise that she can't get away from this, no matter her threats or her plans.

310

'That's the greatest gift you can give someone, you know. Forgiveness. It's what people deserve, when they're dying. Even the bad people. The people who make mistakes. They deserve to die in peace. I gave him that. I let him know. I let him know he was forgiven.'

'What did you ever have to forgive him for?' Heidi snorts. 'You barely even knew him. You stayed away for so long . . .'

She says the words and time slows. I see the look on Kathleen's face. I see it and I wonder how I ever missed it.

Was I so far in denial of my own pain that I couldn't see it written all over someone else's face? I'd missed it with Heidi . . . and now . . .

Kathleen pales, struggles to compose her face again. She knows she's said too much. She's flustered. Her mouth opens and closes, but she isn't saying anything.

'Oh my God . . .' is all I can say and she flashes me a look. A look that pleads with me not to say any more. If we don't say it out loud it isn't real.

A small cry comes from upstairs. Lily must be waking up. I see the panic on Heidi's face.

'I need to get to Lily,' she says. 'She's crying.'

Kathleen looks at her. Steps to one side.

'You can go,' she says, 'but you're not taking your bag with you.'

'Why can't I bring my bag?' Heidi asks. 'Lily might need changing.'

'Then take what you need from it up to her. You're not taking your bag. Do you think I'd risk you calling the police?'

'I want to look after my daughter,' Heidi says, but she doesn't argue further.

She simply pulls out a nappy and wipes from her bag and, with a tilt of her head that seems to ask if I'm okay with her going, she heads towards the stairs.

I nod at her. I'm quite looking forward to getting Kathleen on my own, although my stomach is churning now. How many people did he hurt? How many lives did he destroy?

How many people had he condemned to live a life of shame and self-blame and fucked-up relationships, mental and emotional scars, a fear of intimacy? Nightmares and self-medicating, distrust and hurt.

He has left innocent people, innocent girls, broken and sullied in his wake.

I don't want to be ashamed or scared any more. It has gone on too long. This has to stop. Kathleen needs to know it has to stop.

She is pacing the room now. Agitated. For all her bluff and blunder she knows that she can't really expect to walk away from this.

I look at her, how she looks older than her years. How any vibrancy I remember in her from my childhood is long gone and I wonder how I never noticed it before. It's enough to make tears spring to my eyes once again.

'Kathleen,' I say, my voice soft.

She keeps walking.

'Kathleen,' I say, a little louder this time.

She looks at me, her eyes filled with fear. I take her by the wrists, forcing her to stop pacing, forcing her to look me in the eye.

'Did he do this to you, too? When you were small? You can tell me, you know. You can tell Heidi. You don't have to protect him any more.'

Her eyes widen and she pulls her arms sharply away from me before raising her hand and slapping me squarely across my right cheek with a force so strong I stumble.

'Don't you ever open your filthy mouth to say that again,' she hisses. 'How dare you!'

I put my hand to my cheek, feel the heat as blood rushes to my skin, colouring my face. It stings, but not as much as her words.

'I'm only trying to help. If the police know, they'll understand. They'll help.'

'You can help by keeping your twisted lies to yourself. I don't know where we went wrong with you, Ciara, but if there is any deviant in this family it's you! I don't know how you did it,' she spits at me, 'you and that vindictive bitch upstairs. You want everyone to be as sordid and sick as you? Well, I'm sorry, you're wrong. He never touched me. It was a mercy killing, because I loved him. You couldn't possibly understand. You have never loved anyone but yourself.'

She is screaming and I can see her come at me again. She's small, no more than five foot four at most, but she is strong and before I know it I'm being pushed backwards, losing my footing and slipping, my head banging off the hard wood floor so hard that I bite my tongue. I taste the metallic tang of blood in my mouth, try to scramble backwards to get away or get to my feet or just to shield myself from her.

She pulls a book from the bookcase, a thick, heavy hardback, and throws it at me. The sharp edges of the spine hit me right in the stomach, making me retch, the effort sending blood spraying from my mouth on the floor. I can't speak as I curl up and feel another book land and another . . . and another. And all the while Kathleen is ranting. No, she's not ranting, she's praying. The Hail Mary over and over again.

Pray for us sinners, now and at the hour of our death.
Pray for us sinners, now and at the hour of our death.
Pray for us sinners, now and at the hour of our death.

Chapter Seventy-Two

Heidi

Now

I'm shaking as I feed Lily, finding no comfort at all from the soft warmth of her body.

Can she really make the police believe her? Can she really make it look like Ciara and I could have been behind it all? That we are horrible people? Maybe, I think, with a sinking sensation, we are horrible people. Maybe all those thoughts that come to me in the middle of the night – which have come to me in the middle of the night ever since the first time he hurt me – maybe they represent the truth?

I close my eyes, hold my daughter close to me. Think about her innocence. No, I was just a child. As innocent as Lily is now.

The sound of shouting downstairs jolts me back into reality. Then the sound of a thud, and another and another. I can hear Kathleen's voice, raised, ranting. But I can't hear Ciara. A shiver runs through me as I lay Lily gently back on the bed, her eyes now heavy with sleep, her mouth milky.

As carefully as I can, I tiptoe out of my room, avoiding that squeaky floorboard, listening to what is happening downstairs.

I still don't hear Ciara. Just Kathleen ranting, punctuated by thuds as if she's throwing something. I peer over the bannister, down into the hall. The living room is open and with another thud, I see one of Joe's precious books hit the floor – flung through the door. I look down to see a hand, an arm, prone on the floor as if someone is trying to crawl out of the living room to safety.

Ciara, I think as I start to shake. I have to help Ciara. I need to get help, but I have to think of Lily. I've no phone. I can't call the police except . . . I remember the phone in Joe's room. He barely used it, but it was there 'for emergencies'.

I'd arranged to have it disconnected, but I can't remember when. It might still be in service.

I pray that it's still in service.

Back in that room – his room – I make my way gingerly to the chest of drawers, where the cheap cordless handset blinks at me from its cradle.

I pick it up and press the call button and I pray, as hard as I can, that the line will still be active.

At the sound of the dialling tone I find myself fighting the urge to fall to my knees. Shaking, the numbers on the handset blurring in front of my eyes, I dial 999.

Help is coming.

Help will be here.

I just pray it's on time.

Chapter Seventy-Three

Heidi

Now

I will never take this for granted. I will never not appreciate the strong man who is lying by my side. I will never complain (well, not much) when Lily wakes in the night needing a feed, or a change or just a cuddle. I will never complain about the jammy handprints she has left on the carpet, or the times she manages to make such a mess of herself that a bath for us both is the only way to clean up.

I won't complain about teething. I won't complain about Alex sleeping on while I feed our baby and revel in her pureness.

I will enjoy every moment, because this is my second chance. This is my chance to experience the childhood I should've had back then. The childhood he stole from me.

'You'll have to be careful not to spoil her,' Ciara said the last time we met.

I'd laughed, especially as Ciara, who declares herself to be the least maternal person in Christendom, had brought a teddy bear with her that was at least the same size, if not bigger, than Lily herself.

Ciara and me? Well, we're not best friends or anything. But we're trying. She spent five days in hospital after the attack. Kathleen had managed to break two of her ribs and puncture a lung. Along with the books, Kathleen had kicked her in the stomach several times. There were concerns about internal bleeding, but thankfully she was fine. She is making a good recovery, physically. And mentally, she's getting there. With the help of Stella, of course.

And I'm trying, too. Because we both know what it's like to have been hurt so badly. We carry the same emotional scars. We're getting counselling. Going to support groups. Trying to meet once a week, for a stroll along the quay and then a coffee. It's been four months since Joe died and the winter is giving way into spring. There's a lightness to the air that I don't think is entirely down to the change in the season.

Sometimes Stella comes to join us. Sometimes Alex meets us when he has finished work. He's doing okay. He still feels some guilt about not calling for help for Joe, even though the doctors and the police have told him there was nothing that could've been done for him at that stage anyway.

Kathleen had done a good enough job to send Joe almost all the way to hell – just not quite far enough. She tried, of course, even after the assault, to pin the blame for Joe's death on Ciara and me, and on Alex, too. Even though she knew she was facing jail anyway for the assault on Ciara, she still seemed determined to punish us.

But she underestimated the power of a guilty conscience. Poor Dr Sweeney – living with the secret got too much for him, especially when he saw Ciara, bloodied and bruised in her hospital bed. He's a good man, I still believe that. He was trying to help in his own way, but he'll pay the price for covering up for Kathleen, who seems not one bit sorry for the position she put him in.

Of course Kathleen had also underestimated the value of our testimony. Ciara and I had cried our way through several boxes of tissues as we had outlined the years of abuse we had suffered to the police. Ciara told me how she thought we might not be Joe's only victims. That she thought Kathleen may have been targeted, too – but when the police asked her about it, she reacted with the same anger she had shown Ciara.

Marie was devastated, of course. I believe she genuinely knew nothing of her husband's perversions. She has finally taken her wedding ring off and reverted to her maiden name.

As for Joe, his remains were exhumed and he was buried, alone, in a plot further down the cemetery. I'm not even sure where his plot is, but that's fine by me. I have no desire to visit his grave. I think he'll have a lonely rest there.

Me? I'm determined to move on. Ciara is, too. The house is on the market. There have been a few offers. Young families looking for a place to build happy memories. It will be gone soon and I hope all those painful memories with it.

The rest of our life awaits. Alex stirs in his sleep, turns over and wraps his arm around me. I feel secure. I feel loved.

I feel free.

Epilogue

Kathleen

Then

I didn't like seeing my big brother look so weak. So pathetic. So scared. It was so unlike Joe. Normally he was this larger-than-life character, full of self-confidence. Sometimes he was too full of self-confidence, but we all had our faults.

Joe had always had a swagger about him. A sense that he was destined for bigger things. The first in our family to stay on at school past sixteen, he'd been determined to rise above the fairly basic working-class lifestyle he'd grown up with.

Joe knew things – all the facts in the world. I could listen to him tell me stories about far-flung countries and exotic insects, the great battles in the history, the Greek myths; his knowledge seemed endless.

Being nine years younger than him, I had hero-worshipped him. Loved it when he took me out on the back of his bike to meet his friends. He never saw me as the annoying little sister – not the way my friends' brothers saw them. And he

319

always bought me sweets. A quarter of cola cubes in a white paper bag. I just had to give him the first one, to make sure it wasn't poisoned, he'd say.

Now he was in pain, pale, and his mood was dipping day by day.

'I'm scared,' he'd told me as I sat holding his hand at his bedside.

'What of?' I asked. 'We'll take care of you, I promise.'

'I'm not scared of dying,' he said, 'or even the pain that might come with it. I'm scared of what happens after.'

It wasn't something I wanted to think about too much. I think I was still in denial about his illness. Just the day before, I'd wept in Dr Sweeney's office, told him the thought of seeing Joe suffer and die was almost more than I could take. I couldn't even think about after.

'We'll take care of you then, too,' I said, gently rubbing his hand. 'We'll do right by you.' I couldn't hold back my tears, but nor could Joe.

'I don't mean like that,' he'd said. 'I mean the afterlife. Where I go. My soul, you know.'

'You're a good man,' I told him.

'I wasn't always,' he said and his eyes flickered from mine.

'You repented and you stopped,' I said. 'That's what matters.'

I felt uncomfortable. I didn't want to have this conversation. There are things I had buried deep in the recesses of my mind and Joe's sins, those awful ones, were one of them.

'I could get Father Brennan for you, to hear a confession. It might put your mind at rest a little.'

'I think my sins are beyond what Father Brennan could fix for me,' he said sadly.

'But if I could forgive you . . .' I said, my voice faltering.

'The others haven't,' he said.

'Others?'

I felt a shiver run through me. I knew of one. Heidi. I'd suspected something when I stayed at the house. I'd confronted him and he'd promised that he would stop. He promised me he hadn't hurt anyone else.

'I'm so sorry,' he said. 'I've been so weak. I didn't mean to. I couldn't help it. I really tried, really, really tried.'

'Who?' I asked, my voice firm. I pulled my hand from his.

'Does it matter now?' he said. 'It will all come out when I'm gone. I'm sure of it.'

'Who?' I asked again.

Who else had been told they were Joe McKee's 'favourite'? His 'special girl'. I remembered how confused it had made me feel, but how I loved him. And how he had cried when I was older and asked him about it. How he said he was a bad person and he should just kill himself. And I'd be so, so scared that he would that I told him it was okay. I told him I was okay because that was the right thing to do, wasn't it?

He whispered two names. Ciara and Heidi, of course.

'When did it stop?' I asked him.

'I don't remember . . . maybe Heidi was around thirteen. Something like that.'

I knew immediately that was at least two years after I'd left. Two years after he'd promised me, swore to me that he wouldn't do it again.

He had lied to me. He had betrayed my trust once again. Something snapped.

'They'll tell everyone, after I'm gone, I know it. If not before. Everyone will know I'm a monster.'

I soothed him, because it felt like the right thing to do. I told him that I would sort it out, just as I did before. He wasn't to worry.

What I didn't tell him was that I had no intention of our family secrets being spilled. I had no intention of people asking me questions. Asking me did I know. Asking me if he did it to me, too. Because I loved him, as flawed as he was. As much of a monster as he was, he was still my big brother and if I could do one thing for him I would make sure his reputation was protected.

It *was* a mercy killing of sorts, in the end. I had left him, content, and gone downstairs. I had looked at the faces of the two young women whose lives he had destroyed. I had thought of the child I had been. Nine years old, or was it eight? I thought of all the times he told me it was because he loved me. All those times I believed him. Helped him.

I couldn't stand to have any of us, wounded and damaged as we were, dance attendance on him when he had caused us so much pain. I knew we never had a chance of getting justice for his crimes, but I could make sure it was over. Really over. For us all.

I think I was in a haze when I did it. If I hadn't been, maybe I'd have seen that stupid diary. Taken it with me, made sure no one ever read those words. But you see, I really didn't plan it. I just popped my head around the door to his room and saw him sleeping there, like a baby. Without a care in the world. Sure that he would be protected in this life and the next – that his reputation would remain unsullied while he had destroyed three lives.

That's when I lifted the pillow.

Acknowledgements

Oh, this book was a doozy to write! It challenged me more than any other I've written because I wanted to do the subject matter justice.

There are a lot of people who helped me along the way.

This book's first and biggest cheerleader was my agent of almost 14 years, Ger Nichol, who saw something in the fairly ropey earlier drafts and encouraged me to keep digging and teasing out this storyline. She gave me faith in the book and in myself as a writer when I was struggling to find it myself and I am incredibly grateful.

Also encouraging and cheering, and holding my hand through the scary bits, was my editor Helen Huthwaite whose faith in my writing is massively appreciated, as is her keen eye and her ability to push me to make a book the best it can be.

Along with Phoebe Morgan, who is taking over the reins while Helen is on maternity leave, I know that I have the best editorial team in the world behind me.

So love and thanks to all at Avon and Harper Collins Ireland for all the incredible work they do behind the scenes to get my books looking great, onto shelves and into people's hearts.

Their enthusiasm and dedication is second to none. A special mention to Claire Pickering who has once again made the copy-editing process a relatively painless one.

To my police sources, who offered information on police procedure in such cases, including my sister-in-law Inspector Penny Jones of the Cheshire Police, and Karen – thank you for your guidance.

Also thanks to those lovely Twitter people who offered me advice on autopsies and the release of remains in ongoing criminal cases.

Any mistakes in the above are mine and mine alone.

To sell books, authors need booksellers and huge thanks to all those who get behind my titles and support me and this industry. In particular, love and thanks to Jenni at Little Acorns, Dave at No Alibis, Bob (the giver of the BEST hugs) at the Gutter Bookshop and the team in Eason, Foyleside. Thanks also to the supermarket buyers who put my books front and centre.

Heidi Murphy of WH Smith in Ireland has been a huge support to me, and happened to mention that you don't get many Heidis in books these days. So I'm delighted to have named a character after her in this book.

To my writer friends who have just been amazing and who fully understand how insane this business can be, thank you. You have gone above and beyond. Thank you in particular to John Marrs, Louise Beech, Rowan Coleman, Liz Nugent, Cally Taylor, Sheila O'Flanagan and Brian McGilloway.

Special thanks to Jane Casey and Alex Barclay who took time out of their hectic lives to read this.

Special thanks to my best writing pal, Fionnuala Kearney who did most of the tea-pouring, and wine-pouring, and Diet Coke providing, and listening and hugging. And thanks to her husband Aidan for allowing me to steal his wife every now and again and to the wider Kearney family who always make me feel welcome when I visit the Claire Allan Suite.

To all the journalists and book bloggers who provide invaluable support and who take part in blog tours and offer reviews. You are amazingly generous with your time and praise and I am forever grateful. Special love to Mairead at Swirl & Thread and Margaret Bonass Madden at Bleachhouse Library.

To the friends who have held my hand, Julie-Anne, Vicki, Carey Ann, Erin, Catherine – thank you.

To my readers, Facebook followers, Twitter pals – thank you so much. Our chats and interaction help to make a very isolated profession a lot more bearable. Thanks in particular to Sam Missingham for invaluable industry support and advice.

And lastly to my family who are my everything. Mum and Dad, Peter, Eavan, Lisa, Mark, Emma, Niall, Abby, Ethan, Darcy, Arya, Thomas and Finn – thank you. To my husband, Neil, thank you for giving me the time and space to live my dream. To my children, Joe and Cara – everything is for you both. You are the greatest loves of my life. And to the two frankly disinterested cats, and the one very interested and amazingly cute puppy, Izzy, thanks for the cuddles.

You watched her die.
And her death has created a vacancy . . .

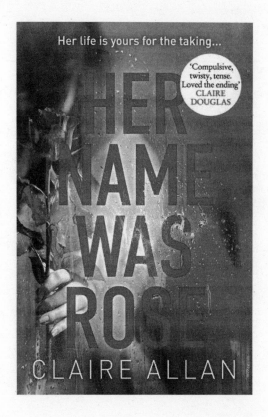

A gripping psychological thriller
that will have you hooked.

Available in all good bookshops now.

Just how far is a mother willing to go?

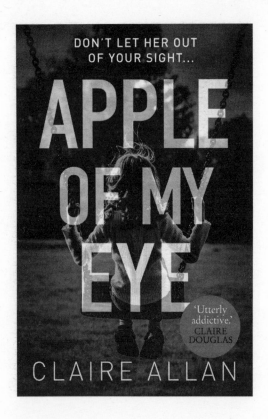

A gripping psychological thriller from
the *USA Today* bestseller.

Available in all good bookshops now.

I disappeared on a Tuesday afternoon.
They've never found my body . . .

A unputdownable serial killer thriller with a
breathtaking twist.

Available in all good bookshops now.